Mouthwatering Prai[se]
Candy-Coat[ed]

FOREVE[R]

"Nancy Coco paints u[s] [a]
charming island setting where the main mode
of transportation is a horse-drawn vehicle.
She also gives us a delicious mystery, complete
with doses of her homemade fudge . . .
a perfect read to wrap up your summer!"
—**Wonder Women Sixty**

OH, FUDGE!

"*Oh, Fudge* is a charming cozy, the sixth in the
Candy-Coated Mystery series. But be warned:
There's a candy recipe at the end of each chapter,
so don't read this one when you're hungry!"
—*Suspense Magazine*

OH SAY CAN YOU FUDGE

"Beautiful Mackinac Island provides the setting for a
puzzling series of crimes. Now that Allie McMurphy
has taken over her grandparents' hotel and fudge
shop, life on Mackinac is good, although her little
dog, Mal, does tend to nose out trouble . . .
Allie's third mystery offers plenty of plausible
suspects and mouthwatering fudge recipes."
—*Kirkus Reviews*

"WOW. This is a great book. I have loved the series
from the beginning, and this book just makes me love
it even more. No one can make me feel like I am in
Mackinac Island better than Nancy Coco. She draws
the reader in and makes you feel like you are part of
the st[ory] [. . . 'fa]ntastic' is
the [. . .] book."

TO FUDGE OR NOT TO FUDGE

"*To Fudge or Not to Fudge* is a superbly crafted, classic, culinary cozy mystery. If you enjoy this category as much as I do, you are in for a real treat. The setting of Mackinac Island immediately drew me to the book, as it is an amazing location. The only problem I had was that reading about all the mouthwatering fudge made me hungry."
—Examiner.com (5 stars)

"We LOVED it! This mystery is a vacation between the pages of a book. If you've never been to Mackinac Island, you will long to visit, and if you have, the story will help you to recall all of your wonderful memories."
—Melissa's Mochas, Mysteries and Meows

"A five-star, delicious mystery that has great characters, a good plot, and a surprise ending. If you like a good mystery with more than one suspect, then rush out to get this book, but be sure you have the time since once you start, you won't want to put it down. I give this five stars and a 'Wow Factor' of 5+. The fudge recipes included in the book all sound wonderful. A gift basket filled with the fudge from the recipes in this book, a copy of the book, some hot chocolate mix and/or coffee, and a nice mug would be a great Christmas gift."
—Mystery Reading Nook

"A charming and funny culinary mystery that parodies reality show competitions and is led by a sweet heroine, eccentric but likable characters, and a skillfully crafted plot that speeds toward an unpredictable conclusion. Allie stands out as a likable and engaging character. Delectable fudge recipes are interspersed throughout the novel."
—*Kings River Life Magazine*

ALL FUDGED UP

"A sweet treat with memorable characters, a
charming locale, and a satisfying mystery."
—**Barbara Allan**, author of the
Trash 'n' Treasures mysteries

"A fun book with a lively plot, set in one of
America's most interesting resorts.
All this, plus fudge!"
—**JoAnna Carl**, author of the
Chocoholic mysteries

"A sweet confection of a book. Charming setting,
clever protagonist, and creamy fudge—
a yummy recipe for a great read."
—**Joanna Campbell Slan**, author of the
Kiki Lowenstein Scrap-N-Craft Mysteries
and The Jane Eyre Chronicles

"Nancy Coco's *All Fudged Up* is a delightful mystery
delivering suspense and surprise in equal measure.
Her heroine, Alice McMurphy, owner of the Historic
McMurphy Hotel and Fudge Shop (as much of a
mouthful as her delicious fudge), has a wry
narrative voice that never falters. Add that to the
charm of the setting, Michigan's famed Mackinac
Island, and you have a recipe for enjoyment.
As an added bonus, mouthwatering fudge recipes
are included. A must-read for all lovers of
amateur sleuth classic mysteries."
—**Carole Bugge**, author of
Who Killed Blanche Dubois?
and other Claire Rawlings mysteries

"You won't have to 'fudge' your enthusiasm for Nancy Parra's first Mackinac Island Fudge Shop Mystery. Indulge your sweet tooth as you settle in and meet Allie McMurphy, Mal the bichon/poodle mix, and the rest of the motley crew in this entertaining series debut."
—**Miranda James**, author of the Cat in the Stacks mysteries

"The characters are fun and well-developed, the setting is quaint and beautiful, and there are several mouthwatering fudge recipes."
—*RT Book Reviews* (**3 stars**)

"Enjoyable . . . *All Fudged Up* is littered with delicious fudge recipes, including alcohol-infused ones. I really enjoyed this cozy mystery and look forward to reading more in this series."
—**FreshFiction**

"Cozy mystery lovers who enjoy quirky characters, a great setting, and fantastic recipes will love this debut."
—*The Lima News*

"The first Candy-Coated mystery is a fun cozy with a wonderful location and eccentric characters."
—*Midwest Book Review*

FUDGE BITES

A Candy-Coated Mystery
with Recipes

Nancy Coco

KENSINGTON PUBLISHING CORP.

www.kensingtonbooks.com

KENSINGTON BOOKS are published by

Kensington Publishing Corp.
119 West 40th Street
New York, NY 10018

All Kensington titles, imprints, and distributed lines are available at special quantity discounts for bulk purchases for sales promotions, premiums, fund-raising, educational, or institutional use. Special book excerpts or customized printings can also be created to fit specific needs. For details, write or phone the office of the Kensington sales manager: Kensington Publishing Corp., 119 West 40th Street, New York, NY 10018, attn: Sales Department; phone 1-800-221-2647.

First printing: October 2019

10 9 8 7 6 5 4 3 2 1

ISBN-13: 978-1-4967-1608-8
ISBN-10: 1-4967-1608-6

Printed in the United States of America

Electronic edition:

ISBN-13: 978-1-4967-1609-5 (e-book)
ISBN-10: 1-4967-1609-4 (e-book)

This book is for the readers.
Thank you for helping to make my stories come alive.

Chapter 1

"You look amazing, Allie," Frances said to me. "Like the scariest of the walking dead."

I laughed. I could feel the makeup cracking, and so I tried really hard to get it together. "At least I don't look like a real dead person. I've got skin flapping off my cheek." I pushed on the latex flap that concealed the gory makeup underneath. "Thankfully, zombies aren't real."

"I love the idea of the zombie walk," Frances said. "The fact that the profits all go to the Red Dress Foundation is fantastic."

"I like the idea that all the bars and restaurants pitched in to supply food for the hungry masses," I said.

"Fudge isn't exactly food," she pointed out.

"I bet there are a lot of people who would argue with you on that," I teased.

Frances was my hotel manager. She'd worked at the Historic McMurphy Hotel and Fudge Shop since before she retired from teaching. Thankfully, she had stayed as an employee after my papa Liam McMurphy died and I inherited the family business.

At this very moment, I was putting the finishing

touches on my zombie pinup girl costume. I didn't usually participate in late night events because I was a fudge maker, and I had to get up very early in the morning to make said fudge. But October was off-season, and I sold most of the fudge online. That meant I didn't have to have fudge ready for when the tourists came in the morning. Yes, sometimes I even got to sleep in as late as 8 A.M. if I wanted.

This event was extra special and benefited a charity close to my heart, the American Heart Association. It was to remind everyone that heart disease is the number one killer of women. The senior center put together the event, called the "Night of the Walking Red." Mrs. Tunisian—one of my favorite seniors—was the head of the committee, and she'd insisted I come to the event and enter the costume contest.

I had made pumpkin chocolate chip fudge for the occasion. "You and Mr. Devaney should come out for the walk," I said to Frances. "You would make great zombies. I know you like to play with makeup."

"Well," she stood in front of me and adjusted the collar on my cardigan. "I did sell Mary Kay for twenty years, so I am trained in makeup application."

"I have a lot of leftover stage makeup upstairs. You can use it. You and Mr. Devaney would look great as a married couple of zombies."

"I don't think Douglas is into that kind of silliness," she said.

"What kind of silliness?" I turned to see Mr. Devaney walking through the door from the basement. He paused when he saw me. "Have you been in a car accident?"

"There are no cars on Mackinac Island," I said. Mackinac Island, Michigan, was known as the fudge capital of the world. We were a small island in the straits between the Upper and Lower Peninsulas of Michigan. The entire island had been combustion engine-free for over a hundred years. That meant the only way to get around was walk, bike, or take a horse-drawn carriage. I loved the traditions of the island. Things were slower here, and the sights and sounds of modern life were left behind.

Huge Victorian cottages with their turrets and gingerbread trim lined the streets. For centuries, the wealthy from Chicago and Detroit would escape the hustle and bustle of the big city to spend the summer season on the island. They usually came by ferries, although some came by private jet these days. My friend Sophie was a private pilot. She worked for the Grander Hotel during the season, but she also had regulars who asked her to fly them on and off the island when the ferries quit running.

Sophie Allison was meeting me for the Walking Red event. My best friend, Jenn Christensen, had left the island for an important job in Chicago. Sophie and Liz McElroy, the editor and lead reporter for the *Mackinac Island Town Crier* newspaper, had stepped in to keep me from moping too much about the loss. Jenn was an excellent event planner, and when she had come to Mackinac to help me through my first season, she'd connected with the islanders like a pro. Me, on the other hand? Not so much. Even though my family had owned the McMurphy for over one hundred years, I had grown up in Detroit and gone to school in Chicago. I kept trying to fit in, but I knew I still wasn't quite accepted as a true local. I was slowly getting there, but there had been a few bumps in the road.

Things had been going smoothly since Jenn left several weeks ago. But it was the off-season, it hadn't been that long, and Jenn had left me with strict instructions on how to make friends. I followed them as closely as possible, but I didn't have the same knack with people that Jenn had. Even with Sophie and Liz, I missed Jenn.

I got a bump on my leg and looked down to see my bichon poo puppy, Marshmallow—Mal for short—nudging me with her nose. She jumped up, and I scratched her behind the ears. "What do you think of my zombie look?" I asked the dog.

She seemed unfazed by the red and white makeup.

"I think I'll skip the zombie look," Mr. Devaney said, pouring himself a cup of coffee from the coffee bar at the far side of the lobby. "But you go ahead and do it if you want to, Frances," he said with a warm look in his eye. "I'd love to see you have some fun."

"Oh, pooh," she said. "I've got to watch the front desk. We have a couple of families coming in for the weekend."

I glanced at my watch. It was getting dark already at 5 P.M. "Did they say if they expected to arrive late?"

"Sophie is bringing them in the next few minutes," Frances said. "I know it's close to Halloween, but I don't want to give them the impression that we aren't a warm and welcoming place."

"What's not warm and welcoming about zombies?" I asked with a laugh, raising my hands like claws. "We only want to eat your brains."

The door to the McMurphy opened and Liz walked in. She was dressed like a ballerina with zombie makeup. Her dark, curly hair was pulled up in a tight bun, and she had fake bite marks created with makeup on her neck. Her leotard was dirty and torn, and her tutu was a bit ragged.

"Oh, my goodness, what happened to you?" Frances asked her.

"Nothing," Liz said with a smile. "I'm a zombie and a prima ballerina. Two things I always wanted to grow up to be. Thanks for sponsoring us."

"It was my pleasure," Frances said. "Douglas pitched in half."

"Thanks, Mr. Devaney," I said. Mr. Devaney was a retired schoolteacher who I had brought on as the new handyman for the McMurphy. It hadn't taken long before Mr. Devaney and Frances had started secretly dating. In a whirlwind courtship, the two seventy-year-olds had gotten engaged, and last month they'd gotten married. You could see the joy on their faces every time they were in the room together. It made my heart fill with hope that someday I, too, might find the love of my life.

Right now, I was sort of single. My ex-boyfriend, Trent Jessop, was in Chicago for the next few months. And my attraction to Mackinac Island's top investigator, Officer Rex Manning, was progressing slowly. The problem with having two handsome men competing for your attention was sometimes they both backed off. I think they were giving me room to decide. Maybe I needed the room.

"Mal can go," Liz said, her eyes lighting up. "They have zombie dog costumes."

"That's creative," Frances said.

"I don't have any doggy costumes," I said with a frown. I could feel the latex on my face crinkle again, so I smoothed out my expression.

"We can give her a black tee shirt with white bones panted on it."

"A black tee shirt?" I said. "We'd need a very small one. Mal only weighs twelve pounds."

"Oh, a onesie will do," Liz said with glee. "I'm going to run over to Doud's and see if they have anything on the shelf."

"I'll go with you," I said. We headed out the door. The McMurphy was on Main Street and only a block or so from Doud's Market, the oldest market on the island. It was almost fully dark outside now, and the air smelled of falling leaves, horses, and the lingering scents of fudge and popcorn. People were beginning to gather. The costumes were equal parts terrifying and funny.

We pushed into Doud's with the doorbells ringing behind us. Mary Emry stood at the cash register dressed as a zombified Minnie Mouse. She was waiting on a burly trucker guy with a cleaver buried in his skull. It almost looked realistic.

"This way," Liz said, drawing me toward the back where they kept a few items of clothing.

"Maybe we should have checked out one of the tee shirt places," I said as I eyed the sparse selection.

"No, this is perfect." Liz pulled a tiny black sundress out of the racks. "Now we need a little blood . . ."

"I have extra makeup." I followed Liz through the store.

"This will do," she said, grabbing some red decorator frosting. "Come on." We approached Mary.

Mary was a regular cashier at Doud's. She wasn't much for talking, at least not to me. "What's this for?"

"We're going to dress up Allie's dog, Mal," Liz said, rubbing her hands together. "With any luck, the red frosting will stain the dress, and the dog will lick it and get red on her face."

"Disgusting," Mary said.

"But effective," I said. "Are you going to be in the Walking Red zombie walk?"

"Sure," Mary said. "It's for a good cause."

I paid for the purchases, and we walked out of Doud's and into the now crowded street. "I didn't know there would be so many people here," I said.

"It's the cause," Liz said. "People care. My mom died of a heart attack."

"I'm sorry, I didn't know that," I said.

Liz blinked back tears, looking away. "This crowd is crazy, let's go around and through the alley." We turned down the side street. It, too, was filling up with zombies and humans alike. People not in costume carried blankets and came out to watch all the craziness.

When we were a half a block away from the McMurphy, in the alley just behind the Old Tyme Photo Shop, I noticed the stray calico who I had named Carmella walking ahead of us.

Carmella had adopted me and the McMurphy when I first came to Mackinac. She wasn't a fan of Mal, who was a bit rambunctious at only six months old, but Mella escaped puppy shenanigans by jumping up on the countertops. My cat was an indoor/outdoor cat. She loved to wander the back alleyways for an hour or so and then return to the McMurphy to receive treats from Frances and attention from the guests.

"Mella," I called to her. "Here, kitty." She walked over to me, and I leaned down to pick her up.

"Wow, looks like you already have a costume started for Mella," Liz said.

I looked at the cat. Her paws were wet and covered with a distinct brownish-red color. Her face had remnants of the same damp substance. "What did you get into?" I asked her. She wiped her feet on my sweater. "Is that blood?"

"Eww," Liz said. "She's coated with it."

I glanced around. It was too dark to see anything in the half-lit alley. We got closer to the McMurphy, and the sensor lights I had installed came on. "It certainly looks like blood," I said, holding her up to the light. "Are you okay, Mella?" I asked. "Did you get hurt?"

She meowed at me as if indignant that I might think she wouldn't win in a fight.

"I don't see any obvious puncture wounds," Liz said.

"That means someone else is hurt," I said. I glanced back down the alley. It was darker now that the lights were on behind the McMurphy. "Let's take her in and have Frances give her a bath and make sure she's not hurt."

"And while she's doing that?" Liz asked.

"I'll get a flashlight, and we can check the alley. Whatever Mella got into has lost a lot of blood. We need to see if we can help it."

Just then, there was a scream from the dark alley. I hugged Mella tight and turned toward the sound.

"Oh, my gosh!" It was Sophie. "Thank goodness you're out here."

"Are you alright?" I asked.

"No," Sophie said with trembling hands. She was dressed as a biker babe zombie. "I think I found a dead man."

"Where?" Liz asked, pulling out her phone.

"Just over there," Sophie said and pointed toward the dark corner of the building that backed up against the alley. We all hurried over to where she pointed. "I was coming around this way to avoid the crowd when I stumbled over something. I got out my flashlight, and there was a crumpled body."

"Are you sure it's real?" Liz asked.

"There's a lot of blood, and paw tracks from Mella," I said, looking at the ground as I walked. "I don't think this is fake."

"But look at us, we're dressed like the walking dead." Liz waved a hand over her costumed self. "What if it's fake blood?"

Sophie paused. "Do you think it might be a decoration? It's pretty gruesome."

We stopped in front of a dark lump. Liz and I pulled out our phones and shone the flashlight apps to get a better look. The lump looked like a man. The head was obscured by a large hat. He wore an old suit coat with patched elbows, and one of his shoes was off. His limbs were at odd angles. A large, dark pool seeped from under his jacket. There were kitty tracks in the blood. It looked like this was the mess Mella had found, after all.

"He looks real," I said. I hunkered down.

"Are you going to touch him?" Sophie asked.

"Should you touch him?" Liz asked.

"It's the only way to know if he's real," I said. "It's what they tell you to do with first aid." I touched his shoulder and gently shook it. "Sir, are you okay?"

His head rolled to the side. His jaw opened, and his tongue flopped out. I jerked back. Mella squirmed in my arms. I held her tight and put my fingers on his neck to feel for a pulse. The body was stone cold, and the blood was dark.

"He's either dead, or he's a very good Halloween effect." I stood and looked at my friend. "But . . . if he is a Halloween effect, why hide him in a back alley?"

"I'm calling 9-1-1," Liz said.

I petted a squirming Mella, who seemed only to want one thing—to leave. The blood she had gotten on her was currently getting all over me, but I didn't want to let her down. She might make things worse. Especially if this poor man *was* dead—it was clear she had already walked through the crime scene.

"Hi, Charlene, it's Liz McElroy," Liz said. "I'm in the alley behind Doud's and the McMurphy, and I think we might have stumbled across a crime scene." She paused. "Yes, I know that the whole island is full of the walking dead right now, but we think this one might *actually* be dead."

Sophie shivered and hugged herself. I rubbed her arm to comfort her.

"Who is 'we'?" Liz said. "Sophie and Allie and me." She looked at us. "Yes, Allie McMurphy."

"I'll call Rex," I said.

"No, don't call him," Liz said. "Charlene is contacting him now. She started calling him the minute I said I was with you." Liz covered the phone with her hand. "She said you're the Grim Reaper."

"Oh, for goodness sakes," I said and rolled my eyes. "I am not the Grim Reaper. Besides, Sophie found him."

"I think Mella found him first." Liz pointed to the dirty paws of my cat. Mella had given up on her struggle and sort of hung there, indignant.

I sighed. "My pets seem to have good noses for dead men."

After what felt like an hour but was more like ten minutes, Rex and Officer Charles Brown walked into the alley carrying flashlights. They were an imposing pair. Officer Brown was tall and square with green eyes, while Rex was about five foot ten with an action-hero physique and a shaved head that was currently covered by a hat. I knew from memory that he had killer blue eyes ringed with black lashes, and that his kiss could curl my toes.

I let out a breath. It was somehow reassuring to have them there.

"Charlene said you had a situation," Rex said.

Liz shone her flashlight on the dead man. "Sophie found him."

Rex squatted down to feel for a pulse.

"We thought maybe it was fake," I said. "But I followed first aid protocol and shook his shoulder and called out. Then I felt his neck, and he was cold as ice."

"What's up with the cat?" Office Brown asked.

"I think she walked through the blood," I said, waving her dirty paw. "I didn't see her do it."

"There are tracks through the blood," Rex said.

"Is he dead?" Sophie asked, biting her nails. There was nervous hope in her voice. "It's probably just a fake, right? You know, put here to scare people. For the zombie walk."

Rex frowned and stood. "I think some of this is makeup, but this man is clearly dead. I'll call Shane out here." He reached for the walkie-talkie on his shoulder.

"Let's step away from the scene," Officer Brown. He motioned us across the alley.

The door on the building behind us opened, and Margaret Vanderbilt stepped out. Maggs was Frances's best friend, and she worked at the drugstore next to Doud's. Maggs had long, curly gray hair, incredible skin, and wide blue eyes. "What's going on?" She asked, looking at us in our zombie makeup. "Are you going to the Walking Red walk? It's starting in a few minutes."

"We were," Liz said, "but something more important has come up."

"What's more fun than raising money for heart disease awareness?" Maggs joked, then turned serious when she saw Officer Brown and Rex. "This doesn't look good." Her gaze went to the crumpled heap on the ground at Rex's feet. "Anthony?"

"Who?" Officer Brown asked.

Maggs pushed through us, but Charles held her. "Anthony? Anthony!"

"Who's Anthony?" I asked.

"My son," she said and covered her mouth with her hands. "Please, tell me—*tell me* it's not Anthony."

Rex stepped across to hide the body from her. Thankfully, the man's hat still covered his face. "We don't know who it is, Maggs." He touched her trembling arm. "Why do you think it's Anthony?"

"He was supposed to meet me here. He was going to dress as a business zombie. I think that's his suit coat. The one with the patches." She started trembling hard.

"You need to sit down," I said, handing Mella to Liz. I took Maggs by the shoulder and helped her sit on the edge of the brick flower bed beside the door. "Does anyone have a blanket?"

The ambulance rolled up to the mouth of the alley. Ambulances were the only type of motor vehicle allowed on the island. EMT George Marron came out. He was a handsome man with high cheekbones and coppery skin. He wore his hair long in a traditional braid down his back. "Charlene called," he said.

"We need a blanket," I said. "I think Maggs might be in shock."

"Got it," George said. He reached into the ambulance, grabbed a blanket, and came over to tuck it around Maggs's shoulders. "Are you hurt?" He asked her quietly and calmly.

"No," she said, gasping for air, "No, I'm okay."

"Are you sure?" He studied her with his dark eyes. His handsome face and copper skin gleamed in the light over the door to the drugstore.

"It can't be Anthony," she said, tears welling in her eyes. "Please, tell me it's not Anthony."

George looked up at Rex. I noticed Rex shake his head subtly and my stomach tumbled. From the look on his face, he was sure it was Anthony. I sat down and put my arm around Maggs's shoulders. She rested her head on my shoulder. I looked at Sophie. "Call Frances."

Sophie nodded. She turned her back to us and got out her phone.

"We're going to find out what happened," I said. Scooching in closer and closing ranks, Liz and I stayed with Maggs, chatting aimlessly until Frances arrived.

Rex cleared his throat. "Margaret, Frances is here. Go with her, please. You shouldn't be here, and we need to work this crime scene and find out what exactly happened."

I helped Maggs to her feet as Frances came over. "I've got her," Frances said. She put her arm around Maggs, carefully and quietly speaking to her as they walked the short distance to the McMurphy.

Shane walked into the alley with his crime scene investigator jacket on and his kit in hand. In addition to being the crime scene tech, Shane was Jenn's boyfriend, so I had become friends with him over the past few months. "What do we have?" he asked.

"A crime scene less than a block away from a crowd of zombies," Rex said grimly. "What's worse, the man's in costume, so it's hard to tell what's real and what's fake."

Shane glanced at Mella in Liz's arms. "Is that fake blood on the cat?"

"I'm afraid not," I said. "Do you need to bag her feet?"

"I need you to put her in a crate and take her to the vet clinic," Shane said with a serious tone. "I need to process the scene, and I need evidence collected off of her before she cleans herself."

"Right," I said, lifting Mella out of Liz's arms. I glanced at Rex. "Do you need me to stay?"

"No, go," he said. "I'll come around later for a debriefing interview. Whatever you do, don't change clothes. It looks like the cat smeared evidence on you, as well."

"Right." I looked down at the bloody paw prints on my pinup girl outfit. "What about chain of evidence? Do I need a policeman to go with me to ensure there isn't contamination?"

"Shane?" Rex asked.

"Probably a good idea until I'm sure I have all the evidence," Shane said from his position beside the body.

"Fine," Rex said. "Officer Brown, escort Miss McMurphy and her cat to the vet clinic, and ensure the chain of custody isn't broken."

"Will do," Charles said. "Shall we?" He pointed toward the McMurphy.

"Okay. Liz?"

"I'm going to stay. I've got a story to write." She started texting on her phone. As the town reporter, Liz took her job seriously.

That left me and Officer Brown to circumvent the crowds and wake the island's only veterinarian. I blew out a long breath. This was a fine kettle of fish. I was becoming an expert in crime scene investigation . . . and so were my pets.

———

DECADENT DARK CHOCOLATE, CINNAMON CHIP, FLOURLESS BROWNIES

1½ sticks (¾ cup) butter
1⅓ cups unsweetened dark cocoa powder
1¾ cups granulated sugar
¼ teaspoon salt
1 teaspoon vanilla
3 large eggs
¾ cup cinnamon chips

Preheat oven to 350° F and prepare 8-inch pan by lining it with parchment paper. I like to use a round pan for thicker brownies.

Melt butter gently. Add cocoa to melted butter and whisk. Then add sugar and salt, and whisk until well combined. Add vanilla, stirring until smooth.

Add eggs. Stir in gently until well combined—do not overmix eggs. I switch from whisk to spatula for this part. Gently fold in cinnamon chips.

Scrape the batter into the prepared pan, and smooth out the top. Bake 20–25 minutes until a toothpick inserted in the middle comes out with moist crumbs and no wet batter. Unlike with cake, a clean toothpick means brownies are overdone.

Your house will smell awesome!

Cool 15 minutes and remove with liner from the pan. Set them on a rack to cool completely (if you can wait). Cut and enjoy!

Makes about 2 dozen brownies.

Chapter 2

Dr. Hampton wasn't too pleased when we knocked on his door and got him out of bed. It was nearly 10 P.M. by this time.

"What's going on?" he grumbled when he answered the door to the vet clinic. He wore scrubs and a striped bathrobe that had seen better days. His gray hair stood up on one side. "Is someone dying?"

"Sorry to get you up," I said, lifting the cat carrier. "But Mella has blood all over her." Officer Brown had let me stop by the McMurphy long enough to put Mella in her carrier. I felt it was safer for her, me, and everyone else.

"Come in." Dr. Hampton usually worked on horses and large animals, but that didn't mean he didn't take emergency visits for cats and dogs—especially in the off-season. He waved Officer Brown and me through the door. We walked from the tiny back porch into the back of his home, where he had a small waiting area and an exam room. "Sorry the place is so small. I usually work in the stables. There's no way I'm bringing a horse into my office."

"No problem. I'll stand right here." Officer Brown stood in the exam room doorway and left the procedure to us.

"The cat's quiet—doesn't sound like she's in obvious pain," Dr. Hampton said. "That's either good or bad. Some animals go quiet when they're hurt. It's a survival instinct."

"I'm not certain she is hurt," I said. "You see, we think she walked through a puddle of blood. Mella found a dead man in the alley. Shane Carpenter, the crime scene tech, said to bring her to you. That way, he can collect any evidence off of her safely, and you can check to see if she's hurt."

"I see," the veterinarian said. He put on his glasses and eyed me. "You look like you're covered in blood."

"I was getting ready to attend the zombie walk," I said. "But Liz and I were in the alley and found Mella with bloody paws. I picked her up, and . . . well, she covered me in whatever she walked through. That's why Officer Brown is here. To ensure any evidence on Mella and my clothes can still be used in court."

"That true?" Dr. Hampton asked Officer Brown.

Charles simply nodded and crossed his arms as if to protect the doorway.

"All right. Let's get her out of the box so I can have a look at her," Dr. Hampton said. I opened the cat carrier door, and he reached in and gently extracted her.

"Shane was hoping to collect evidence before she cleaned herself," I said as he gave my cat a careful examination.

Mella liked the vet and let him examine her without a peep. He put his stethoscope ends in his ears and listened to her heart, then checked her temperature.

"I think she's fine," he pronounced. "It looks like all this blood is from something else."

"More like someone," I said, glancing at Officer Brown. "But I probably shouldn't talk about it."

"Sounds like something I'll learn about in the paper tomorrow," Dr. Hampton said. "I think I can wait until then."

The sound of the bells and a sudden gust of wind signaled the opening of the back door. Mella reacted by trying to claw her way out of the vet's grip, but he had her nice and tight by the back of her scruff.

"Hello," Shane called.

"We're in here," I said. Shane pushed past Officer Brown with his kit, and the room shrunk considerably. He was a thin guy, but it was a tiny room. I could feel Mella's tension rise. "I think I'll step out."

"Officer Brown, they want you back at the site," Shane said. "This should only take a minute."

I grabbed the cat carrier and hurried to the waiting room. Having had evidence collected from me, I had a pretty good idea of what Mella would be going through, and I didn't want to be there for her reaction. Officer Brown trailed beside me. "Wait, do you need to stay with me if I'm out here?"

"The exam room door is open, and I'm sure Shane will verify your custody," Charles said. Then he nodded, tipped his hat, and left.

A few minutes later, Shane walked out wearing heavy gloves, a fresh scratch on his cheek. He held Mella out at arm's length while she wiggled and tried to get free.

"Were you able to collect any evidence from her?" I asked, standing. I opened the metal door to her cat crate, and Shane poured her inside. I quickly closed the door, and Mella made a mewling noise as she curled up tight in the back of the crate.

"I think I got enough." He peered at me through thick glasses with his calming blue eyes. "She got me good a couple of times, but I was able to clip her nails and get some evidence from underneath them."

"You have a battle wound," I said, pointing to his cheek. He pulled off the glove on his right hand and touched the dried blood on his face.

"Just a scratch," Dr. Hampton said. He walked out of the exam room, wiping his hands on a towel. "It might swell up a bit, but nothing too bad."

"I don't blame her for being scared," Shane said. "After all, she was just minding her own business, and bam! She's being hauled away and tested for forensic evidence."

"I suppose it has to be a shock," I said. "Isn't that right, Mella," I cooed into the locked door of the cage. "I'm sorry she got you so good."

"It's fine," Dr. Hampton said. "It means that if she gets out, she'll be able to defend herself."

"Mella likes to roam. She adopted me, you know. One day she showed up and never left, so I let her inside. She still likes her freedom to roam the alley when the crowds are small."

"Has she scratched other people?" Shane asked with concern in his eyes.

"Gosh, no," I said. "As far as I know, she's never hurt anyone before." I studied his face. "That's why I think she has to be stressed out."

"I recommend that you take her home and let her rest," Dr. Hampton said. "Of course, you might want to give her a bath first."

I winced. "Jenn was the one who gave her a bath

last time. I'm good with Mal, but I've never had the pleasure of bathing a cat."

"You never know," Dr. Hampton said. "She might like it."

"Or you could end up with the nickname 'Scarface,'" Shane teased, touching the scratch on his own face.

I ignored Shane's silly comment. "Thanks for letting me in and checking on Mella," I said to the doctor. "How much do I owe you?"

"We can settle the debt in chocolate," he said. "My daughter is having a baby shower next week. It would be great if you could get Sandy Everheart to make a sculpture for the event."

"Sounds like a deal," I said. "Call me in the morning with the details, and I'll get Sandy right on it."

"You do that," he said and waved me off. "Take care of that cat. She's pretty special."

Shane walked with me down the street to the McMurphy. He was very quiet.

"You processed the crime scene quickly," I said as I hauled Mella's crate. "I expected you to be at least an hour."

"I made you a priority," he said. "Cats can lick themselves clean pretty quickly."

"Oh, then are you on your way back to the scene?"

"I waited for them to transport the body," he said. "Most of the evidence will be collected from the victim in the lab."

"Did you know Anthony?" I asked. "You seem particularly grim tonight."

"I did," he said. "He was a nice guy. Didn't deserve to have his head bashed in."

"Do you have any idea who might have done this?"

"No." He shook his head. The sound of a rowdy crowd ahead of us filled the air. We were close to Main Street.

"I thought the Red Walk would be over by now," I said. I glanced at my watch—it was 11 P.M.

"People usually stick around until the bars close. I'm sorry you didn't get to participate."

"Don't be sorry. You didn't do anything. I'm worried for Maggs, you know? She just lost her son. I want to get whoever did this."

"I know you know this, but you shouldn't be investigating," Shane said. He pushed his glasses up. "Jenn encouraged your sleuthing, but she was wrong. There are some pretty horrible people in the world. Some of us choose to hunt them and bring justice for the victims. You aren't one of us."

That hurt a bit. "I don't mean any disrespect. I really am only trying to help."

He stopped me with a gentle hand to my arm. "You could 'help' by volunteering at the police and fireman's ball. Amateur investigations make us question our own training. Trust me, we go to school for years to be prepared for this stuff. Imagine if some random kid off the street came into your fudge shop and started making fudge."

"What? No! That takes years of classroom work and apprenticeships . . . oh, right." I sighed. "Fine. I'll try to keep my help to a minimum."

"Thanks."

"Do you hear from Jenn very often?" I asked. It had been a few weeks since she left the island to take a great job in Chicago, and if I was missing her, Shane must be, too.

"We talk every day," he said simply. There was a quiet

sadness in his words. "I'm going down there next weekend for a day or two. They keep her pretty busy."

"Yes, she seems either tired or excited every time she calls me. But she seems to be learning a lot."

"There's certainly more to do in Chicago than on Mackinac in the off-season."

We arrived at the McMurphy's back door. "Oh, wait. Do you need to collect my costume?"

He glanced at me. "I think what I got off of the cat will be fine. No need to take your clothes this time. But don't wash anything for a while, just in case."

"Great. Good night, Shane." I left him and went inside. The new backdoor locks on the McMurphy were tough to negotiate holding a cat carrier, but I managed. I set the carrier down and locked the door.

"Good, you're back," Mr. Devaney said from behind me. I jumped a little, surprised at the sudden voice and still edgy from the events of the night.

I turned to see him standing at the mouth of the hallway. Mal ran past him and jumped on me for her greeting. I gave her a pat on the head and a scratch behind the ear. "Is everything okay?"

"The whole of Main Street is overrun with zombies," he stated grumpily. "But that's beside the point. Frances is spending the night with Maggs. It was a horrible shock for her to lose her son like that. I promised Frances I'd check on you and the McMurphy since it happened so close." He paused and watched me pick up the crate and move out into the lobby. "It sounds like the Wild West out there."

"Thanks for letting me know," I said. "The McMurphy is locked up tight, so you can go home."

"You sure?"

"I'm sure," I said. "I have to go up and change and then give my first cat bath. Unless you want to?"

He looked slightly terrified. "I believe I'll be heading out. Glad you ended up getting the security system and the new locks. Frances and I don't like the fact that a murder happened so close."

"We had a murder inside the McMurphy," I said. "Remember?"

"Not on my watch," he grumbled.

"True," I said with a smile. "Not since you were here. Hey, before you go, tomorrow I've got a meeting with the historic committee to get the permits for the rooftop deck."

"So you have the money?"

"We made more than I thought this season."

"Remind me to ask for a raise," he said, tugging on his coat.

"You might want to go out the back," I said. "There are a lot of zombies hungry for brains out there."

"Good thing I carry my zombie spray," he said as he left. Mr. Devaney was mostly gruff and rarely had a comeback, but when he did, it always made me smile. I locked the front door behind him and caught my reflection in the glass. I was one sad-looking pinup.

The crowd outside was rowdy, but they weren't interested in the hotel since we didn't have a restaurant or bar inside. The people partying on the streets must not know that a crime had happened so close. I had a feeling the police presence got bumped up, though. It was going to be a long night for the Mackinac Island police force.

The McMurphy was quiet. I ensured the lobby was all closed up. Had it really been only five months since I moved in to the old building in May? This past summer was supposed be my first season working in the hotel's fudge shop with Papa Liam, but he died before I was able to work with him, leaving me to learn the ropes on my own. The thought of my beloved Papa's death made my chest constrict. It still hurt so much to have lost him. I can't imagine what it must be like to lose your child.

I turned off the light in the fudge shop, leaving only a soft glow through the window from the street-lights outside.

Pride filled me as I looked over the fudge shop once more. The McMurphy had changed a lot since I had taken over. I had enclosed the shop in glass so that people could watch the fudge being made, but I still wouldn't have to worry about my pets getting hurt from hot sugar. I knew from experience how badly it could burn.

Across from the fudge shop was a small sitting area with free Wi-Fi. I thought that it might bring people in to rest or work and enjoy the smell of the fudge and the view of the people walking past the front windows. Before the season had started, I pulled up the old flowered carpets and refinished the wood floors. The walls of the big lobby were covered in pink-and-white striped wallpaper that I matched to a piece of the original that I'd found in the attic. Behind the sitting area was the reception desk, where Frances usually sat when she wasn't helping with room turnover and cleanup.

The hotel used to have old-fashioned room keys hanging from hooks behind the desk, but the locks had gotten a bit tricky, so those keys were now for decoration only. Instead, we had the very latest in room keycards. Even the front door was now unlocked with keycards. Across from the receptionist desk and behind the fudge shop, the coffee bar by the group of settees was another new addition. We made it fresh every hour until 9 P.M. With it being this late, Mr. Devaney had shut it all off and cleaned it up a couple of hours ago now.

At the very back of the lobby, a double staircase rose on either side of the old-fashioned, open-gated elevator to take guests up to the second and third floors.

Mal followed me around as I turned down the lights, leaving only the lowest of lights meant to guide patrons up the stairs to their rooms. October was the off-season, and I currently had only five rooms filled. That meant it was extra quiet. I picked Mella's carrier back up, and the three of us went up to the fourth floor, where my office and apartment were. I unlocked the two locks on the apartment, flicked on the light, and locked the door behind me. I hated to think that I needed so much protection, here on Mackinac Island, after all I'd been through, but it was best to keep things locked.

I put down the carrier and pulled Mella out. She protested a bit, so I didn't let her go right away. Mal ran around my legs, excited that the cat was back. I wasn't looking forward to it, but I needed to drop everything to give Mella a bath. There was no way I was going to let her get away with licking blood off or trailing it through the apartment.

Thirty minutes later, I had a clean cat sulking in the closet. I took a shower and cleaned off the zombie makeup that Frances had so carefully applied hours earlier. I was a bit sad that I missed the Walking Red zombie walk, but at least I was home safe. Still, the second bedroom, now empty of Jenn and the vibrancy she had brought when she stayed with me this summer, left the apartment strangely dark and quiet.

I was almost ready for bed when I got a text from Rex. *Are you up?*

Yes, I texted back. *Just got out of the shower.*

It can wait until morning.

I looked at the time—past midnight. *It is morning. What do you need?*

There was a pause. *Just thinking about you,* he texted. *I liked your zombie outfit.*

I smiled and curled up on my bed with Mal beside me. *Thanks.*

Don't find any more dead bodies, okay?

You keep saying that!

You keep not listening.

It's certainly not intentional.

Good night, Allie.

I slipped down into the covers, happy to have my pets surrounding me. October was my favorite time of year. I usually loved all the ghosts and witches and zombies. Now the fun will be forever marred by the memory of Maggs's face when she saw her son with his head bashed in.

Chapter 3

The next morning was a Sunday, and I was up early making fudge. With fewer crowds than summer, it was a great time to experiment. Today's experiment was apple pecan fudge with cinnamon chips inside.

At 5 A.M., there were still a few zombie stragglers on the street. I waved at them when they stopped to watch me work the fudge. The fudge shop portion of the McMurphy was built to show off fudge making to people outside, so the windows to Main Street were large and clear. I cooked the candy in a big copper pot in one corner of the shop, then carried it over to the cool marble table near the windows. The hardest part about making fudge by myself was lifting the heavy pot. I'd gotten stronger this past season, though, and I hefted it up on the table like the pro that I was, spilling the candy onto the buttered surface.

Next, I scraped out the pot and put it into the deep, stainless steel sink so I could wash it. This gave the liquid fudge time to cool a tiny bit. After that came the long-handled scraper that I used to mix the fudge and beat air into it. It was a repeated scrape and pour, scrape and pour motion that was as familiar to me as the back of my hand. I grew up watching my grandfather turn fudge, and I had learned to do the same, working the fudge demonstrations as a high schooler on the island during summer vacations.

As the fudge began to solidify, I sprinkled on the cinnamon chips and the nuts and, using a short-handled scraper, folded them into the fudge. Then I carefully cut one-pound pieces and added them to the candy tray that goes in the counter. Finally, I cut a small piece for myself as a sample. It turned out pretty well, I thought. I wiped my hands on a towel I had hanging from my waist and noticed that the zombies had all gone, leaving Main Street dark and empty.

I worked through three more batches so that I had four total trays of fudge ready for the tourists who would come in by ferry. Saturday and Sunday were the busy days now that it was off-season, and I expected to see all my guests leave this afternoon. I didn't mind the down time, though. It gave me time to work on the proposed roof deck and to plan out next year's promotions.

I washed up and headed back into the lobby, leaving the glass door to the fudge shop closed behind me. Mal climbed out of the dog bed that we kept by the receptionist desk. She stretched and padded up to me, wagging her stump of a tail. "I bet you want to go for a walk," I said, taking my apron off and hanging it up on the pegs by the door. I put Mal into her halter and leash and stepped out into the chill morning air.

There had been no sign of Mella this morning. I think she was still mad at me for giving her a bath last night. My pup made straight for her regular grassy patch with no worries, but I glanced down the alley. The crime scene was four blocks away, and even from this distance I could make out the yellow tape that cordoned off the area. It was too early to call Frances and see how Maggs was doing.

I was beat. Four hours of sleep did not sit well with me. I was used to going to bed by 9 P.M. and up by 5 A.M. Nothing like a murder to mess with your routine.

I turned and walked down the alley in the opposite direction. It opened up into parallel streets. Mal and I took the street down a block to Main and walked out toward the shore.

The wind off the straits rustled the brilliant orange and red leaves. Not many people were out yet today. An early morning jogger passed by. He clearly hadn't been out all night partying as a zombie. There were a few boats out on the water, too. Fishermen never seemed to need to sleep.

"Hey, Allie." I turned to see Mrs. Tunisian biking toward me from the alley. Mrs. T was one of several senior citizens who kept me informed of the latest gossip. Truthfully, any sleuthing I did always included the seniors. They seemed to know everything that went on.

"Mrs. Tunisian, good morning. Are you out biking by yourself?"

"Yes. I was supposed to go with Mary, but she isn't feeling well. There was no way I was going to let that stop me."

"But there's been a murder," I said. "It's not safe to be out alone."

"You're out alone," she pointed out as she stopped and got off her bike.

"I'm not alone," I said. "I've got Mal." I gestured toward my pup, who was already greeting Mrs. Tunisian.

"Ah, the famous body finder," Mrs. T said, bending down to pat Mal's head with her free hand. "Did she find the latest dead person?"

"No," I said. "This time it was Mella, my cat."

"Ah, so both of your pets are involved in detective work."

"I suppose that's true. I should put out a shingle on my door that says 'Pet detectives inside.'"

Mrs. Tunisian chuckled.

"On a more serious note, we are pretty sure the dead man is Anthony Vanderbilt."

"Oh, no. Maggs's boy?" Her expression was stricken. "That's horrifying. How did it happen?"

"I'm not sure," I said. "It was dark. Liz and I were walking from Doud's to the McMurphy when we found Mella. The poor cat was covered in blood. Then we heard a scream—it was Sophie. We ran to her and found the body. Mella's footprints were all around him."

"That's horrible," Mrs. Tunisian said. She was a shorter woman with steel-gray hair, which she wore pulled back from her face. Today, she was wearing a corduroy jacket, a flannel shirt, and pair of jeans.

"We called 9-1-1 right away. Then Maggs came out into the alleyway and recognized the victim as her son Anthony. It was awful."

"Poor dear, is she home now? Is anyone with her?"

"Frances took her home and spent the night with her. It was quite a shock."

"I bet it was," Mrs. Tunisian said, her expression grim. "I've got to go tell the ladies. They need to know so we can start the food brigade."

"Food brigade?"

"Whenever anyone dies or is seriously ill, we all take turns cooking for the victim's family. Maggs may not want to eat for a few weeks, but we will continue to cook and bring her food. That way, Frances can push her to take a few bites. Keeping your strength up is important when you're faced with tragedy. Any idea when the funeral is?"

"No," I said. "I don't think they will release the body for a few days. I know they wanted to do an autopsy and collect as much evidence as possible. Until they do that, there's nothing Maggs can do."

"Poor Maggs," Mrs. Tunisian shook her head. "She was supposed to help out at the art fair today."

"Oh, I nearly forgot about that."

"Don't forget," Mrs. Tunisian said with warning in her voice. "It's one of the best things about Mackinac in the fall. The art fair brings artists from all walks of life. Frances tells me you will be redecorating the guest rooms at the McMurphy soon."

"I hope to, yes."

"Then you have to come to the fair. I bet you can get some very good, original Mackinac Island art for the rooms. We have many plein air artists who paint with watercolors and acrylics. Plus, it's good for the local economy."

"Sounds wonderful," I said. "I'll make sure I'm there. You said that Maggs was supposed to help. With her and Frances out, do you need me to step in?"

"Would you? That would be great. Come by at one. Stop at the information booth and tell them you're a volunteer."

"Great, I'll see you then."

Mrs. Tunisian got back on her bike and pushed off

down the alley toward Market Street. I watched her go, thinking that if I were a better person, I'd be on a regular exercise program like hers. But I was too busy doing the things I loved—creating new fudges, growing the McMurphy, and becoming a part of the island community. I gave Mal a scratch behind her ear. At least I had to take her on regular walks.

Rex stopped by the McMurphy at 10 A.M. I had a few guests checking out when he arrived. With Frances out taking care of Maggs, I had to handle the checkout process. Sandy Everheart, my friend and resident chocolatier, was using the fudge shop to make small chocolate sculptures for the art fair. She had been creating miniature pieces for the past week to display and sell at her booth at the fair.

Sandy had studied in New York, and she was crazy good at making chocolate miniature versions of animals, buildings, and whatever object you could think of. The only reason she worked in my fudge shop instead of for some fancy chocolatier in a big city was because she had returned to Mackinac Island during the summer to take care of her grandmother. All of the other local places had hired for the season but, lucky for me, I still had my "help wanted" sign out. Once I realized how good she was, I knew I couldn't pay her what she was worth. So I offered her time in my kitchen to run her own business. It had worked out very well for us both so far.

"Allie, do you have a minute?" Rex asked. While I finished up with the guests, he had stepped to the side and taken off his hat, tucking it under his arm.

"Sure," I said. "Mr. Devaney, can you watch the front desk?"

"Watch the front desk, repair the squeaky door, unclog a toilet . . . sure," he said. "Seems I'm more than a handyman."

I shook my head. "Let's go up to my office," I said to Rex. "I'm sure you're looking for a statement from yesterday?"

"Yes," he said as he followed me up the stairs.

"Does Shane need my costume for evidence?"

"If you have it handy, I'll take it, but he hasn't asked for it yet."

"I bagged it last night and put it in my office. I figured you'd be coming by." My office was on the fourth floor, near my apartment. File cabinets and bookshelves covered the office walls. My laptop computer sat on one of the two heavy oak desks that faced each other in the center of the room. The other was sadly empty. It had been Papa Liam's desk before he died, and then Jenn's while she was here. I tried to ignore the sad pang in my heart.

"Please have a seat," I said, waving toward the extra desk chair. "What do you want to know?"

He pulled out a small notepad and pen. "Let's go over last night, step by step."

I told him everything, from going to Doud's for a zombie outfit for Mal to finding Mella covered in blood and then seeing Anthony crumpled on the ground. "His head was bashed in."

"Yes, but we haven't released that detail," Rex said.

"I haven't said anything to anyone about that," I said. "I saw Mrs. Tunisian this morning when I was walking Mal. I told her about Anthony and Maggs, but I didn't say anything about cause of death—other than I doubted it was natural."

"Good," he said with a short nod.

"Were you able to determine anything else?"

"Blunt force trauma," he said. "Most likely from a bat or pipe. So, you know Maggs Vanderbilt well?"

"Yes, she's Frances's best friend. We see her quite a bit."

"Did she give you any reason why someone would want to hurt Anthony?"

"No." I shook my head. "I have no clue. All I really know about Anthony is that he was Maggs's son and in his early thirties."

"He grew up on the island," Rex said, filling me in. "He was star quarterback on the football team and worked as bartender for the Nag's Head Bar and Grill for a short time after high school, then worked through college. Best I can tell, he was well liked."

"Did he have a wife or children?" I asked. I cringed at the thought of little kids losing their father.

"No, he was single," Rex said. "Although it was rumored he had a new girlfriend. Maggs couldn't tell me who it was."

"Bashed in the head means a fight of some kind, right? Maybe he was mugged. Did you find his wallet? His phone?"

"It didn't look like a mugging," Rex said. He frowned. "We don't have those on the island."

"Wait. With all the tourists, you never get a complaint of pickpockets?"

"Careful, your fudgie is showing," he said softly, smiling. *Fudgie* is the name islanders warmly call the tourists who venture here for fudge. "Clearly, you've lived in the city too long. This is a small town.

A mugger couldn't get off the island without someone knowing something."

I crossed my arms. "So you're telling me that there has never been a robbery? I've seen several murders, but there are no robberies?"

"I didn't say we didn't have the occasional miscreant. I do have a job on the island, after all. What I'm saying is that this community is a big family. And it's unusual for a mugging."

"That means it was probably someone Anthony knew who killed him."

"I'm checking into that," he said, sitting back. "How is the new security system working?"

"Fine," I said with a casual wave of my hand. "So far, I've caught a few bats and Mrs. Johnson's cat on camera."

"Good," he said. "Have you heard from Jessop lately?"

"Trent? No," I said with a shake of my head. "His mother's keeping him and Paige close. That last adventure was a final straw, as far as she's concerned. As far as I know, it will be next spring before we see any of the Jessops."

"I wouldn't let my mother get between me and the woman I love," he said softly.

"That's easy for you to say. Your mother isn't alive."

"No," he said with regret. He stood up. "But I still wouldn't do it."

I stood, too, and walked him to the office door. "You never did get to finish making me dinner."

He lifted one corner of his mouth into a half-smile. "I'm waiting for the crime rate to go down. The next time I have you over, I don't want anything to interrupt us."

"Let's hope this is the last body I find."

"I couldn't agree more."

I arrived at the art fair fifteen minutes early, leaving Mr. Devaney with front desk duty. I'd sold most of this morning's candy already, so we closed the fudge shop before I left. I'd also stripped sheets and towels from the rooms that had been vacated. No one was coming in until next weekend so I could take my time cleaning them out, but it didn't hurt to get a head start.

Having completed most of the hotel work, I dressed in a simple, floral maxi dress with a cropped cardigan. I added hoop earrings to the ensemble in the hope that I would look a little creative, since I was working the art fair.

"Hello, I'm here to volunteer," I said when I stepped up to the information booth. Mrs. Oslow was checking people in

"Great," she said. "Yes, I see Mrs. Tunisian has created a badge for you. Please wear it so customers know that you're working."

I took the badge and lanyard and put it on over my head. "So what do you need me to do?"

"Go around the booths and find out if anyone has any questions or needs any help. Here's a walkie-talkie." She handed me the small plastic radio. "If you don't know the answer to a question, just call over. Here's a pamphlet with all the booth names and a map. Make sure all of the artists are setting up in the right spots. Also, take this wagon with water bottles. Each exhibitor gets two bottles of water. Any questions?"

"Not yet," I said.

"Good, now go. Start at the far end and work your way back here. The people closest to this booth are more likely to pop up here with questions."

"Got it." I grabbed the handle of the little red wagon filled with ice and water bottles and headed across the lawn. The fair was set up on the wide park lawn at the foot of Fort Mackinac. The island had been a stronghold for first the Americans and then the British during the War of 1812. During the summer season, reenactors played the part of soldiers from both sides every day. They fired the cannons at the fort on the hour. I had grown quite used to the sound. It didn't even seem to bother Mal anymore.

This time of year, the fort was closed except for the weekends. Today, the flags flew and whipped in the air. The fort was built on a bluff and rose high above the front of the lawn. People climbed the sloping entranceway to go inside and visit the tea shop and museums. Some of them would stop by the art fair on their way back, once everyone was set up.

The art fair had twenty booths. Most of them had canopies to keep the artwork protected from the weather, although today was sunny so far. I walked through the bustle of setup to the far booths and carefully stopped by each one, handing out water bottles and lending a hand when needed.

At one booth, Max Avery's watercolors of scenes from the island included the fort, the marina, Main Street, and pictures of the Grand Hotel and the new Grander Hotel.

"Wow, these are gorgeous," I said.

"Thanks," Max's wife, Ann, said. "Max has been

working on these for years. I think he's perfected his technique."

"You aren't asking too much for them," I said, checking the price tags. "I may be looking for something like this for my guest rooms."

"People love to see these scenes, especially once they visit," Ann said.

"Hmm. If you want, maybe I could hang them in the rooms and offer them for sale," I suggested. "They really are quite good."

"I'll have to ask Max," she said. "But I think he'll like that idea. It would be good exposure." She handed me his business card.

"You know where to find me. I'm at the McMurphy."

"I know. I adore Frances Devaney. I'll ask Max to stop by and at least look at your renovation ideas."

"Great," I said. I handed her two waters. "Let me know if you need any help or have questions about setup."

The next two booths were fiber arts—vintage patterns and contemporary subjects. The booth after that held beautiful pottery with melted glass in the bottom. I couldn't help but pick up a piece to get a better look at the glass.

"Do you like those?" The voice belonged to a lovely young woman with rosy cheeks and long blond hair in a thick braid down her back. Her cornflower-blue eyes sparkled in the afternoon sun. With her denim jacket, white tee shirt, and long denim skirt, she had a Western look.

"I love pottery," I said. "I always have. You can feel the energy of the potter when you touch them. The textures are so incredible."

"That bowl you have is one of my favorite pieces," she said, sticking out her hand. "I'm Haley Manx."

"Allie McMurphy," I said, shaking her hand.

"Ah, the famous fudge maker turned sleuth. I've heard a lot about you."

I winced a bit at the description. "I hope what you've heard is all good. I'm actually a lot more of a fudge maker and hotelier than I am a sleuth. It's been a strange few months. I take it you're local?"

"Yes, I am."

"Oh, boy. I'm sorry I haven't met you before now."

She looked like an elf when she smiled. "It's okay. I spend the summer moving from fair to fair selling my pieces. I'm around more in the winter. I teach at the high school. So I know you, but I'm easy to miss."

"Oh, then I feel a bit better. What do you teach?"

"I teach art, of course. I've been working on pottery for at least ten years."

"Well, these are perfect," I said. "I'd love to own one."

"Great," she said. "Shall I wrap it up for you?"

"Yes, please." I handed her the small bowl and got out my credit card. "I'm supposed to be helping, not shopping, but I can't help myself."

"I tell you what, you put away your credit card. I'll wrap this up and keep it for you. When your shift is over, come back and buy it then. I promise it'll still be here."

"Sounds perfect," I said. "I've got two bottles of water for you, and I'm meant to ask if you have any questions."

She put the bowl away and took the water bottles. "I do have questions," she said. "Is finding a dead body as horrible as I think it is?"

"Yes," I said sincerely. "I hope you never find one."

A man walked up to the booth and kissed Haley's cheek. "Hey, babe, are you drumming up some business?"

"Rick, this is Allie, Allie McMurphy. Allie, my husband Rick."

"Hello," I said, shaking his hand. He was tall, at least six feet, with wide shoulders and windblown, caramel-colored hair. His hands nearly engulfed mine. "I was telling Haley how lovely her pieces are."

"They should be—they cost a fortune to create."

"Well, they make up for it in happiness," Haley said.

"Are you an artist, too?" I asked Rick.

"I'm in construction," he said. "I suppose that's an art form."

"It certainly is," I said with a nod. "I had the lobby of the McMurphy renovated in May. It made a huge difference. I have plans to renovate the guest rooms next."

"I work mostly on roofs and structural things," he said.

"Oh, good to know," I said. "I'm trying to get permits to create a rooftop deck. Since the McMurphy is on Main Street, it does have a flat roof, but it's simply not structurally sound enough for a deck right now."

"I'll send my boss your way," he said. "I work for Faber Roofing."

"Oh, yes, I had Elmer come and do an initial inspection. He's one of the guys who are giving me a quote."

"Good," Rick said. "It'd be nice to have some work before the snow comes."

I looked at my watch. It was getting closer to the time the art fair was scheduled to open. "I better keep moving," I said. "It was nice to meet both of you. I'll be back later for my bowl."

The next booth was contemporary oil paints. Betsy Shaw was at the one after that. She did a lot of inking and calligraphy. I studied the handwritten signs that said "Best Friends" and "Live, Love, Laugh."

"Hi," Betsy said. She was an older woman with strong facial features and steel-gray hair. "Allie, isn't it?"

"Yes." I reached down and gathered her water bottles. "It's Betsy, right? I think we met at one of the senior center events."

She took the water. "Yes, that's right. How are you?"

"I'm good."

"I heard you found another body last night."

"Terrible," I said with a shake of my head.

"Is it really Margaret Vanderbilt's son?"

"I believe so," I said. "She identified him."

"Whoever did that should be shot. He was a good boy. Doted on Maggs, and she doted on him. You aren't supposed to outlive your baby, you know?"

"I know, I'm heartbroken for her," I said. "Frances is staying with Maggs for a while."

"Well, I certainly hope you will help figure out who the killer is. A thing like that just isn't right." She shook her head.

"Do you have any questions about setup? Anything else I can help you with?"

"Oh, no, dear. You go on now," she said, waving me on. "I'm going to be doing demonstrations. Draw them in, maybe teach one or two the art."

Five more booths brought me back to center and the information tent, where I refilled my wagon. The crowds had started arriving off the docks. The sky was the crisp, clear blue of fall. The flags above the fort snapped in the wind. I wished I could have brought Mal. She would have loved the crowds and the attention from all the tourists. But I volunteered to work, and you didn't get much work done with a pup getting all the attention.

The rest of the art fair booths were well in hand by the time I arrived to pass out water. I answered a few questions and said hello to some of the people I knew from the summer season. Mackinac Island was a real art colony. Many of the artists lived on the island at least half of the year.

I got a few more cards for artists whose work I might feature in my renovated rooms. My plans firmed up with each artist I talked to. I could do each room around a different artist and offer their art for sale. Several of them seemed to love the idea. Finally, after my two hours of volunteer time were up, I went back to collect my pottery bowl.

My own apartment at the hotel was filled with things that had belonged to my grandparents. I loved having their things around me, but it didn't give me much room for my own things. I thought the little bowl would make a great candy dish on my office desk. Perhaps I could entice people to come up to my office and visit. Ever since Jenn had left and I had broken up with Trent, there weren't a lot of reasons for people to visit. Even Frances and Mr. Devaney didn't stick around for drinks or dinner anymore. I guess I didn't blame them. They were newlyweds, after all.

Perhaps the excitement of being new to the island and the rush of the summer season had finally worn off.

Haley saw me walking up and reached to get my
bowl. She had wrapped it in paper and put it inside a
pretty, patterned blue bag. I handed her my credit
card to process. "Thanks for saving this for me."

"I'm sure you're going to enjoy it." She gave me
back my card, and I signed the receipt before picking
up the bag. "You know, I offer pottery classes at the
senior center. You should think about signing up."

"Me? No, I'm not an artist."

"I beg to differ," she said, leaning against the table
where she wrapped up her goods. "I saw the way you
handled that bowl. You might actually be good at
slinging mud—that's what I like to call making pottery. It's soothing to the soul."

"As long as I'm not expected to do more than coil
clay, I might give it a shot."

"I think you'll be surprised," she said. She crossed
her arms. "You should free your inner artist. I know
that fudge making is an art, too, and sometimes when
we make art our work, it's good to switch to other
forms."

"I'll keep that in mind," I said. "Thank you."

"My pleasure."

An elderly couple walked up and started talking to
Haley about her work. I walked down the busy lawn
that separated the booths. Maybe it wouldn't hurt to
take a pottery class. It could be a good way to meet
more people. Maybe then I wouldn't be so lonely.

Chapter 4

"I need to talk to you," Sandy said when I entered the McMurphy.

"Sure." I took off my jacket and hung it on the pegs by the back door. I brought in my package and pulled the little bowl out of the bag. "I thought you had a booth at the art fair."

"I did, but I sold out early. I have pictures up as sample work, so I left my mother there to take orders. I thought it was important to talk with you right away."

"What do you want to talk about?"

"I've been offered the position of head pastry chef at the new Grander Hotel for next season," she said.

"Oh." I put the bowl down on the receptionist desk and turned toward Sandy. Her face didn't reveal any expression so it was hard to tell what she was thinking. "Are you excited?"

"It was what I was hoping for when I went to school to study pastry and candy making."

"Will you be able to make your chocolate centerpieces?"

"The manager, Roy Williams, told me that I would

be able to keep my business going. I could even schedule time off to work on pieces for local events. Roy saw my work this summer and thought I'd be perfect for when they host weddings and special events."

"You would be perfect," I said. I tried not to let my disappointment show on my face. "Are you going to take it?"

"I told him I'd think about it. The pay is nearly double."

"Of course," I said. "I always knew I couldn't pay what you're worth. I know he said you could keep it, but would you have time to expand your business?"

She shrugged. "I would most likely have to give it up. But people would buy from the hotel."

"It sounds like a good opportunity," I said, trying to remain positive. "That kind of money would help your grandma, and having a place like the Grander Hotel on your résumé wouldn't hurt."

She eyed me with a tilt of her head. "Are you okay with it?"

"If that is what you want," I said, hugging my waist. "I want you to be happy. I really appreciate you and all that you do to help. The McMurphy won't be the same without you, though."

"So you don't want me to take it?"

"I . . . I want what's best for you."

"I'll think about it," she said, turning on her heel and heading off into the fudge shop. I didn't know what I had thought would happen in the off-season. But I felt as if I was losing all my friends.

I spent the rest of the day cleaning up the rooms that guests had checked out from. I didn't replace the sheets, as I would be closing rooms on the second floor for remodeling soon. I had one guest staying on the third flood this week. That left a lot of time and space to plot and plan.

Frances came in toward evening. "I came to check on you," she said as she entered my office.

I was busy paying bills.

"How's Maggs?"

Frances sat down in Jenn's chair. "She's hurting pretty badly. I can't imagine what it's like to lose your baby like that."

"Do you need more time off?"

"No, Maggs's sister Anne came up from Lansing. I'm going to go home to Douglas and take a nice hot bath. I'll be back in the morning."

"Okay." I sighed. Mal got up from the dog bed beside me and put her paws on my thigh, as if she knew I needed a reminder that I haven't lost all of my friends.

"You sound blue," Frances said. "Are you doing okay?"

"Yes, sure," I said. "It's just that sometimes Papa's death weighs heavily on me. It was supposed to be him and me together for a few years, you know?"

"Yes, I know," she said, putting her hand on mine. "But you're doing so well by yourself. Liam must be so proud."

"He's probably too busy running around meeting as many famous people as he can while he's up there."

"No, I think he's looking down on you. I swear it's how you've remained safe during most of the awful adventures you've had this season."

"They have been awful, haven't they?" I picked up Mal, petting her for a few moments in silence. "Do you know Haley Manx?"

"She's a potter, right?"

"One and the same," I said with a nod. "She said

she gives pottery classes. I was thinking I should go and try my hand at making a bowl."

"You should go," Frances agreed. "It would do you good. When's the class?"

"I don't know," I said. "I'll check the website to see what's scheduled. I think she gives them at the senior center."

"You know, you're too young to be hanging out at the senior center as much as you do. You should try the church hall. There are lots of classes and friends to be made there."

"That's a thought," I said. "What else goes on during the off-season? I mean, besides snowmobiling and the Santa fun run?"

"It's very laid-back here in the winter. I usually only go out to get groceries. Otherwise, it's puzzles and books—lots of books. I'm glad the library gets regular shipments. I must have read almost every book in there. Douglas gave me an e-book reader on our honeymoon. There are thousands of books you can download and read, all on one handy little tablet."

"I'll try to remember that. Listen, before you go, I've got an appointment with the permit office to start the second-floor room remodel."

"Oh, good. Do you know what themes you're going to decorate with?"

"Well, I spent a couple of hours today volunteering at the art fair, and I got the great idea to highlight local artists. Let them put paintings and such in the rooms, and offer them for sale. I wouldn't take a commission."

"Why not? I think that's a great idea," Frances said. "You know, it's really too bad you didn't get out and do that Walking Red zombie walk. You were very cute in your pinup girl outfit."

"Thanks?" I said, slightly bemused. Frances was a dear, but she rarely commented on what I wear.

"Don't look at me that way. I just think you don't get out enough."

"Well, Trent and I broke up, and Jenn's in Chicago—"

"All silly excuses," Frances said. "Rex is right here, you know. Plus, there're a lot more men on the island than women—especially in the off-season. You're young and lovely. You should be having the time of your life, not staying holed up in a hotel kitchen making fudge."

"But making fudge is having the time of my life," I teased.

"You should have beaus left and right," she said.

"You just want me to fall in love because you're in love."

"Well, maybe a little bit," she said with a shy smile. "But I know we aren't spending as much time with you like we used to, and you shouldn't be alone."

"I'm fine," I said. "Really. I have Mal and Carmella and the McMurphy."

"All that is not enough for a young woman."

"Well, I'm not really the bar-going, party-girl type," I said with a shrug. "I guess I'm more of an introvert. Jenn's better at socializing. I always feel strange walking into a bar by myself, and I'm horrible at pool and darts." I shrugged again. "We all know I can't play chess. Is there something I'm missing? A card club, or something that isn't tied to the senior center?"

"Oh, dear," Frances said. "Yes, I guess I see the problem. Maybe I can fix that."

"No, no," I said, raising my hand to stop her. "I'm fine. Really. I don't need any matchmaking."

"We'll see about that," Frances said.

"Changing the subject back to business," I said. "I've got the permits to make the room updates, so starting Monday, I want to rope off the second floor and put all guests on the third. Once the second floor is done with fresh paint and fresh flooring, then we'll start on the third."

"What about the rooftop deck?"

"I've got a meeting with the historical society today."

"On Sunday?"

"Yes, they meet Sunday afternoons. I think it's more of a social club than a quote-unquote 'society.' They're having a tea this afternoon with a speaker on the War of 1812."

"And you'll get your approvals at this tea?"

"At the meeting before the tea," I said. "It's sort of a formality. I've presented all the plans and gathered all the permits. I just need the mayor and the society to bless it, and then I can schedule out the work."

"We need to get that work done before the snow flies," Frances warned. "Once it freezes, there will be little they can do to the roof until next year."

"Well now, see, that's the beauty of the roof deck," I said. "It's all about reinforcing the studs, and those can be done from underneath, through the attic. The roof itself is covered in rolled asphalt for now. Once the structural work is done, we can wait until spring to have them refinish the roof with wood planks and then stain it. And as far as the historical society is concerned, there will be no change to the front of the building and no change to the look of Main Street. It's not like the lobby remodel, where they had to approve colors and such. No one will see the deck unless they're up on the roof."

"Sounds like a good plan," Frances said. "Are you prepared to have workmen coming and going through your home during the day to work in the attic? After all, you sealed off all of the entrances other than the one in your apartment."

"I'm certainly not looking forward to it, but the chance to offer rooftop events is worth it. Don't you think?"

"I think it's a novel idea. Lots of people would love the view, certainly. I can attest to how lovely it is. I'm just worried you might be in over your head with such a project."

"I've got some good contractor quotes. I've actually decided which one I want to go with," I said. "I had a structural engineer out here and he drew up the plans. It will be fine."

"I know it will," she said, patting my forearm comfortingly. "I just was playing devil's advocate. Asking all the questions Liam would have asked." She hesitated, then said, "I heard that Sandy got an offer from the Grander Hotel."

"Yes," I said, trying not to sound upset. "I can't match the salary—even if I didn't spend money on the remodel."

"I know."

"I can only be happy to see her getting such a good job. Think about all the things she could do to take care of her family."

"She does have a large family."

"I worry that it will take away from all the work she did building her own business this summer, though," I said.

"Did she express any hesitation over that?"

"No," I said with a shrug. "But it's tough to really get a good read on Sandy's emotions. You know that." I paused a moment. "I guess I'll be looking for a new assistant next spring." I winced. "Mostly I'm going to miss her company, and all of her family members who come in and help. Especially with Jenn gone, too."

Frances patted my arm. "Life is full of changes," she said. "Look at everything you've done since you arrived in May."

"I thought I was building a family," I said. "Now they're scattering to the four corners."

"That's what families do," Frances said. She stepped back around the reception desk and looked through the mail. "Fall is a good time to regroup before the harsh winter. It probably is the best time to do your roof repair."

"Speaking of which, I have to go. I'll let you know how the approvals go." I hurried up the three flights of stairs to my apartment and changed quickly. I petted Mal, gave her a treat, and grabbed my purse. Time to find out if the mayor was going to help me with the permits. Mella showed herself for the first time today and slipped outside with me onto the staircase that led from my apartment at the back of the hotel down to the alleyway below. It had been twenty-four hours since we found the body, so it was probably safe for her to play outside again. After all, she was originally an outdoor cat who adopted me and allowed herself to be brought inside. I supposed it couldn't hurt to let her go visit her animal friends who lived near the McMurphy. I left her on the landing at the top of the stairs, calmly licking a paw.

DARK CHOCOLATE CINNAMON FUDGE

1 (14-ounce) can sweetened condensed milk
2 cups dark chocolate chips
1 teaspoon vanilla
1 cup cinnamon chips for a milder flavor
    or Red Hots to make it spicy

Put sweetened condensed milk and chocolate chips in a microwavable bowl. Microwave on high for one minute, then remove and let it sit for one minute before stirring until chips are completely melted and chocolate is smooth. (It might take another 30 seconds of microwaving, depending on your unit).

Add vanilla and mix until combined. Add cinnamon chips or Red Hots, stir, and pour or pat into a buttered, parchment-lined, 8-inch pan. Score into ½-inch chunks. Place in refrigerator until completely cool. Once cool, remove from pan, cut along scored lines, and serve. Leftovers should be kept in a covered container in a cool place.

Makes about 32 pieces of fudge.

Chapter 5

"Congratulations!" Frances said.

"Let's celebrate now." Mr. Devaney opened up a bottle of champagne. "But not again until the work is finished," he added sternly.

"Okay," I said. I opened a cupboard in my apartment's kitchen and took down several glasses for him to fill. I had managed to secure the permits needed to create the rooftop deck. When Mr. Devaney handed me a now full glass, I lifted it into the air with a grin. "This is one small step for me, and one giant step for the McMurphy hotel!"

"Here, here," Frances and Douglas both said, and we all sipped champagne. I wore a sundress, but I had taken my dress shoes off at the door.

"Have some crackers and cheese." I urged them to eat from the party tray I'd picked up at Doud's Market on my way home from the historical society's tea. The salty pepperoni and cheeses looked appealing after an afternoon of cake and cookies.

Mella thought so, too. She had come in from the alley and now sat on the counter, eyeing the platter. I picked her up and put her on the floor. Mal barked with joy and chased Mella up her cat tree. Mella sat in the top carpeted box and twitched her tail at Mal, who looked excited to have gotten the cat's attention.

"You know, if you played with her for a bit, she might leave you alone," I said to the cat.

"Cats are solitary creatures by nature," Frances said. "Although I once had a cat who would greet you at the door like a dog does."

"This one has a mind of her own," Mr. Devaney said. He walked over to stroke Mella's fur. The cat liked the old man and didn't make a fuss over his attention. "I heard she's the one who found poor Anthony last night."

"She did," I said. "She wasn't happy with Shane when he collected evidence—or with the bath I had to give her."

"She's pretty smart," Mr. Devaney said. "I'd bet you anything she'll figure out who the killer is."

"I won't take that bet," I said. "You never know with my pets. But I hope she's not going to be doing as much roaming for a while. I really worry that my fur babies will end up on the wrong side of a criminal. I need to keep them safe."

"We should go," Frances said. "But we'll be back to help in the morning. Congrats again on getting the permits." She hugged me and gave me a kiss on the cheek. I knew they were itching to be home and enjoying their Sunday evening as newlyweds. It was kind of them to come up for champagne.

"Congrats," Mr. Devaney said. "You realize you just made my job harder, right?"

"I'm sure you can handle it." I closed and locked the door behind them. I was going to get my rooftop deck. Money was going to be a bit tight, but I was certain it would all be worth it in the end. I cleaned up the kitchen and texted Jenn to share the good news.

She answered with *Congrats!* When she didn't text more, I knew she must be busy with something for her new job. So I poured the final glass of champagne and sat on the couch with my pets beside me and toasted to myself. One thing was for sure: People would come and go, but my fur babies would never leave me.

There was a knock on my back door. It was Liz. "Hey," I said as I opened the door. "Come on in."

"I was going to text you," she said as she came in, carrying a tablet computer. "But then I thought, what the heck? I'd just see if you were home." She glanced at my glass of champagne. "Are you busy?"

"No, come on in." I opened the door wide. "Frances and Mr. Devaney just left. This is the last of the champagne, but I have a nice cabernet. Can I get you some?"

"That would be great," she said. She walked through the kitchen into the living room and greeted Mal with a few pats on the head. "I'm sorry, I should have called first. I guess I got excited and ended up here. Why the champagne?"

"I was able to get the permits to start work on the rooftop deck." I poured her a glass of cabernet sauvignon and handed it to her, waving for her to sit. "It was a nice win, especially considering the mayor isn't all that happy with me. I'm really glad for the company. What has you all excited? Do you have news?"

She laughed and sat down in Papa Liam's chair. "I was going over the pictures we took at the Walking Red walk, and I thought I saw our victim."

"But you were with me when we found him dead."

"Yes, but I was taking pictures for an hour before," she said, turning on her tablet. She scrolled through the pictures. There were shots of different people in costumes posing for the camera and random crowd shots as well. "See? Look at the crowd shots. Here's that suit coat he was wearing." She turned the tablet to me. I studied it.

"Yes, that looks like Anthony's suit coat. Can you tell who he was with?"

"It's hard to really tell," she said as we looked through the crowd shots. "Here he is with Justin Alders and Steve Radick. But in these shots, he seems to be with someone else."

"Stop," I said, studying the pictures. "Those are two different people."

"No, they're not," she said. She took the tablet from me and blew up the photos. "Wait. You're right. They are different. They could both be Anthony, though." She looked at me. "This one with the stranger has lighter hair. Maybe it's a trick of the light?"

"I don't think so. The two guys are with different people, too, although I'm not sure which one is Anthony," I said. "Look, this guy seems to be constantly with Justin and Steve. While this guy is with . . . is that a girl?" It looked like the second person was with someone who wanted to keep very close, and I noticed something else. "This one looks like it might be pregnant. It's hard to tell because of the zombie makeup and torn, baggy clothes. But still . . ."

"Well," Liz said. "I could see that, so maybe they are female."

"And look at this other guy in the corner of the picture," I said. "He seems very upset about Anthony and this girl. Oh, wait, it doesn't really matter."

"No?"

"No, look. I'm pretty sure this one isn't Anthony.

See? This looks like the sleeve of Anthony's coat." I pointed to a tiny spot in the picture that held a man's elbow.

She looked at it. "It could be anyone's elbow."

"No, it has a patch on it. It's like the guy in the main part of the picture, but it has a leather patch. I remember distinctly that Maggs recognized Anthony's jacket because of a leather patch."

"Right. Okay, well, let's see if we can distinguish which guy is which by the patches."

We looked through all of the pictures and put them into two categories. Finally, Liz said, "This guy, the one with the lighter hair, seems to be mostly with this woman, while Anthony is consistently with Justin and Steve. I think we need to visit with Justin and Steve."

"I agree," I said. "But not tonight. It's late. Thanks for sharing this with me."

"Sure. Before I go, though, let's plot out how we're going to talk to them."

"Okay," I said, sitting back. "In the morning, I'm going to award the roof job to a contractor. After I do that, I can go with you to visit Justin and Steve."

"Justin works at the Nag's Head," Liz said. "We can go there around 3 P.M."

"Great. What about Steve?"

"Steve and Anthony worked together at the Grander Hotel. He's a talented chef."

"Who? Anthony or Steve?"

"Steve, silly," she said. "Anthony was a lawyer. Maggs put him through law school. She used to say she was investing in her retirement."

"Oh," I said. My heart hurt for her anew. "That's

terrible. She won't have any children to ~~care~~ for her
when she's older . . . well, she's older now, but you get
my meaning."

"I think she has a niece in Green Bay, so she should
be okay when the time comes that she needs con-
stant care."

"Come to think of it, there isn't a nursing home on
the island, is there?"

"No, just the senior center. Once they need nursing
care, they usually go to family or to Traverse City."

"I don't want to think about Frances or Maggs
needing nursing care. They seem so young."

"Yes, but in ten years they'll be in their eighties.
That's prime time for nursing care."

"Speaking of, how's your grandfather?" I asked.
Liz's grandfather, Angus McElroy, had been hospital-
ized with a stroke the month before. I liked Angus. He
sometimes joked that he was nervous around me
with so many old guys turning up dead. But I think
he really liked the fact that I brought interesting news
to the paper.

"He's doing well," she said. Then she sobered a bit.
"He's not coming back to the island." She looked from
her wineglass to me. "The clinic doesn't have good
enough care."

"It must be so hard to leave him in Traverse City."

"He's with my mother." She sipped her wine. "I miss
him, though."

"Have you considered closing the paper for the
season? I think everyone would understand. You could
continue the blog from below the bridge. I could feed
you stories of what's happening on the island."

"What, and miss your first winter here?" She shook

her head with a resigned smile. "No, my place is here." She glanced around. "I hear that Sandy got a big offer from the Grander Hotel."

"She did," I said.

"How's that make you feel?"

"I don't want her to go, but I can't pay what they can. Plus, they have a richer clientele who would pay for Sandy to design centerpieces and such for their events. She could be flying into Detroit or Chicago. I can't expect her not to take the opportunity."

"So they're going to let her run her own business?"

"No, that's the only shame. When she starts working there, she won't have time."

"I wouldn't take it," Liz said, surprising me.

"What? Why not?"

"I like to own my own work. I wouldn't want to give that up. And Sandy's an artist. Artists should never sell out."

"I wish that were true, but she's supporting her grandmother and several other family members. That's hard to do on the salary I pay her."

"Maybe, but she makes quite a bit on her own."

"Yes, and pays self-employment tax—she's looking at a thirty-five percent tax rate. No, it's better to work for someone else. You don't have to worry about marketing to bring in clients, and you don't have to pay so much in taxes."

"But then the Grander Hotel will make money off of her work, and eventually her name. I still wouldn't take it. Won't you miss her?"

"I will," I said. "I'll miss her desperately. With Jenn gone, and now Sandy leaving, my connection to the community is dwindling. I missed you so much when you were gone for a whole month. I swear, if it weren't for you and Sophie, I'd be really lonely. I mean, even Frances has Mr. Devaney now. They don't have as much time for me as they used to—and I don't blame them."

"What about Trent?"

"What about him?" I asked with a shrug. "He and Paige are in Chicago for the winter. I get the occasional text, but out of sight, out of mind."

"Oh, I highly doubt that you are out of his mind. Didn't he just send flowers? Doesn't he text or call? Or are you two . . . you know."

"What?"

"Sexy texting."

"Liz!"

"Well, I had to ask. He's a handsome man and you're a pretty young woman." I made a face at her, and she paused. "Unless you have your eye on someone else."

I felt the heat of a blush rush up my cheeks. "I don't kiss and tell."

"Oh, you are so old fashioned."

"Don't laugh at me," I said. "I do still have feelings for Trent, but I can't let that get between me and my dream—and inheritance—of running the McMurphy."

"Oh my goodness, you're far too young to lock yourself away all for an old family tradition. And what about Rex? Hmm? He's right here on the island, *and* I happen to know for a fact that he likes you."

"He's been busy. A man was murdered just yesterday."

"There are a couple of other guys who have their

eye on you, too, you know. I think that Steve is one of them. You should go out on a date . . . on more than one date. The island is teeming with young guys who have families here and want to live here forever. They would be happy to help you with the McMurphy."

"Okay, not you, too! I really don't need a match-maker," I said. "Frances was in here earlier today trying to convince me that I needed to get out more. I'm fine. I'm quite busy, actually. I've got the second-floor remodel going on, and now I've got to work on plans for the roof refurbish, too. Plus, I'm ramping up the fudge marketing for the holiday online sales and pulling together next season's calendar."

"Well, aren't you quite the busy bee," Liz said with a lift of her glass. "I, on the other hand, am quite lonely now that Grandpa Angus is away. Here I was, hoping we could spend some time together doing cool Mackinac Island stuff. But if you are too busy . . ."

"Oh, for goodness sakes," I said, frowning at her. She started to laugh, the sound clear as the tone of a bell. "What?"

"I got you good," she said, lifting her glass again. "I propose that we meet on Mondays and Wednesdays for dinner. That way, we won't go stir-crazy this winter. I can teach you card games, and you can teach me . . . What can you teach me?"

"How to make fudge."

She laughed. "I don't need to learn how to make fudge. I'd rather just buy it from you. We'll work on something for you to teach me."

"I love the idea of girls' nights, though. Let's start with tomorrow. I'll make us a nice pot of chili for dinner. You can bring the cards. But I have to warn you, I do go to bed early. I like to be up at five to get the fudge started and just in case I have a hotel guest who wants to check out early."

"Sounds great," Liz said. "But first, we will meet with Steve and Justin and see what we can learn about Anthony and why someone might want to kill him."

"It wasn't a robbery, was it?"

"I don't think anything was missing," Liz said.

"I remember that Anthony was still wearing a watch. If it were a robbery, they most likely would have taken that, right?"

"Unless we somehow interrupted the robbery, he would have taken the watch," Liz agreed.

"Do you think it was a 'he' who killed Anthony?"

"Well, I suppose it could be a 'she.' We'll have to wait to see what Shane says about the blows to the head. Whether they were from someone taller than Anthony or shorter."

"There are tall women on Mackinac Island," I pointed out.

"Yes, but Anthony was six feet tall. There are only the McCoy women who grow tall enough for a downward blow to someone of that height."

"I suppose knowing the trajectory of the blows would certainly help identify the killer. We can assume that the person wasn't five foot two or under," I said. "They would have to be able to reach Anthony's head to bash it in, right?"

"I would assume so," she said. "So—a reasonably tall person bashed Anthony in the head for reasons unknown. We didn't see anyone in the alley, right?"

"Just my cat."

"Then, if we did interrupt the killer, they had to be very fast in leaving the alley."

"They could have gone into the back of the Old Tyme Photo Shop."

"We should ask Kim," Liz said. "I happen to know she was working that night. She was telling me that a lot of people came in to get tintype pictures from the shop of themselves in zombie costume." Liz stood and put her glass in the sink. "That gives us three people to talk to—Steve, Justin, and Kim. We can narrow down our search and find more leads by asking them the right questions."

"I'm glad you took those pictures of the crowd," I said, walking her to the door. "Thanks for sharing them with me."

"No problem. I figured you have a good eye for these things. In fact, you're the one who noticed that the coats were different, not me. I would have kept wondering who the woman was with Anthony. I'm glad to know that it was someone else with a similar costume."

I laughed. "Maybe that was the motive—women hate it when they show up somewhere wearing the same dress as someone else."

Liz laughed and shook her head. "On that note, I'm off."

"Are you okay to walk home alone?"

"Sure, it's not that far."

I winced. "A man was murdered four blocks from here. I think I'll feel better if you let me walk you home."

"What, so you can walk yourself back home alone in the dark from my place? That's silly. I'll be fine. I have the police station number on speed dial on my phone, and I'll video the entire walk, okay?"

"Let me call Rex—"

"Oh goodness, no. Seriously it's only a few blocks."
She leaned down and gave Mal a few goodbye pats.

"Fine," I said. "But stay on the phone with me,
please."

She laughed. "Now you know how others feel about
you walking around the island on your own. It's perfectly safe, you know. The crime rate is very low."

"Except for the murders."

"Those are a recent phenomenon. I swear, before
you came, the island was a sleepy little place. The
news consisted mostly of what Mrs. Bashka's cat was
doing the night before." She opened the door. "I
should know. I grew up here. I think my grandfather
did report on a missing persons case once. But the
news was mostly about festivals and parades and who
would be named Lilac Festival Queen."

I smiled. "Tell me the truth. Were you ever Lilac
Festival Queen?"

"Me? As if that was something I ever wanted to be,"
she scoffed, opening the door. "I was on the court,
though." She shrugged. "There were only a handful of girls in my class. Someone had to step up to
the plate."

When she reached the bottom of the stairs, she
called me. Out of habit, I said hello into the phone
when I answered.

She waved. "You can practically watch me walk
home from up there." She set off down the alley, then
disappeared onto the road.

"I can't see you now," I said.

"I'm nearly at my door."

"I'm glad you live close."

I could hear her unlock her door and enter her

place. "Alright, I'm home, and my place is locked up tight. Good night, Allie."

"I'm looking forward to tomorrow," I said. I went inside with both of my fur babies. "I am curious if Justin or Steve can tell us anything about who might want to harm Anthony."

"Thanks for helping me decipher the photos," she agreed. "My question is, why did Anthony leave Justin and Steve and go out—presumably alone—into the alley?"

"Maybe he left with his killer," I said thoughtfully. "How amazing would that be?"

"So amazing, I'm sure Rex is all over that one already."

I sighed. "Of course, he would be."

Chapter 6

The next morning went smoothly. I checked out my final guest and made two batches of fudge for the candy counter. Frances and Douglas had things well in hand, so I decided to walk to Faber Roofing near the airport. I had decided on Faber for the roof deck at the McMurphy, and I wanted to let them know in person that I chose them.

Pete Faber was an old friend of my Papa Liam's. He and his sons worked a construction business that took care of the old Victorian cottages and painted ladies–style buildings. They also helped build the new places along the biking path at the edge of the forests. Pete's son Elmer owned the company now. He was my dad's age, and his sandy hair was interspersed with gray. Elmer was a big man with wide shoulders and large hands that had worked with a hammer at construction his entire life.

"Allie McMurphy," Elmer said when I entered the office. "I heard you got the permits and the historical society's blessing. How the heck did you manage that?"

"People like Frances," I said with a shrug while he came toward me and wrapped me in a big bear hug.

Elmer's ancestors were loggers and builders. He came by his muscular build through generations of hard work.

His deep laugh reverberated through my spine. I hugged him back, then stepped away. "I received three quotes for the job."

"Ha, where did you get the other two? Off island?"

"You're not the only contractor on Mackinac."

"But we are the only ones you've worked with before, and you were satisfied by the job we did. As all our customers are."

"Why is it that construction workers measure twice, cut once, but when you get a quote, you should double the time and add a third to the price?" I teased him. Elmer loved to haggle. That was in his blood as well, I suspect, but Papa Liam had taught me how to haggle, too. It was a skill I was glad to have.

"Now, now. We came in on budget this spring."

"But two weeks over the time," I pointed out. "The only reason you came in on budget is because I helped strip the floors and put up wallpaper."

"You had nothing better to do." He went over to his big desk, sat behind it, and pulled out a contract and two pens. "We're going to create the best rooftop deck in all of Mackinac."

"I have permits to remodel the second-floor guest rooms, too," I said. "But I only have money for half of what you quoted. I figured you could give me a discount if I put up a sign on the rooftop deck letting everyone know you created it. You could make the plaque in bronze. Think of it as a lifetime of free advertising."

"Five hundred off for a lifetime of free advertising," he said. "That's all I can offer."

"Fifteen hundred, or I'll go to my second choice."

"I don't believe you have a second choice," he crossed his arms over his chest. "Eight hundred."

"Two thousand dollars off, and I'll cater your daughter's wedding."

"How did you know about Hazel?"

"It's a small island," I said. "And Sandy Everheart works for me. She would do an amazing chocolate sculpture." I didn't tell him that Sandy was leaving. I had my fingers crossed that he hadn't heard it yet.

"Hazel does love Sandy's sculptures."

"Come on," I said. "I know you don't have much work now that winter is coming."

"It's only October. There's a lot of winterizing and other work to do around the island." He shrugged. "Besides, I like the slower winter months. I get to go ice fishing and snowmobiling."

"Fine," I stood. "Maybe next year, I'll get you to quote my third-floor remodel."

"You're going to redo the McMurphy from head to toe?"

"All of it," I said. "It's too bad you only did the lobby. I'll go to Augusta Hammer. She underbid you the first time around. I'm sure she and her crew will be excited to have a remodel on Main Street, where they can advertise with a sign in my window."

"Augusta Hammer has only been in the construction business for five years. You need an expert to do that roof remodel."

"She has a civil engineer on staff with fifteen years of experience."

"If you're talking about Robert Packs, he worked for me first. I taught him everything he knows before he jumped ship and went over to Augusta's place."

"I came to you first," I pointed out. "It's not my fault you weren't in a bargaining mood. I only have a few profits left. I want to spend them wisely." I turned to go.

"All right, all right. I can't let anyone but the best remodel the McMurphy. We'll do it for fifteen hundred off *and* you cater my daughter's wedding. Deal?"

"You drive a tough bargain," I said, but I stuck out my hand. "Deal."

I walked out of the building happy to know they would be starting on the roof remodel on Wednesday. My bank account was also a thousand dollars lighter, but I was ready to take the risk.

At least this much was going right in my life. I was halfway home when I saw Mella strolling down the street. "Mella?" I called. She stopped and looked at me over her shoulder and meowed. Then she walked faster away. Was it a different cat? "Mella, what are you doing out?" I hurried after. The cat took me for a merry chase before finally slowing down enough for me to catch up.

Yes, it was Mella, after all. A mom knew her fur babies. Plus, I had put a collar on Mella when I first brought her inside the hotel, and now that I was close up, I could see the pink of the collar peeking out through her fur. It had her name printed on it. I didn't want to give her metal tags, which would rattle and make it difficult for her to be her sneaky self, but a name and phone number were important in case she ever got lost. Or someone decided she needed picking up.

"Come here, you little scamp," I said and snagged her. She snuggled against me and meowed. "How did you get out? I'm not sure it's safe for you to be this far away from home."

"Is that your cat?" It was Haley Manx. She was dressed in a tight black tee shirt and black leggings under a flowing, rainbow-colored skirt. "She's quite lovely."

"Yes, this is Carmella," I said as Haley reached over and petted her. "She doesn't usually stray this far from the McMurphy." I was still two roads up the hill from Main Street.

"My studio is right here," Haley said, pointing to a small purple guesthouse with white trim. Large, leafless lilac bushes stood in front of the door. A series of three pumpkins carved with intricate, fantastical Halloween scenes sat on the tiny porch. "Why don't you come in and have some tea?"

"Sounds wonderful." I followed her into the tiny shop. There were two rooms in the front. One was a small parlor with a settee and two chairs, all covered in blue and white florals. The room across from it was her studio. It was filled with pots, plates, and all manner of pottery in various stages. Her potter's wheel sat near the corner, where sunlight streamed in from two sides. "This is lovely."

"It's just enough for me," she said with a smile. "There's a nice little kitchen for making tea and serving guests. Sometimes, I have evening wine tasting and showings. People like it."

"Do you live here?" I asked, a bit confused. I thought she was married to Rick. There didn't seem to be more than four rooms. The two in front, two in back and a tiny bathroom in the middle.

"Oh, no, not anymore," she said. "This used to be my place before I married Rick. I've kept it for the shop." I followed her into the tiny kitchen and watched her put a teakettle on to boil. "It's close enough to Main Street that I get fudgies wandering in."

"You mentioned pottery lessons the other day." I watched her take down two mugs and a tin filled with lavender tea.

"Yep. Most of them are at the senior center."

"What about places besides at the senior center? Frances, my office manager, thinks I spend too much time with old people."

She laughed and led me out to the living area. "Please, sit." The kettle went off in the kitchen, and she headed back in for a minute before coming out and pouring hot water in both mugs. "You don't have to go to the senior center. I can give you lessons here."

I put Mella down to explore and picked up the tea. "That would be great. Apparently, I need to get out more."

"I get that," Haley said, settling into one of the two flowered chairs. "Have you ever worked in clay?"

"I think I made a soap dish in high school art class . . ."

"Perfect."

"How much for lessons?"

"For you . . . bring wine, and all you have to do is pay for your clay and such. I'll donate the time."

"Oh, I don't want you to see me as a charity."

"No, really, you'll be doing me a favor. You're quite popular on the island, you know."

"I am?" She must have been kidding. I knew that most still considered me an outsider.

"Yes, you are," she said. "And if people hear you're taking pottery lessons from me, then they'll want pottery lessons, too—so you see, I'm quite selfish in asking you to take them."

"I think that's nonsense, but I'm not going to turn down free lessons. When can I start?"

"As soon as you would like," she said. "I've got to make a clay run off the island, though. What would you like to make first?"

"I think a pair of mugs might be easy. Or maybe a bowl?"

"A pair of mugs it is," she said with a smile. "I'll pick up some good quality clay for mug throwing."

"Oh, I don't want to throw them—unless they're awful, of course. I'd really like to keep them." She laughed again, a lovely sound that made me smile. "What?"

"I don't mean throwing as in 'throwing them against a wall.' When you make something on a pottery wheel, it's called throwing the pot."

"Oh." I felt the heat of embarrassment rush into my cheeks. "I told you I made a soap dish, tight? I don't think there was a pottery wheel involved. Although there might have been some literal throwing around of clay."

Mella jumped up in my lap. She pawed at me a few times, playing a little patty cake with my thigh before snuggling down in my lap.

"Someone knows how to get comfortable," Haley said with a tip of her tea cup toward the cat.

"She's the best cat ever. That reminds me, did you get out for the Walking Red zombie walk?"

"Oh, yes," she said with a twinkle of mischief in her eyes. "I love a good zombie walk. I also earned five hundred dollars toward the American Heart Association. I assume you walked?"

"Well, I tried," I said. "Mella and I found Anthony before I could actually do the walk, but I was dressed the part. Lucky for me, my sponsors felt sorry for me and donated anyway. I made one fifty."

"Not bad for not walking."

"I think it was a consolation for finding a dead man in the alley."

"That is a pretty unique find—even with all the zombies running around."

Chapter 7

Mella and I left Haley's art studio full of tea and laughter. Well, the cat had less of the tea. I was excited for my lessons, too, which Haley said I could start in the next few days. I thought about the mugs I would make, and how I would share a cup of hot cocoa with someone later this winter once the mugs were made. I decided to create blue mugs with white snowflakes.

A glance at the time on my phone told me I had only ten minutes before I was scheduled to meet Liz at the Nag's Head to see if we could get some insight into Anthony's last moments. I rushed home, dropped Mella off in my apartment, gave Mal a treat and put her in her crate, and headed out. Knowing my pets were safely locked up freed my mind to think about Anthony.

The Nag's Head Bar and Grill was intentionally divey. It sat on Main Street with its back to the water. The interior was dark wood, a large, nineteenth century bar with just a few tables for customers. In the back were two pool tables and a door that opened out to a deck over the water. On the deck was a second bar, and that was where I found Liz.

"Sorry I'm late," I said as I gave her a hug. "I ran into Haley Manx. Do you know her?"

"Sure," Liz said, walking me to the bar. We climbed up on two empty stools. "She does pottery, right?"

"Yes, I'm thinking of taking lessons."

Liz gave me the side-eye. "Why?"

"We discussed this," I said. "I need to get out more."

"Pottery lessons are not the way to meet people." Liz waved down the bartender. He was a tan man with blond hair and blue eyes. He had a casual beach look that suggested he spent a lot of time on the water.

"What can I do for you, ladies?"

I studied the drink menu. "It's a little early for alcohol. I might have an iced tea."

"It's five o'clock somewhere," he said with a wink. "How about a chardonnay?"

I pondered for a moment. "Okay," I said, putting down the menu.

"Make that two," Liz said. He moved away to fill our drink orders. "That's Justin," Liz said. "You start the conversation. Otherwise, it will feel like I'm interviewing him for an article."

"But everyone knows I investigate crimes . . ."

"He's a good-looking, single guy, and you're cute. He won't be thinking about your sleuthing."

"Fine."

"Great," she said. She leaned back. "I was thinking we should have a girls' weekend, not just girls' night. We could go wine tasting, get facials, fun stuff like that."

"I'm in," I said. "It's been a long season."

Justin came back with our drinks. "Here you go, ladies."

"Thanks," I said and took a sip. "Good choice. You

know, we're actually thinking of doing a girls' weekend with wine tasting. Do you know of any good places to go?"

His eyes twinkled at me as he leaned on the counter. "There's this winery near Traverse City that makes cherry wine. Pretty good stuff."

I sipped my wine, floundering for how to start the conversation about Anthony. "Have you ever gone on a girls'—er, I mean, guys' weekend there?"

"My friends and I would go for the weekend sometimes. There's a couple of good places to fish around there in the summer. Have I seen you somewhere before?"

"I'm not sure."

"Were you at the zombie walk?" he asked.

There was my chance. "I planned on going, but something came up. It sounded like a lot of fun. Did you go?"

"Yeah," he said. Then his expression sobered. "Then I found out that my friend Anthony had died."

"I heard he was murdered," I said. "Liz is doing a story on the investigation."

She sent me the stink eye.

"Yeah," Justin said. "I read the first story. I hope they catch the guy who did this."

"Were you with Anthony that night?" Liz asked.

"Yeah, sure. Steve and I were hanging out with Anthony. Then his mom called, and he left to go meet her." He paused and wiped his eyes. "Guess he never got there."

"Do you have any idea who would do such a thing?" I asked.

"That's the thing," he said. "Anthony was a great

guy. Everyone loved him. If I find out who did this before the cops do, the guy had better watch out."

"I understand there was another guy at the zombie walk that had a costume similar to Anthony's." Liz pulled a picture up on her phone. "Do you remember this guy?"

Justin studied the picture for a moment. "Yeah, sure. We commented on how he was wearing the same suit. But his makeup was subpar, you know? We had a guy do ours who's heading out to Hollywood to do movie makeup."

"You're a bartender here. I bet you know practically everyone. Do you know who the other guy was?"

"No," he said. "But then, I didn't really try. I mean, it was lame, right?" He frowned and looked at Liz. "Do you think it's important?"

"Not necessarily," Liz hedged.

"We think there's a chance Anthony was killed by mistake," I said, ignoring the look Liz gave me. "That means this other guy might be in danger. If you figure out who it was, would you let Rex know?"

"Sure," he said. "Anything that might help catch the killer." He left to take an order from three men who walked into the bar.

I turned to Liz. "Well, that wasn't as helpful as I had hoped. Do you think Steven might know who the guy is?"

"There's a chance," she said. She finished her wine. "I'll go see if I can talk to him."

"I'd come with you, but I need to get back to the McMurphy. Frances is with Maggs, and Mr. Devaney gets grumpy if he has to do my job as well as his."

"I'll keep you posted on what, if anything, I learn from Steve."

"Great," I said. "Could you send me those pictures, too? I'd like to look at them some more."

"Sure." She pulled out her phone. With a few taps of her screen, she said, "Done."

We left a big tip on the bar and walked out. I thought about Justin and his beautiful eyes. Maybe getting a drink at the bar on occasion wasn't a bad thing.

"Allie, thank goodness I've found you," Mrs. Tunisian said as I rounded the corner of Main Street toward the McMurphy.

"What's wrong?" I asked. Mrs. Tunisian wore a tracksuit in turquoise and new running shoes. She looked like she was out for some casual afternoon exercise.

"It's Maggs. She's beside herself with grief. We don't know what to do. Frances said to get you and have you stop at Doud's to pick up some ready-made meals."

"I don't need ready-made meals," I said. "I make a mean lasagna." I picked up my pace to match the older woman's power stride. "I'll grab things from Doud's and then head over to Maggs's place. Is Frances with her?"

"Yes," Mrs. Tunisian said. "Bring some cat food as well, if you don't mind. Maggs has two beautiful kitties that need as much care as she does. The whole house is upside down with grief. We've all done our best, but we can't seem to knock her out of this. Frances thinks that you can help calm Maggs by telling her you'll solve the murder."

"Well, I can bring food, but I don't know about solving the murder."

"It's okay dear, we know you can do it. Maggs is counting on you."

Great.

I texted Mr. Devaney and asked him to watch the McMurphy for a few more hours than expected because Frances asked me to go see Maggs. He texted back quickly: *Okay.*

Then I texted Frances and let her know that I was coming over with ingredients to make a meal.

Mary Emry was working at Doud's again. She looked up from her tabloid magazine as I walked into the store.

"You here to find another body?" she asked.

Mary was tall, with brown hair and blue eyes. She rarely spoke to anyone but locals. I stopped for a moment and took in the fact that she was talking to me. I guess I was beginning to be seen as a local.

"I'm going to make Maggs a casserole," I said. I gathered noodles, sauce, and cheese to make Grandma Alice's lasagna recipe as well as some cat food for Maggs's kitties. I didn't like the idea of pets missing out on their regular meals. I put my items on the counter.

"There's a special on fresh French bread," Mary said, nodding toward the rolling shelf with the day's baked goods. She rang me up as I grabbed a loaf plus some butter and garlic.

"Did you know Anthony?" I asked.

"He was in the class below me in school," Mary said, continuing to ring up and bag my items. "He was a nice guy. Didn't deserve to die so soon." She looked at me as she totaled my purchases. "I hope you catch the killer."

"I'm sure that Rex will see that whoever did this is caught."

Mary watched as I swiped my debit card and paid my bill. "You catch this guy," she said. "Everyone's counting on you."

"Everyone?" I asked, drawing my eyebrows together as I gathered up my bags.

"Everyone on the island loves Maggs," she said. "If I were you, I would make sure you catch him soon."

"No pressure," I said under my breath.

The walk to Maggs's place was quick. She lived in an old Victorian a few blocks from Main Street—right in front of the place where we had found her son's body just a few days ago. No wonder she was having trouble. I stepped up on the wraparound porch and knocked on the door.

"Allie, come on in," Frances said as she opened the door. "What did you bring?"

"Lasagna fixings," I said, entering the hallway. This was my first time in Maggs's home. There was a parlor on the left and stairs to the right. Frances led me down a hall that went straight back to the kitchen. Off the hall to the left, between the parlor and the kitchen, was a cozy den and a bathroom. On the right was a long dining room. The kitchen covered the entire back of the house. I put the bags on the counter and started to take things out of the bag. "How's Maggs?"

"Things have been difficult today," Frances said. "I understand, though. A mother should never have to bury their child. Anthony was her world, you know."

"No, I didn't know," I said, pulling out a bottle of red wine. "But I can imagine." Frances took the bottle, uncorked it, and left it to breathe as I started putting the casserole together. "I'm so sorry this happened. How else can I help?"

"We need to find this killer and bring them to justice."

"I wish I could help, but Rex hasn't told me anything. I didn't really see anything in the alley."

"No," Frances said. She poured three glasses of the wine. "But I heard you and Liz were looking at pictures of the zombie walk."

"Yeah. Anthony was with his friends Justin and Steve. Liz and I were just at the Nag's Head this afternoon talking to Justin about it."

"What did you learn?" Maggs asked from the kitchen doorway. She hovered there, unsure and trembling, as if the slightest breeze might knock her over. She was dressed in sweatpants, a tee shirt, and a bathrobe that had seen better days. Her eyes were swollen, and her nose was red. She wrapped her arms around herself, her fists filled with used tissues.

"Not much," I said. I went over to give her a hug. "I'm so sorry for your loss. This is terrible. Everyone loved Anthony."

"We're going to find this killer," Maggs said. "I'm going to get justice for my boy."

"Yes, ma'am," I said.

"Come on, let's go sit down in the den," Frances said. She handed me a glass of wine. I shepherded Maggs down the hall and into the den. The walls were painted a pale, calming green, only covered in a few places by tall wooden bookshelves and several pieces of art. Four easy chairs huddled around a fireplace where a fire crackled softly.

I set my wineglass on an end table next to one of the chairs before helping Maggs into her own chair. Frances handed her a glass of wine, then tucked a plaid blanket around her knees. I sat in the chair next to my wine and waited for Frances to settle into the chair beside Maggs. The only sound was the crackling of the fire. I noticed a statue of a black cat wearing a witch's hat by the fireplace—a single nod to the Halloween season. Finally, I broke the silence. "I made a lasagna. It will be ready soon. You should try to eat."

Maggs nodded. "Maybe."

"It'll freeze well," I said. "You can get a few good meals out of it."

"Anthony was looking forward to the zombie walk," Maggs said, her tone low. It was clear food was far from her mind. "He was one of the people who suggested the event to the senior center. I helped him with his costume. The man was thirty years old and still loved to dress up. When he was excited about something, he was like a little kid again."

"Who did his makeup?" I asked.

"His friend Eric," Maggs said. "He's heading to Hollywood to do movie makeup soon. Anyway, he did a lot of people's makeup. He'd been designing looks for the last six weeks. The guys made Eric come to their homes one at a time so they could keep their looks secret until they met up at one."

"The walk wasn't until seven," I pointed out. "That was a long time of gathering and drinking beforehand."

"The kids loved having a reason to get together," Maggs said. "Anthony was in the middle of making a career move, you know. He was going to head to Saginaw for a job in a school district down there."

"A school district? I thought Anthony was a lawyer."

"He wanted to be a fourth-grade teacher," Maggs said. "He loved kids. His undergraduate degree was in mathematics and he went on to law, but he preferred teaching. He was so excited to get this new job, you know? The teaching jobs on Mackinac are few and far between. Teachers come here and they don't leave."

"I can attest to that," Frances said. "I was lucky to get my job when I was twenty-five, and I stayed until I retired."

"Anthony got his teaching certificate last summer. He was substituting here on the island when he got the call. The job in Saginaw happened when their fourth-grade teacher was in a car accident and broke both legs. That poor man has a lot of surgeries in front of him, plus physical therapy. Anthony was going to finish the year out for him."

"I'm so sorry, Maggs," I said. What else could I say?

"What did you and Liz learn when you went through some of the photographs from that day? You have to have seen something."

"Yes," I said. "At first, we thought he was with a girl in some of the pictures, but then we realized that the person with the girl just had a similar costume on. We were able to separate the two and could track some of the hours before he died."

"Do you think he was killed by mistake?" Maggs asked. "I mean, if someone else had a similar costume, couldn't the killer have mistaken Anthony for the other guy?"

"That's what we're wondering," I said. "Liz is looking to see if she can figure out who the other guy was. In the meantime, do you know of anyone who might want to hurt Anthony? Was he fighting with his friends? Did he have a girlfriend? What was his regular life like?"

"Rex already asked me if I thought anyone would want to hurt Anthony. There's simply no way. He was going to be a teacher, for goodness sakes. He loved kids. He was a God-fearing man who went to church with me on Sundays. Who would want to kill him?"

"I don't know," I said with a shake of my head. I reached over and hugged her. "I'm going to try to find out."

"Thank you. I know Rex won't like it if you interfere," Maggs said. "And I would be so upset if anything happened to jeopardize the case. But you won't do that, right? You'll help find my Anthony justice?"

"I promise I'll help, and I won't do anything to jeopardize the case."

"Thank you, Allie," Frances said. "I'll help, too. I can talk to the senior citizen network. Someone will know something. "

"Frances and I can go to the senior center in the morning. I hear they're having a card tournament. Frances and Mr. Devaney can play in the tournament, and I'll serve refreshments. I think people will tell me things just because I'm there, without me even having to ask many questions. That way, Rex can't complain that I'm investigating or ruining his case."

"It might just work," Frances said. "I'm sure Douglas would love to join the tournament. We're pretty good. We'll keep our ears open. That place is a hotbed of gossip."

"Someone knows something," I said. "Don't worry, Maggs. We'll make sure whoever did this pays."

Maggs started to look overwhelmed again. "I'm tired," she said, a waver in her voice. She stood up. "I'm going to go lie down."

We watched her slowly move to the bedroom. "I'll stay with her," Frances said. "And see that she eats a little something. Thanks for making lasagna. I'll text Douglas to make sure he's part of the tournament tomorrow."

"Are you sure she's going to be all right?"

"I don't know," Frances said. "She lost her only boy."

"I feel like there must be something else I can do."

"You're doing enough," Frances said. "Make some fudge for the seniors. The tournament starts at ten."

"I'll be there."

APPLE CINNAMON WHITE CHOCOLATE FUDGE

2 cups white chocolate chips
1 (14-ounce) can sweetened condensed milk
½ cup diced dried apple
1 teaspoon apple cider
1 cup cinnamon chips

Prepare an 8-inch pan by lining it with parchment paper and buttering the paper. In a microwave-safe bowl, combine white chocolate chips and sweetened condensed milk. Microwave on high for one minute. Stir. Microwave for 20 seconds more if needed to create a smooth mix. Add apple pieces and apple cider, and mix until combined. Finally, add cinnamon chips and pour into the prepared pan. Place in refrigerator until completely cool. Take out of pan, remove parchment, and cut into ½-inch pieces. Enjoy!

Makes about 32 pieces of fudge.

Chapter 8

The next morning, I left the McMurphy in Sandy's hands. She wouldn't start at the Grander Hotel until the spring season, so for now, she was still cooking in my kitchen. Mr. Devaney was seeing to the last two guests. The hotel would be fully vacant until Friday night. That meant that the remodeling crew could start on the second-floor remodel today without waking any of the guests.

I arrived at the senior citizen center a little early, three batches of fudge in hand. The place was decorated for the season with pumpkins, black cats, and witch hats.

"Hey, Allie, did you bring the fudge with nuts?" The question came from Mrs. Addison, one of my favorite seniors, almost as soon as I walked through the door.

"I have dark chocolate cherry and walnut," I said. "I also have pecan pie and pumpkin. So I brought two kinds with nuts."

"Sounds wonderful," Mrs. Tunisian said. "But not for you, Jenny." She swooped in and took the tray of fudge away from me, moving in the opposite direction from Mrs. Addison. "You're allergic to nuts, remember?"

"Doesn't mean I don't like them," Mrs. Addison pouted. She was a heavyset woman with a face full of freckles and red-orange hair.

"Allie, did you come to watch the tournament?" Mrs. Platty asked. She was the event coordinator for the senior center. She was all of four foot ten, with bright white hair curled tight around her head and wide, cat-eye glasses.

"I did," I said. "Frances and Mr. Devaney entered. I came to cheer them on."

"Oh, good," Mrs. Platty said. "It would be nice if more young people came to cheer us on."

"Where's Mal?" Mrs. Tunisian asked. "I hope she is okay."

"She's fine," I reassured her. "They're starting construction on the second floor of the McMurphy, and my cat, Carmella, is bothered by all the coming and going. So I left Mal with her to help her feel safe."

"Leaving a puppy for company does not make a cat feel safe," Mrs. Tunisian said.

"At the very least, Mal will distract Mella and give her someone to tell her troubles to."

"Who's doing the remodel work on your place?"

"I'm having Elmer Faber and his crew do the second-floor work and the roof."

"Oh, I like Elmer," Mrs. Addison said. "He did a nice job on my niece's place."

"I like him, too," I said. "He subcontracted some of the work on the lobby when I remodeled it this spring."

"Are you redoing your roof, too, honey?" Mr. Bluto said. "I thought that Liam just put that roof on ten years ago."

"He did," I said with a smile at the memory of my

Papa. "But I'm going to add a rooftop deck space. I've got a great view of the straits, and I can rent out the space for events. The only trouble is that the deck isn't supportive enough for more than five people on it, so we have to do a bit more than just add a deck on top of what we've already got."

"You need to have the trusses redone," Mr. Bluto said with a nod. "I know a guy who can do that for you."

"Faber Roofing?" I said with a smile.

"That's the guy."

"His crew starts work tomorrow."

"Oh my goodness, you're going to have the roof worked on and the second floor remodeled at the same time?" Mrs. Tunisian asked. "I hope you don't have any guests."

"Only a few, and they'll stay on the third floor," I said.

"What about the fudge?" Mrs. Addison said, a look of horror on her face. "Don't you have an online business to take care of?"

"What about Sandy Everheart's business?" Mrs. Tunisian asked, her hands clasped in front of her.

"Our businesses will be fine," I said. "The crew shouldn't bother the lobby or the fudge shop kitchen."

"I heard Sandy was going to take her grandmother to Florida next month," Mrs. Addison said. "She should move down there in the winter. That woman deserves to be a snowbird. My Emmerson and I are heading down that way next week, too. The winters up here are lovely, but I'm too old to deal with all that snow." She made a motion with her hand as if she were done with the whole business. "You should come with us, Irene."

"I've got train tickets to Texas to visit my kids," Mrs. Tunisian replied with a half-smile. "Look around, Allie. This is the last visit to the senior center for most of us this season. We all travel south for the winter, except for the diehards. Are Frances and Douglas going south, too?"

"I don't think so," I said with a slight frown. "They haven't told me they were going."

"Well, maybe they'll stay for your first winter, but after that they should go. It's hard on old people—all that snow and ice. No one want's to be a shut-in."

"I'm sure they'll go if they want to," I said. "But last I heard, they were planning to help me keep the McMurphy open in the off-season."

"It's okay, dear," Mrs. Tunisian said, patting my arm. "Everyone thinks they should be open in the off-season at first, but you'll learn that your grandfather was right. Closing for the winter is best. Why, you might even go down to Chicago to spend time with your friend Jenn."

"Thanks," I said, "but I want to make Mackinac my year-round home."

"Suit yourself," she said with a shrug and a smile. "You'll learn."

Mrs. Tunisian put my fudge down on a table laden with treats and snacks. A scan of the room had me honing in on Frances and Mr. Devaney at one of the card tables near the center of the room. The games had started. I worked my way over to see how they were doing.

"Oh, Allie, you're here," Frances said when she spotted me. "I was just telling Ethel how we're helping Maggs by investigating her son's murder."

"I heard that there were two zombies who looked

alike," Ethel Thigbee said while studying her cards. "My guess is that whoever killed Anthony killed the wrong zombie."

"We're sort of thinking the same thing," I said.

"So the real question is who could the other zombie be, and why would someone want him dead?" Ethel went on to say.

"Exactly."

"Do you have those pictures?" Ethel asked as she put down cards and made her move. Douglas moved in swiftly to pick up her hand and discard something he didn't want. Ethel didn't seem too concerned about the blunder. "Did you bring them?"

"She did," Frances said. "I told her to. Show her the pictures, Allie. Ethel might know who it is."

I pulled the pictures I'd printed out for today's event from my jean jacket pocket. "We can only see the back of the guy's head, so I'm not sure you'll be able to tell who it is . . ."

Ethel took the first picture out of my hand and studied it through her bright orange, cat-eye glasses. "That's Josh Spalding," she said. "I'd know those shoulders anywhere." She glanced up at me. "Not to mention that butt."

"Ethel!" Frances looked shocked.

"What? A woman can look," she said, handing me the picture. "I'm old, not dead. I'd bet my life that it's Josh Spalding."

I studied the picture and frowned. "How do you know? I mean, look at this other picture. The silhouette is so similar."

She grabbed the photo of Anthony out of my hand. "That's definitely Anthony," she said immediately, handing the picture back to me. "It's the backside.

Josh's is a little higher and tighter. You're young. You should be able to see the difference."

I studied the pictures and frowned. They looked too much alike. "I guess I'm no expert on men's backsides."

"Let me guess, it's their eyes that draw you," Ethel said.

"Um, yes . . ."

"Figures." She played her next round just as quickly as the last. Douglas took advantage of her recklessness and finished the hand.

"Well, shoot," Ethel said.

"You need to keep your head in the game," her partner, Cecilia Rig, chided her. "Let me look at the pictures."

I moved around the table and presented both pictures to Cecilia. She studied them closely. "I agree with Ethel. This one is Anthony and the other is Josh Spalding." She looked up at me and handed me the pictures. "You need to find out who wanted to kill Josh."

"See!" Ethel said.

"Okay, I believe you," I said as Douglas dealt the next hand.

There was a commotion at the door. I looked over to see several of the seniors gathering near the front of the building. "What's happening?" Frances asked.

"I'll go find out." I left them to their game. The front of the senior center was filled with windows. The seniors had gathered near the windows, and a few were still looking out while a small group were standing near a table. "What's going on?"

"Sally noticed a strange box near the door," Mrs. Tunisian said. "She and Alice went out to look around and bring the box in." She pointed, and I noticed the wooden box the ladies had put on the table near the door. Mr. Rucker was trying to pry it open with a crowbar.

"Wait!" I shouted, pushing my way through the crowd. "Don't touch that!"

"Whyever not?" Mr. Rucker asked.

"It might be a bomb."

"A bomb? Don't be ridiculous," he said, studying the box. "It looks like one of those man crates. Why would your first thought be bomb?"

"I'm serious," I said as I pushed the ladies back. "You don't know who left that. It could be a bomb." I knew from firsthand experience how serious a bomb could be.

"Oh, my," Alice Edson said. "I carried it in."

"Everyone get back," I said. I dialed 9-1-1.

"9-1-1, what's your emergency?"

"Hi, Charlene," I said into the phone.

"Allie McMurphy. Who died?"

"No one died," I said. "Yet."

"What do you mean 'yet'?"

"There was a package left outside the senior center," I said. I went over to listen to the box. "It doesn't have any address label. I don't hear any ticking, but things are digital now."

"You think it's a bomb."

"Yes," I said and the crowd took another step back— all except Mr. Rucker. He frowned at me.

"Let me open it," he said, waving the crowbar. "It's probably some good whiskey."

"Tell him not to touch it," Charlene said. "I'm contacting the officers on duty."

"She said don't touch it," I said, pulling him back.

"Rex said to evacuate the senior center now!" Charlene said.

"On it," I said. I turned to the crowd. "Ladies and gentlemen, we need to get out of the building now. Don't panic, but leave in an orderly fashion as quickly as possible."

"At our age, nothing is quick," Mrs. Tunisian said as she helped an elderly lady with a walker.

"I'll get the door," I said, guiding several seniors to the side door near the back entrance. "Please, everyone leave." I reached over, grabbed the fire alarm, and pulled it. The sound penetrated the noise of the card tournament. The men stood and started to escort the ladies out. Mr. Devaney and Frances helped a few of the slowest out of the building. I went to the box and ensured no one went out the front door. The chaos seemed to last forever. My heart raced. What if the box *did* contain a bomb? It might take out all of the seniors at any moment.

Rex and Officer Pulaski arrived and assisted the last of the stragglers outside. "Are you getting them far away?" I asked Rex when he came back in after emptying the building.

"Why are you still in the building?"

"I wanted to make sure everyone stayed away from the box." I felt my lips tremble. I had been near an explosion around the Fourth of July. I knew the power of a blast.

"Is that the box?" he asked, nodding toward it.

"Yes."

"Okay, let's get you out of here." He put his arm around my shoulders and walked me quickly out through the door. I could see the seniors still trailing off across the parking lot and into the church that sat a block away.

Rex and I were on the opposite side of the parking lot when the blast hit and the senior center went up in pieces. He dragged me to the ground and covered my body with his as pieces of wood, glass, and hot nails rained down on us.

My ears rang from the sound of the explosion. After the initial blast, Rex pulled me up, and we ran to the church. Two senior ladies had been knocked from their feet near the front stairs. My hands shook as Rex and I helped them up and into the church. A second blast went off right as the church door closed behind us. Debris hit the front of the church and I ducked, an automatic reaction. Some of the older ladies screamed.

Frances and Mr. Devaney comforted some of the other seniors. I looked at Rex. Suddenly, my heart clenched in panic. "Where's Officer Pulaski?"

"Here," he said, emerging from the vestibule with the preacher.

"Oh, thank goodness," I said, putting my hand on my racing heart. "For a moment, I thought you might be caught outside."

"You're bleeding," Rex said. He gently wiped a spot on my face. "Are you all right?"

"I think so," I said with a frown. "You took the brunt of the blast." I noticed the scrapes on his face. But then I gently turned him around and saw that shrapnel had sliced and burned holes through the cloth of his uniform to his back. "Oh no!"

"Is it bad?" he asked, glancing behind him.

"You need to sit down," I said, gently pushing him

into a pew. "I lost my phone. Officer Pulaski, call for the ambulance, please." I turned back to Rex. "We need to get you taken care of." I winced. "Does it hurt?"

"Adrenaline," he said. "I don't feel anything. Is everyone else all right?"

"Some got a bit banged up in the rush to get to the church," Mr. Devaney said.

"I'm so sorry," Sally Mender said. She wrung her hands and stood close to Rex. "I'm the one who saw the box and helped Alice bring it into the center."

"Mr. Rucker was going to open it with a crowbar," Alice said from a pew two rows up. "Can you imagine what would have happened if he had opened it while we were all inside?"

The room was deathly quiet for a few seconds as the reality of what might have happened hit us. Rex stood. "But he didn't open it, and we are all safe."

I could hear the ambulance sirens coming our way. "I imagine the entire island heard those explosions."

"The bomb squad is flying in from Traverse City," Officer Pulaski said. "They want to check the site before anyone else gets close to it."

"How long are we going to have to stay here?" Mr. Rucker asked.

"I have to use the restroom," Mrs. Tunisian said.

"I can help anyone who needs the facilities." Pastor Henry stepped forward and took Mrs. Tunisian by the arm. "I'll call the phone tree and get the women's committee to bring some food and drinks."

"So we do have to stay here?" Mr. Anderson asked.

"Yes," Rex said, still seated. "We need to take statements, and the bomb squad needs to make sure there are no more bombs. Did anyone see who delivered the box?"

"No," a number of people in the crowd said, with a few headshakes and frowns.

"We had a card tournament going," Mr. Devaney said. "Most of us were busy playing cards."

"Whoever did this knew that the place would be packed," I said. Dizzy at the thought, I had to sit. I was shaken by the idea that someone wanted to kill the seniors. Why? Was it because I used them to help solve murders? I covered my mouth with my hand.

Rex studied me with careful eyes. "This is not your fault," he said, his tone serious. "This is the fault of whoever put the bomb together."

"But—"

"This is not your fault," he said again. "Say it."

"This is not my fault," I half whispered.

"It isn't."

The side door of the church opened, and George Marron walked in with a stretcher and emergency kit. He pulled the stretcher behind him. On the other side of the stretcher was a female EMT who I hadn't met before. She looked to be about my age, with a sturdy frame and light brown hair pulled back into a no-nonsense bun. Her name tag said Seal.

"Rex needs looked at," I called, waving my hand to signal George. "He took the brunt of the explosion."

"Who was outside when it went off?" George asked.

"Allie and me. So where Mrs. Handle and Mrs. Mender," Rex said, noting the two women who we had helped. He winced when George pushed him to lean forward so he could see Rex's back.

"I need to examine anyone who was outside," George said, opening his medical kit.

"I'm fine," Mrs. Handle said in a gruff voice. "Just got startled and lost my footing."

"You were subjected to shockwaves," George said. "You need to be checked out."

"Shockwaves can hurt you?" I asked.

"They can cause damage to your brain and your lungs," he said. "Concussion is number one. That's what I need to check for first. I need to listen to your breathing and check your head."

"Great," Rex said. "Be quick. I don't have time to be down for the count."

"There's a bomber and a murderer on the loose," I agreed.

Chapter 9

"Thank goodness no one was badly hurt," Frances said. We sat in the lobby of the McMurphy. It was nearly 8 P.M. Frances, Mr. Devaney, and I had finally gotten home and were sitting around the fireplace. I had my hands wrapped around a mug of cocoa from the coffee bar.

The remodeling crew had left for the day. The foreman, Elmer Faber, had stuck around until we returned to give us an update on their first day. They had torn out all the carpets and taped off the rooms and hallway for painting. The room furniture was all covered in plastic drop cloths. After giving us a progress report, he bowed out quickly. We all must have looked as exhausted as I felt.

"Just a few cuts and bruises," I said. I touched the three stitches in my forehead. "At least no one had a shock concussion."

"We won't know that for sure for a while," Mr. Devaney reminded me. "These kinds of incidents can have long-term effects."

"I want to know who sent that box," I said. "What were they thinking, attacking the senior center?"

"It could be the killer trying to get rid of the senior gossip line," Frances said.

"I had the same thought," Mr. Devaney said.

"It's criminal, and I hope they catch him," I said. "A murderer was bad enough. Now I'm even more determined to figure out who did this." I paused and sipped my cocoa. The sweet hot chocolate had a nice marshmallow foam. Then I switched topics to address something else that was weighing on my mind. "Are you two planning on leaving for the winter?"

"What? No, where did you get that idea?" Frances asked. She looked at Mr. Devaney. "Douglas?"

"No," he said with a definitive shake of his head. "We planned on staying through the winter to help you. You're keeping the McMurphy open, right?"

"Yes, at least a few rooms," I said. "Mostly I'll be making fudge and supervising the remodels."

"Then we're staying," he said. "Why are you asking?"

"It came up at the senior center this morning. The ladies were pretty sure you would go south when the weather got bad."

"Not this year," Frances said. "There's too much to do at the McMurphy."

"I plan on helping the general contractor for the roof and second-floor remodels," Douglas said. "Contractors will be in tomorrow morning to talk about the roof, too, don't forget."

"Right, thanks for the reminder," I said. "They're starting most of the work on the underside, right?"

"Yes, but they do have to pull off sections of the

roof decking to build the trusses underneath. So you will have a few days of tarps."

"But I thought they said they could take care of the structure in the attic without pulling off the roof."

"They can do it that way," Mr. Devaney said. "And they'll try, but with any kind of construction on a building this old, we have to be prepared for any contingency."

"Like a snowstorm," I said. "Which means they can't take off the roof."

"We're not expecting snow for another three weeks," he said. "We'll get it done by then."

"Okay," I said, suddenly exhausted. "We have no guests tonight, right?"

"No one until Friday night," Frances said.

"Good, I'm tired. You both must be exhausted, too. I'm going up to the apartment. I'll see you in the morning."

"Are you okay?" Frances asked. She stood with me. "Do you have a concussion?"

"George said he didn't think I did," I said. "I think it's just the adrenaline wearing off. I've got plans for fudge in the morning. Why don't you two go home and take care of each other?"

"If you're sure you're all right . . ." Frances said.

"I'm sure."

I walked them both out of the McMurphy and locked the door behind them. I turned back and picked up my pup Mal, who was sticking close by my heels. "Come on, let's go upstairs and go to bed."

I turned off the lights and made my way up the stairs. Poking my head into the second floor, I saw what looked like a ghost town. The wood floors on the hallway were exposed and stained dark with age. I wondered if it was smart to refinish the wood and not put carpet back on top. I guess I would learn that answer after next season when the guests came through on a regular basis again.

Mella wound her way around my legs to encourage me to go up to the apartment. Both fur babies were used to heading to bed with me by nine. They were tired, too.

I skipped the third floor and went up to the apartment. Inside, a new flower-patterned couch that I'd picked up at a garage sale sat next to Papa Liam's chair. I was slowly but surely moving my grandparent's belongings and replacing them with things more my own taste. Right now, the place was an eclectic mixture of old and new.

My phone rang. It was Rex. "Hello?"

"Hey, Allie." His rich deep voice sounded tired.

"You aren't still working, are you?" I asked. "You took the brunt of the explosion. What did you get, fifty stiches?"

"Not in the same place," he said ruefully. "They're scattered, with three or four stitches per spot. I feel like my back is full of gravel."

"You should wear a bulletproof vest," I said. "That would have caught a lot of the shrapnel."

"It's hot, heavy, and not part of the standard uniform."

"Oh."

"I called to check on you," he said. "Are you doing okay?"

"I'm fine," I said, looking around the empty room.

Things were so quiet without Jenn and everyone. "Any more information on who did this?"

"The fire chief says it wasn't the box that exploded," he said.

"Wait, what?"

"The box was still relatively intact after the blast. They found it digging through the rubble."

"I don't understand."

"The fire chief thinks the blast was set outside the center, in the rafters. Whoever set the explosion off knew that everyone was out of the building."

"That means they didn't want to hurt the seniors," I said. "They only wanted to scare them. To keep them from talking?"

"We don't have a motive," Rex said. "But the fire chief and I do agree that they were trying to scare people, not hurt them."

"There wasn't anyone left in the building, was there?" I asked. "I mean, I'm pretty sure we checked . . . but . . ."

"No bodies were found," he said quietly. "But the bomber had to be within sight of the building to know that. And even then, they took a huge chance when they set off the explosions."

"I'm just glad no one had a heart attack. That explosion was loud."

"George told me that he has the clinic on call. There could be some delayed reactions to today."

"What about you? You could have a delayed reaction."

"Same with you," he said. "Is there anyone there keeping an eye on you?"

"Just Mal and Mella."

"I don't think they could call 9-1-1 if anything happened to you."

"You shouldn't be alone either, then," I said.

"I agree."

There was a knock at my outside door. Mal barked and wagged her tail happily. I peeked out through the peephole in my back door. Rex stood outside. "You're here," I said as I opened the door. My tone came out surprised and breathy.

"I'm here," he said, stepping inside. He closed the door, pulled me against him, and kissed me hard. I sank right into the moment.

The next morning, I was up at 5 A.M. making fudge for several online orders. With the remodeling going on, I decided not to open the fudge shop to anyone on the street. I glanced out the window. The sun had not come up yet, and the streets were cold and empty except for a cleaning crew coming around to sweep up the horse droppings from the night before.

I thought about last night with Rex. It was completely unexpected, but it left me feeling very happy and warm inside. Something about facing death together brought us even closer. He'd left around four to go home, shower, and prep for his day. I could be wrong, but it seemed that neither of us had any residual concussions from the blast.

I made dark chocolate fudge with macadamia nuts and cranberries. The process was the same whether anyone watched through the shop window or not. I cooked the base, and when it was at the "softball" stage, I poured it on the marble cooling tables, which had coolant running underneath. Then it was time to stir the liquid as it cooled and thickened. When it was ready to fold, I reached over and added the nuts and cranberries. Then I took the small metal scraper, folded it all into a long loaf, and expertly cut one-pound pieces, adding them to a tray for boxing later.

The online orders had tripled since the reality show. Even though I hadn't won the fudge-off, it seemed I had still been a fan favorite, and viewers went to the website and ordered fudge for themselves. And now it was time to gear up for the holidays, too.

I made five different kinds of fudge and placed them on trays for boxing. When I was done, it was 7 A.M., and the first rays of sunlight had finally started to creep over the street in streaks of pink. Frances unlocked the front door and came in with Mr. Devaney in tow.

"Is there coffee?" Mr. Devaney asked. He rubbed his hands together to warm them.

"What's the temperature?" I asked. "Should I start a fire?" I was hot from cooking fudge and working. But it was clear from the red on Frances's nose that the outside world was cold.

"It's thirty-five degrees," Frances said as she unbundled herself from her coat, scarf, and hat to reveal a long denim skirt, sturdy black boots, and a sweater with a black cat on it. Mal jumped up and begged her for pets. "You'll need to layer up when you take the pup out for her walk."

"When was the coffee made?" Mr. Devaney asked. He sipped it and made a face.

"Oh, I guess it's the first batch. I made it at five. I

forget to freshen it when we don't have any guests. I'll have to start making it later so we can share one batch. When do the construction workers come?"

"They'll be here at eight," Mr. Devaney said. "Did you get a look at the floor?"

"I poked my head in last night, but I didn't take a good look. Do you think we can refinish the wood and skip carpets?"

"I'll assess it and let you know." Mr. Devaney gave Frances a kiss on the mouth and went upstairs to the second floor.

I made fresh coffee, and Frances started a fire in the fireplace, creating a warm and cozy atmosphere. "Well, we certainly look ready for guests, even if we don't have any," I said. I handed Frances a cup of coffee. "What are you going to work on?"

"The new booking system we ordered," she said. "It came yesterday, and I need to install it and then transfer our files from the old to the new."

"I know it's hard to start up new software, but I think that it will be much better come next year. It allows us to have online reservations and put specials on those travel sites when things get slow."

"I doubt things are going to get slow next year," Frances said. "You've been pretty popular since that reality show. It's a shame you didn't win."

"I'm kind of glad I didn't. If I had, I would have had to go on a speaking tour, and I'd rather stay on the island."

Frances went to her desk and studied her screen for a moment, then looked up at me. "Rex was here late last night."

I felt the heat of a blush race up my cheeks. Perhaps having cameras on the outside of the building wasn't always a good thing. My private life was pretty public among my team, and there was little that they didn't know. I shrugged.

"Yes, well. We wanted to make sure neither of us had a concussion."

"Right," Frances said with a smile before going back to work.

The doorbells rang as the remodeling crew walked in, in painter pants. They were talking and laughing and pounding their arms because of the cold. Some had Carhartt jackets on, but others wore only a light shirt with their painter's pants. It was clear the cold had caught a few of the men off guard. "Mr. Devaney's upstairs." I pointed the way.

"Is Elmer here yet?"

"Not yet," I answered.

"Coffee?" One of the young guys looked familiar.

"Over there. Rick Manx, right?" I asked. "Haley's husband?"

"Yeah."

"I didn't know you were part of this crew, too."

"Yeah, I'm good, so Elmer brought me on."

"This guy's an expert painter," one of the other guys said, putting his arm around Rick and pounding his chest. "Glad to have him."

The doorbells rang to signal the entrance of Elmer Faber. He wiped his feet on the doormat and pulled off his hat. "All right, you motley crew, let's get to work." He turned to me. "Morning. Did you have a chance to look at the work so far?"

"I'll go up with you," I said. "I was wondering if refinishing the floors instead of laying carpet would be an option."

"That could work. Refinishing is an option for most places," he said. "Not sure about that spot by the window that had the chicken blood from the prank those kids did last month. Stuff's hard to get out."

"I thought we got it out of the carpet?"

"Maybe the carpet, but it stained all the way through to the floor. We can try to sand it out."

"Will that work?"

"It depends on the thickness of the floorboards. These are old boards, so they may be able to take a deep sanding."

"Keep me posted," I said. "I really think that polishing the original floors could be the way to go."

"We can coat them a few times with poly to really make them shine, but then you have to be careful with your older guests. They slip on rugs and slick floors."

"I hadn't thought about that," I said, biting my bottom lip. "I'll talk this over with my staff. In the meantime, the walls will be painted and stenciled, right?"

"Yes, ma'am, if that's still what you want. Most people put up wallpaper."

"I know," I said. "Your crew did great work removing the old paper. I'd like to try the paint and stencils, though. I found a photo from the opening of the McMurphy, and the rooms were painted then."

"Whatever you like—you're the boss."

"Thanks," I said. Mella came strolling out of one of the open rooms being remodeled. I picked her up. "Silly kitty. The second floor is off-limits." I turned and made my way back down to the lobby when the bells over the front door rang again.

Rex walked into the lobby. My heart picked up. It

wasn't fair, really. He looked like he'd slept eight hours, and he was showered and wearing a freshly pressed uniform. I knew I was a bit rumpled, with my hair put up in a messy bun and my white shirt and black slacks smelling of fudge. In fact, I was a bit sticky. Mella was licking my arm, her tongue like sandpaper. Her fur stuck to me in the places where I hadn't washed off the hardened sugar. His eyes took in the messy sight of me, and he grinned. "Hi."

"That kind of look got me into trouble last night," I said.

"I hope to get you into trouble more often," he said, walking right up to within an inch of me. Mella rubbed up against him and pawed at his arm, as if to ask him to take her from me.

"What's up, Rex?" Frances asked, breaking the tension between us as she came down the stairs. "Any news on the bombing at the senior center?"

"Whoever did it set the charges in the roof."

"What? I thought the bomb was in the box."

"You were supposed to think that," he said. "The bomber wanted to incite panic, but then they waited. As soon as they were certain everyone was out of the building, they literally blew the top off of it."

"Well, that's still terrible. Did they leave a note or something? Anything to give us a reason why they would do such a thing?"

"We have no motive at this time," Rex said. He looked at me. "Why did you think bomb when you saw the box?"

"I've been wondering that myself," Frances said.

"I don't know," I said. "It seemed suspicious, and the first thing that came to mind was *bomb!*"

"Good thing you're suspicious," Frances said.

"I think the bomber was counting on it," Rex said. "I'd like to see the pictures you and Liz went through from the night of the zombie walk, if you don't mind."

"Sure." I put Mella down. "They're up in my office. Do you think the two things are connected?"

"I don't, but you do," he said as he walked up the stairs behind me.

I turned to him. "I never said anything."

"You didn't have to say. I could see it in your expressive eyes. You thought they were bombing the senior center to threaten people who might give you some clues."

"Maybe you're right—that would mean they had to know that I was investigating, and only Liz and Frances knew that. Neither of them would have bombed the center."

Rex gave an inelegant snort. "Honey, whenever there's a crime on the island, everyone figures you're investigating. They also all know you don't hang out at the senior center for the company. The senior gossip line is ground zero for any investigation. I know because that's what I use when I'm trying to figure out who might have a grudge against whom."

I turned forward again and resumed climbing the stairs. We passed the second floor, and Rex looked curiously at the group of men working away. "I'm remodeling," I said.

"I knew you were going to redo the room that the prankster ruined, but I didn't realize you were redoing the entire floor."

"Now's the best time," I said. "I don't have guests this week, and next week is also pretty empty. Except for Friday and Saturday, and the guys won't work those days."

"It's nice you're adding to the local economy."

"It needed to be done." We made it to the fourth floor and walked into my office. Mal barked and ran across the room, flinging herself at Rex. He picked her up and rubbed under her chin. "I see you have more than one fan," I said.

"Are you a fan?"

"I was referring to my dog and my cat," I teased, walking into the office. The pictures were in a packet on the top of the desk. "Here are the photos I printed off. Liz will have a fit if you take them into evidence, though."

"There's nothing to take into evidence," he said as he put Mal down and went through the pictures quickly. "I can see why you think it might have been a case of mistaken identity. These two guys have the same build and the same jacket. The killer could have been nervous. The alley was dark. He might have taken his opportunity and left in a hurry without checking that he had the right person."

"Except we didn't find the murder weapon," I pointed out. "So they had enough forethought to take it with them and get rid of it. Did you look in all the garbage bins along the alley?"

"Of course. My guys thoroughly combed the area, and no weapon was found. Most likely, the killer took it out into the street with them. It was a zombie walk, after all. A bloody weapon wouldn't have been paid any attention."

"It sounds like it was premeditated," I said. "The killer had to have been planning it to pick that night."

"I agree," he said. "But we still haven't found a motive yet." He pulled a photo out of the group. "I'm going to take this one and send it to a friend who's good with pictures. Maybe he can help us figure out who the other guy is."

"Oh! After the chaos of yesterday, I completely forgot," I said. "Before the bomb, I was talking to Ethel Thigbee. She said that this other guy was Josh Spalding. I can't be sure, though. She said she recognized him by his butt." I blushed.

Rex, frowning, moved right past that last detail. "Is that what you intended to do at the senior center? To ask seniors if they could identify the other man in these pictures?"

"Yes."

"Who knew that?"

"Liz did, of course, and a few of the seniors who thought I should investigate. I have no idea who they might have told." I studied his handsome face. His expression was cool. "You think it could be connected, then? That the killer knew what I was going to do and bombed the place?"

Rex sighed. "Could be. Either way, those bombs took time to place. How long did you have those pictures?"

"Only since the night before. Liz and I looked at them the day before that, though. Did anyone see a person on a ladder at the senior center? It took a ladder to get the explosives up there, right?"

"I've asked that question myself. Most of the seniors were pretty shaken up by the bomb and don't have a clear memory of that day or the day before. Officer Brown is chasing that angle, but he hasn't had much luck."

"I'd like to go back to the senior center," I said.

"Why? It's a pile of rubble. Once the fire chief releases the scene, we've got volunteers set to come and haul the busted piles away. It will be next summer before we can build a new center."

"Then I'll have the seniors come to me."

"What do you mean?"

"I mean I'll volunteer the McMurphy's lobby for the senior activities. Most of them are leaving for the winter months. It won't be crowded, and I will get some use out of the McMurphy in the off-season. Other than the Christmas tourists and the snow-mobiling enthusiasts, of course."

"Are you sure that's a good idea?" Rex asked. "You are in the middle of renovating, after all."

"I think it's a great idea," Frances said from the doorway. "I was going to ask you if we could do that."

"I'm all for it," I said. "Why don't you go tell Mrs. Tunisian and Mrs. Anderson to spread the word? I'll have boxed lunches a few days each week. We can put up card tables and have artists come in to do different crafts."

"It's a plan," Frances said.

"Is that why you came up?" I asked her when she stayed in the doorway.

"Oh, actually no. Brenda Baker is downstairs. She says she might know something about the bombing."

"I'll head right down."

"Wait," Rex said after Frances had left. "Why would she come to you with information, and not go to the police"

"I don't know," I said with a shrug. "Maybe I feel safer."

"Are you saying the police aren't safe?"

I leaned closer toward him. "I think you're pretty dangerous, myself."

That comment took him off guard, and he grinned.

"But, in all seriousness, most people seem to find it easier to share gossip with me. You need facts and proof, right?"

"Right."

"Then I'll gather gossip until we have facts and proof."

"Just be careful, Allie."

"I'm always careful," I said with more confidence than I felt. I turned to my puppy. "Come on, Mal. Let's go down and greet our new guest."

Brenda was short, with long brown hair and a pixie face. She had large green eyes that looked at me expectantly.

"Hello," I said, sticking out my hand. "Allie McMurphy."

"Hi, Allie, I'm Brenda." She shook my hand. "I stopped by because I heard from my grandmother that you were there for the senior center bombing."

"Yes, I was. So was Rex—er, Officer Manning, I mean," I said, awkwardly pointing behind me toward Rex.

"Rex Manning," he said, extending his hand as well.

Brenda shook his hand. "Thank you for helping to save my grandmother and the others from the bombing. It's horrible that someone did that. What were they thinking?"

I put Mal down. She went to Brenda and jumped up, begging for attention. "Why don't you come and sit? Can I get you a coffee or a cocoa?"

"Coffee will be fine," she said, sitting down in one of the flowered, wingback chairs.

"I've got to be on my way," Rex said. "Allie, we'll

talk later?" I nodded and tried not to blush. "Nice to meet you, Ms. Baker."

We both watched as Rex left. There was something about the way he moved that exuded power and control. I turned and poured two coffees. "Cream or sugar?"

"Cream, please."

I added half-and-half to both mugs and carefully brought them over to the chairs, where I sat down across from her. Mal jumped up on the settee and snuggled in beside me. Mella was already curled up on the back of a third settee sleeping. "How's your grandmother?"

"She's okay. A little shaken up, and some bumps and bruises. I was wondering if you had any idea who did this?"

"I don't," I said, shaking my head.

"But you're going to find them, right? I mean, everyone knows you're good at finding killers."

"Well—"

"You're investigating Anthony's death, right?"

"Yes." I shifted uncomfortably. "But it's not official or anything. Rex has his men investigating. They have all the resources to do a good job."

"But you *are* looking into it," she pressed.

"Yes, I promised Maggs I would. In fact, that's why I was at the senior center. I mean, in addition to supporting Frances and Mr. Devaney in the card tournament."

"You are so funny," she said with a slight chuckle.

"What do you mean?" I tilted my head.

"You just said, Frances and Mr. Devaney. She's Mrs.

Devaney now, you know. I think you can call him Douglas. Everyone else does."

"Do they?" I felt the heat of a blush. "I'm so used to thinking of him as Mr. Devaney, but I guess you're right. Since Frances is Mrs. Devaney now, it might seem disrespectful to only call him Mr. Devaney. I'll have to ask them how they feel about that."

"Feel about what?" Frances asked as she came down the stairs to join us.

"Brenda pointed out that I call you Frances and your husband Mr. Devaney. It's kind of disrespectful."

"Oh, I'm sure Douglas wouldn't mind you calling him by his first name," Frances said. "And no, it's not disrespectful. We work for you, dear."

"Okay," I said. I settled back in the chair. "Then that's what I'll do. Brenda, Frances thought you might have some information for me."

"I might. I think I know who might have wanted to hurt Anthony," she said.

"Wow, who? Why?"

Her mouth became a thin line. "I think it was Philip Lemkin."

"Who?"

"Philip Lemkin has an adventure tours group that comes to Mackinac to run the outer trail and climb Arch Rock."

"I've never heard of him before," I said. I looked to Frances to confirm his identity. She nodded.

"He's about Anthony's age. Didn't Anthony take one of Philip's adventure tours?" Frances asked.

"Yes," Brenda said. "There was some kind of incident during the tour. The two had a disagreement, and Anthony left a bad review for the tour."

"Well, that doesn't sound like a reason to kill a man," I said.

"Google it. It was a really rough review. It was the talk of the island for a full month. You see, people loved Anthony, and they took his side. And the review was pretty negative, so even strangers took it seriously. Philip hasn't had a tour on the island since."

"How long ago was that?" I asked.

"Three months ago," Brenda said. "Check out the reviews for Northwest Adventure Tours."

I grabbed my phone and did a search for a few review sites that Brenda told me to check. "Wow," I said after going to the fourth review site. "Anthony made sure each site had a bad review." I looked at Brenda. "This hurt his business even off the island?"

"That's the rumor," Brenda said. "Philip grew up in Petoskey and spent summers working on Mackinac Island before he started his adventure tours business."

"It's a small world," Frances said. "What does the review say?"

"It says that Northwest Adventure doesn't respect the environment on their tours. They do unethical things and leave trash wherever they go."

"Oh, that's not good," Frances said.

"It seems that Philip was just going to leave the tour group's trash on the ground in the park, and he walked away and left a fire going. People around here pride themselves on stewardship of the parks and the land. Everyone is a fan of Smokey Bear." Brenda shook her head in disgust.

"Having that get out would ruin him," I agreed. "Now, he could have answered it and done restitution, and put in place some guidelines for his tours, but I'm not seeing any response at all to the reviews."

"The word is that Philip thought the review wasn't worth addressing. Then his business fell off, and he started blaming Anthony and told everyone who would listen."

"Was Philip on the island that night?"

"Yes," Brenda said. "I have proof." She pulled out her phone. "I was taking pictures that night. That's me in the zombie waitress outfit. See this guy here? The one with the Day of the Dead face paint and the Beetle-juice costume? That's Philip. Now look." She thumbed through the photos until she got to the one she wanted. "This is Philip watching Anthony. See that look on his face?"

"Yes, he looks angry," I said. "You can tell even through the makeup."

"Now look at this picture."

The next photo was one of Philip lunging at Anthony. Two of Philip's friends held him back. It was clear angry words had been said. I don't know how Anthony's friends missed this altercation."

"Looks pretty bad," I said. "You should take these to the police. Maggs would really appreciate it."

"Well, see, I brought it to you because the police have already talked to Philip. He's telling people that the cops have ruled him out. That's not right."

"No, that's not right," I said. "Do you want me to dig into this?"

She nodded. "Yes, it's why I came to you. I'll send the photos to your phone." She swiped, and they showed up on my phone. She stood. "Thanks for the coffee. I know if Philip did it, you'll be able to prove it. Thanks Allie."

"I'll do my best," I said. After she left, I studied the pictures more carefully. It was a lead. Unfortunately, we thought the killer planned the murder. Yet this looked spontaneous. Maybe we were looking at things all wrong.

Chapter 10

"Do you know Philip Lemkin?" I asked Liz later that night. Liz had been working on the story of the senior center bombing and stopped by after Frances and Mr. Devaney—I mean, Douglas—had gone home. We were upstairs in my apartment with Mal sleeping at my feet and Mella curled up on Papa Liam's favorite chair.

I'd poured us both a glass of wine. Liz was draped across the couch, and I sat in my second-favorite chair.

"I know *of* Philip Lemkin. He tried to get his tours in the newspaper. Grandpa told him that he had to pay for an ad. Lemkin refused, and that was that."

"Did you know of the feud between him and Anthony?"

"I wouldn't call it a feud," she said. She sipped her wine. "Seriously. If it was a feud, don't you think Philip would have been the first person I suspected?"

I frowned. She was right. "So if it wasn't a feud, why did Brenda think it was? Why were they fighting the night of the zombie walk?"

She sat up. "What do you mean, they were fighting?"

"Brenda had pictures." I pulled out my phone and thumbed open the pictures. "See." I turned my phone to Liz.

"Okay. I see Philip looking angry, and here I see Philip being restrained, but who is he trying to fight? This guy?" She pointed to the back of Anthony's head.

"Yes, Anthony."

"I don't think that's Anthony," she said with a shake of her head. "I think it's the other guy. Do you still have the pictures I gave you?"

"Yes, keep scrolling."

She swiped through my phone photo album until she came across the pictures from the zombie walk. "See, look, this is the other guy. He has a wedding ring on and so does the Wannabe Anthony or should we call him Anthony two-point-oh?"

I took my phone back and studied the photos. Sure enough, Philip wasn't lunging at Anthony. He was lunging at the guy who was dressed the same, maybe Josh Spalding. "I see what you mean. It really is easy to get them confused. If we made that mistake, and Brenda did, too, it's looking more likely that the killer thought this guy was Anthony."

"I agree. Do you think we can rule out someone killing Anthony on purpose?"

I shrugged. "I don't know. Brenda also said that the police have already questioned Philip and let him go. Rex would have told me if they had a suspect."

"Would he, now?" Liz said in a singsong voice. She waggled her eyebrows. "Why would he do that? Unless the island scuttlebutt is true."

"What scuttlebutt?" I asked, trying to remain calm.

Did someone besides Frances see Rex leaving in the wee hours?

"That you and a certain hunky police officer are enjoying each other's company."

"I mean, everyone knows we tried to have a date last month. But then with everything that happened, the date didn't end up actually being a date."

"And now?"

"Why are you so curious?" I asked, trying to dodge the question.

She shrugged. "I'm a reporter. I'm nosey by profession. Plus, I don't have a love life of my own right now, so I have to live vicariously through you. And the word is that Rex was seen leaving your apartment pretty darn late last night—or very early this morning, if you know what I mean. And you know what I mean. What happened to Trent?"

"Trent and I are broken up," I said with a sigh. "He's spent the last month in Chicago helping his father transfer control of the businesses to his children. And Trent's mom pulled both Trent and Paige off the island. Can you blame her, after what happened to them both this year?"

Liz shook her head and leaned back against the couch, swirling her wine. "No, I can't blame her. Lots of people are concerned about the recent rise in crime. It's bad enough we have an aging population living on the island full time. Now we're bombing them? People are going to leave here in droves."

"I don't think so," I said. "Mackinac Island is filled with very strong, sturdy people. They've seen wars and terrible storms, droughts, fires, severe cold, and snow. An exploding building isn't going to keep them down.

In fact, I'm having them come to the McMurphy twice a week for cards and crafts. I'm going to bring the senior center to me. I've even called and gotten the go-ahead to cater lunches on those days."

"That's cool," she said. "But aren't you worried you'll just bring the bomber to the McMurphy?"

"No," I said, reaching down to pet Mal. "I don't think the bomber would strike twice. Why would he? He's already sent his message. Besides, the McMurphy has cameras everywhere and a darn good security system."

"I did notice you're a bit of a Fort Knox around here."

"Experience has taught me to be prepared. If a bomber tried to take down the McMurphy, I'd catch him on camera."

"So what's our next step in the investigation?"

"I don't know," I said. "Did you have a chance to talk to Anthony's friend Steve? Sorry again for bailing on you."

"Yes," she said and blew out a breath. "He told the same story as Justin. They noticed the double, but not enough to identify him. They were drinking."

"And he doesn't know who might want Anthony dead?"

"No. Again, it's the same story. Anthony was a great guy."

"Sounds like the investigation is stalled. That said, tomorrow is Thursday, and the seniors will be coming for the first 'lunch and learn.' Maybe I'll learn more about Anthony or the bomber."

"What's the 'learn' part? Are you going to teach fudge making?"

"No, I've asked Haley Manx to come and show them how to make glass-bottom pottery."

"That sound like fun," Liz said. "Maybe I'll come and do a story on it for the newspaper. It could be a nice follow-up to the story about the bombing."

"That would be wonderful," I said, sitting up. "It would be good for the island to see that others still care."

"Yes, well, I'd better head out if I'm going to get any work done tonight." Liz stood. Mella got up with her and stretched. She came with me to walk Liz to the outside door of my apartment.

"I almost forgot to ask. Any more news on your grandfather?" I asked.

"They've moved him into a nursing home."

"Oh, no!"

"Oh, it's not permanent. It's to give him a month of full-time therapy and rehab. We hope to have him back at my mom's house in early December."

"Oh, good." I relaxed my posture as she opened the door and stepped out into the cold, clear night. I reached down and picked up Mal before my pup could run outside. "Thanks for stopping by. Keep your eye out for Anthony's double, okay? I'd love to talk to him about what happened that night."

"I will," Liz said with a smile. "I'm sure there are a lot of people who would like to talk to him." Mella slipped out the door with Liz and raced down the stairs and into the alley. "Oh, no!"

"It's okay," I said. "Mella likes to go off and explore at night. She always comes back."

"Be careful feeding strays," Liz said with a quick grin. "You might get too many coming back." She waved, and Mal and I watched as she walked down the alley the half a block to Main Street, where she turned right and disappeared into the night.

There was a party going on somewhere. I could hear the "Monster Mash" being played and excited chatter mixed with laughter and the clink of glass. It was a surreal reminder that there were still tourists on the island—and that not all zombie parties ended in death.

Mella didn't come back right away the next morning, which worried me a little. She usually showed up after a night of prowling when I took Mal out for her quick walk first thing each morning.

I called her name. "Mella, Mella girl. Here kitty, kitty." I made kissing sounds with my lips, and Mal joined in with a bark or two before I stopped her so she didn't wake the neighbors. After all, not everyone was in the habit of walking their dog at 5 A.M.

Sadly, Mal and I went back inside to start our day alone. I trusted that Mella would return eventually. She always did. But I also made a mental note to keep an eye out for her. The longest she had ever stayed away was twenty-four hours, and that was when she first started to come around.

The rest of the morning went by quickly. Frances had spread the word that I was having the senior center meeting at the McMurphy, so we needed to get the space ready for that. The workmen were busy on the second floor, painting. They had spent yesterday taping off corners and pushing furniture to the middle of the rooms. The mattresses had all been pulled out and hauled away. Papa Liam liked to change them out every three years, which was a good hotel business practice. At least painting wasn't much noise or bother for the seniors. They were shaken up enough from the explosion—they didn't need more construction noise.

I had finished making and shipping my fudge for the day by 9 A.M., and Frances had everything covered with the catering service, who would bring in two kinds of soup, salad, and plates filled with sandwiches, from turkey to roast beef and even vegetarian with cheese. By ten-thirty, we had two long tables set up near the coffee bar, waiting to be filled with food.

Then Frances, Douglas, and I worked to organize the rest of the lobby for the event. Frances covered the tables near the coffee bar with white tablecloths. Douglas and I moved the chairs and settee over to the other side of the lobby, near the seating area by the front window. We grouped all of the furniture together like a lounge area to sit.

"We had better make the aisle wide," Douglas said. "We have a few using wheelchairs and walkers."

"Got it," I said, scooching the settee a little closer to the other chairs and widening the aisle. I figured the seniors would move them to their liking, anyway.

I pulled out my phone and texted Haley to see what she needed for the demonstration. She texted back that she just needed a table. She was going to bring everything else, including a microphone and speakers.

Great, I texted back. *Speakers are a good idea. I didn't think of that.*

"I've got a demonstration table set up in front of the elevator," Douglas said.

"Haley's bringing speakers, too," I said.

"Good, I'll set them around the room so that everyone can hear."

We then brought four more long tables up from the basement and unfolded the legs, setting them up in two rows. It filled the lobby with just enough room for wheelchairs to get around. The doorbells jangled, and Mal barked and ran to greet our guest. It was Haley. She carried a big box and pulled a wagon behind her. I hurried over to help out. "Hi, Haley. Thanks for coming. That's a lot of stuff, what can I do to help?"

"I've got everything packed in the boxes, but they keep tipping off the wagon." Her wagon was a little pull cart with no sides.

"I'll hold on until we get you all the way in. We have a table set up in the back for your demonstration."

"Perfect," she said. "Oh, hello, Mr. Devaney. How are you?"

"Good," he replied gruffly.

"Do you know each other?" I asked as we stopped in front of the table.

Haley put the big box on the table and opened it. "Mr. Devaney taught English when I was a senior in high school," she said. "That was a long time ago."

"Oh, come on. You're pretty young," I protested.

"I'm thirty-five," she replied as she pulled out speakers and set them up.

"I would have never guessed," I said.

We took her materials and tools out of the boxes. She had brought a table cover, clay wrapped in plastic—which I assumed was to keep it from drying out—and smaller boxes filled with tiny shards of colorful glass.

"I'm going to have them make pinch pots," she said. "I'll take them and fire them in my kiln. This time next week, we can meet again and distribute the pots."

"Oh, how nice," I said. "I can't wait to learn how to make them."

"Pinch pots are the simplest introduction to pottery. They may be far too easy for some of your participants," she warned.

"But not for me!" I said.

The doorbells rang. I turned to see Mrs. Tunisian and Mrs. Elliot come in.

"Hi, ladies, thanks for coming. You're a bit early. We're still setting up."

"Well, that's why we are here," Mrs. Tunisian said. "To help you set up. But it looks like you have most things done."

"You can put a small packet of clay in front of each chair," Haley said. "I've also got placemats to help contain any mess."

"Very smart," Mrs. Elliot said, taking the pile of placemats. The two ladies and I helped Haley finish. It went very quickly, and I showed the seniors where the coffee was and waved them toward the sitting area near the door. By this time, more people had started showing up. By 11 A.M., we had a packed house.

While Frances emceed the event, I took Mal outside for a short walk. She was enjoying all the attention from the seniors, but her presence was taking attention away from Haley's teaching. I checked the alley for Mella while Mal did her business. "Here kitty, kitty," I called. "I've got some treats!" That made Mal's ears perk up, but it didn't draw out Mella. We walked our usual route down the alley, along the road toward the lake. I kept my eye out, but there was no sign of my wily cat.

"Well, at least she isn't finding dead bodies," I said to Mal. "Come on, let's go home."

"Allie."

I turned to see Mr. Beecher walking toward me. A dapper dresser, today Mr. Beecher wore a fedora and a waistcoat, jacket, and pants. He had also begun using a cane recently, and I hadn't seen him out walking for a while. We stopped, and Mal sniffed two jack-o'-lanterns while I huddled in my jacket. Fall was truly upon us.

"Hi, Mr. Beecher," I said. "How are you?"

"I'm well, thanks. I hear you found another poor dead soul. Was it Mal who found him again?"

"No, this time it was Sophie and my cat, Mella," I said. "You haven't happened to see her, have you? She's a lovely calico. She went out last night and hasn't returned yet."

"No, I haven't seen a calico. There was Percy—a gray-striped fellow who belongs to Mrs. Anderson—and Rex, a nice brown cat, but no Mella." He looked at me. "I've been on the lookout for a cat, too. I like to say hi to the cats when I walk, and I've been looking for Angel. I'd also like to see a black cat—black cats are special this time of year."

"You certainly know everyone and their pets," I said. "Wait, perhaps you can help me with identifying someone."

"Well, I can try." He reached into his waistcoat pocket and pulled out a small dog treat, which he offered to Mal. She wagged her stub of a tail in puppy happiness and took it eagerly.

I swiped up the pictures of the guy who we thought might be Josh Spalding and turned my phone toward

Mr. Beecher. "Do you recognize him? I mean, under the zombie makeup?"

Mr. Beecher pulled a pair of reading glasses out of his front pocket, placed them on his nose, and looked at the picture carefully. "I'm not sure."

I scrolled to a second picture. "What about here?"

"It's the same man, that's for sure," he said. "The same wedding ring. Quite unique. Sorry I can't be of more help."

I pulled the phone back toward me and looked at the ring. It *was* unique. It was silver, with a diamond and a blue stripe in the center of the band. "That's a big help, actually. I was so busy trying to identify the zombie, I didn't look closely at the ring. But someone will know who wears a wedding band like this."

"Why do you need to know who he is?"

"Because he's wearing the same costume as Anthony Vanderbilt."

"The dead man."

"Yes. I think this guy was the intended victim, and I need to find him and let him know that his life might be in danger."

"Well, there are only a handful of fellows with that build and hair color," he said. "I'm sure you'll narrow it down soon."

"I certainly hope so," I said.

Chapter 11

After walking Mal, I wasn't sure I would have enough time to make my own pinch pot. Luckily, Haley was still walking everyone through how to make simple pots, and I was able to catch up. They were so much fun to make. After we made the ones Haley helped us with, she distributed pencils so we could create our own designs. When we finally finished, we put our artwork on the demonstration table and then washed up for a late lunch. I was surprised at how resilient the seniors were. Most of the members who were at the card tournament two days ago were here. Some wore their cuts, scrapes, and bruises with pride.

"I've never been in an explosion before," Mr. Merger said. "Hope to never be in one again."

"I heard the culprit used the box to get us out of the building and then pulled the trigger on explosives in the roof," Mrs. Anderson said.

"That's the report in the paper," Mr. Merger replied. "Don't know why anyone would want to blow up a bunch of old people, though, so it rings true."

"Maybe it was someone who wanted a new building," Mr. Worther suggested. "We've been asking for improvements for years, and the city council never gets around to funding them. Gotta fund them now."

"Well, that would certainly be one way to get their way with the counsel," Mr. Merger said. "Who in here was wise enough to think to blow up that old tinder box?"

"No one in here blew up the place," Frances said, giving him her best teacher stare.

He crossed his arms over his chest and grumbled a bit. "Well, someone decided to blow the place up. All's I'm saying is that the insurance money will help us rebuild, and I bet the new building will be even better."

"Better stop talking like that, or the cops will think you did it," Douglas admonished him.

"As if I could climb a ladder," Mr. Merger said.

"You can't even climb out of your easy chair," Mr. Worther teased, and the room erupted in laughter.

"Well, the word is they'll release the building to the city in a couple of days, and the city will have to hire someone to haul off the debris."

"Out with the old, in with the new, I guess," Mrs. Anderson said.

I brought coffee and fudge around while Haley cleaned up and packed her stuff away. Some of the seniors started to straggle out. As I distributed each cup, I brought out my phone and asked if they knew anyone who wore that type of wedding band. But senior after senior shook their head.

"Ain't never seen nothing like it," Mr. Worther said. "Nice, though."

"Well, thanks everyone," I said. "Haley will fire these and bring them back tomorrow. We'll finish the pots then, at the same time as today."

"Yes, we'll work on glaze and glass placement next time," Haley said.

Mal was worn out from all the excitement by this time. She curled up in her bed by the receptionist desk, which conveniently placed her out of the way as we worked on cleaning up. Douglas began to break down tables while Haley carefully packed the pots to take back to her studio. They were very small pots and more flat than round so that it would be easier to see the glass bottoms, so they weren't too difficult to pack up safely.

"What can you do with such a small pot, anyway?" Mrs. Tunisian asked as she watched Haley pack up the pots.

"They make good ring or change holders," Haley said.

"Won't the glass bottom break?"

"Oh, no. They will be quite durable."

"Huh," Mrs. Tunisian said, then turned to me. "Show me those pictures again. Maybe I can guess who it is."

I showed her the pictures.

"Nope, still don't know," she said. "Looks like the killer was wrong to bomb the senior center. We really don't know anything this time. But now we're going to work to find out. Come on, Eleanor," she said to Mrs. Elliot. "Let's get going."

I watched as the two old ladies left. They were the last to go, other than my staff and Haley. Douglas was already hauling the tables back down to the basement, so I grabbed a broom to sweep up. Having a bunch of seniors in the lobby was about the same as hosting a bunch of kids, I thought with a smile. Things got spilled.

"I'm ready to go," Haley said. She picked up her box and grabbed the wagon handle. "See you tomorrow."

"Bye, Haley. Thanks again for coming."

It took another half an hour to restore the lobby to its former self. By the time we were done, it was nearly 3 P.M. I stuck my head out the back door and looked up on the fire escape from my apartment to see if Mella was in the alley or up on the landing, ready to come home. She wasn't.

"What's the matter?" Frances asked.

"Mella hasn't come back today," I said. "I think I'll take Mal and go look for her again. Are you okay with holding down the fort until I come back? You can text me if the construction crew needs anything."

"Are you sure she didn't slip back in with one of the seniors?" Frances asked. "You know how tricky she can be."

I smiled at the memory of how Mella first came into the McMurphy. While Rex was walking in, she had slipped past him and run through the lobby and up the stairs to the guest rooms. "I guess it wouldn't hurt to take a look inside first." I made my way up the floral-carpeted stairs to the second floor and saw that the hallway was freshly painted pastel blue. It was very welcoming. Elmer Faber, the foreman of the construction crew, had done his homework and matched paint colors to the original paint very well. My heart swelled with a sense of pride at restoring the McMurphy to its original beauty. I think Papa Liam would have been proud.

I stuck my head into the first room and found two guys finishing up painting a rose color on the walls. "Did anyone see a cat today?"

"No, ma'am," the one guy said.

"Are you sure?"

"I'm allergic to cats," the second guy said. "If one was nearby, I'd be breaking out in hives."

"Wow." I drew my eyebrows together in concern. "I have a cat. Will you be all right working here?"

"I'll be fine unless the cat gets into breathing distance," he said cheerfully. "I've got an EpiPen if I need it."

"I'll try to keep her in the lobby or the apartment," I said. I went looking for Elmer Faber. He was in the final room, talking with a guy who was adding finishing touches of lavender paint. "Hi, Elmer. How are things going?"

"We're on schedule," he said, coming toward me. "All the rooms and the hallway have fresh paint. We're going to let that set for forty-eight hours before we touch the walls again. Which means tomorrow will be a short day. We'll come and move the furniture out of the back half of the rooms so that we can sand the floors and stain them."

"Great. Hey, I didn't know one of your guys is allergic to cats. I've got Carmella. He said it shouldn't be a problem, but I need to know my cat won't put anyone in danger."

"He isn't that allergic," Elmer said. "Haven't seen the cat, though. Are you sure you have one?" he joked.

"I've got one, but she seems to be missing."

"Funny thing about cats is they always show up. You'll find her."

"I hope so."

"Oh, I just remembered. The supplies came in to start on the roof. Is it okay if I bring my roofing crew in starting tomorrow? They'll have to go up through your apartment."

"Sure," I said. "I'm usually up by five. Just don't hire anyone allergic to cats or dogs, I've got both."

"Deal," he said. "We'll be in around seven."

"I'll be ready." I did a cursory check of the remaining rooms for Mella, but as Elmer said, she wasn't there. Next, I tried the third floor, but all of the rooms were closed and locked. So was the utility closet. I opened it, just in case, but my cat wasn't inside.

That meant she was either in the office or not home yet. I climbed the last set of stairs and peered inside my office. Dust motes floated through an afternoon sunbeam, the only movement in the room. My heart squeezed a little at the emptiness, an unexpected pang at the fact that Jenn wasn't sitting at the second desk. I really needed to get used to her absence. She seemed to be happy with her new job in Chicago. I couldn't wish her back. What kind of friend would I be then?

Mal came up the stairs looking for me. I opened the apartment and went straight to the back door. There was no sign of Mella. "Come on, girl," I said to Mal. "Let's go for a walk and see if we can't find your sister."

I put Mal's harness and leash on and texted Frances that I was going out. She texted back a thumbs up emoji. Frances had taken to texting like a duck to water, and she loved sending emojis and pictures. She had even used an app to create a cartoon version of herself and often sent messages that way. It always made me chuckle.

Locking the back door as I left, I checked to see that the security cameras I installed were still covering the back of the building. They were. Which meant that anyone who studied my security footage would know who leaves my apartment at 4 P.M.

Mal and I searched a mile in each direction from the McMurphy. The pup had a field day sniffing the ground in some spots she didn't normally get to visit, but my fingers were crossed that she didn't find anything—not with her nasty habit of turning up dead bodies.

When we walked by the senior center, I couldn't help but stop and stare at the rubble. I glanced around, trying to figure out where the bomber might have stood when he hit the detonator. The center was surrounded by bed-and-breakfasts and other small business. Thank goodness nothing else caught fire.

A thought occurred to me. I decided to check out every bed-and-breakfast in sight of the center. Officer Brown had most likely already done that, but Mal and I could go meet neighbors just the same. Right?

First I went to the Dragonfly Inn, across the street and two houses down from the senior center. I'd met the proprietor once three months ago at a chamber of commerce event. She was around Papa Liam's age, but she had mentioned that she hoped I would take over the business. I thought for a moment and pulled her name out of my memory vaults: Agnes James.

The front porch of the Dragonfly was painted in blue, green, and white, and the house itself was white. The ceiling of the porch was blue, as was the decking, while the window trim was green. These old Victorian cottages were often called painted ladies because of the vibrant colors their architectural elements were painted in an effort to help them stand out.

The Victorians were a bit ostentatious, I thought.

"Come on in—the door is open!" a woman shouted from somewhere inside. I opened the door to a main foyer with a receptionist desk in the corner. A large staircase ran up one side, and the doorway to a parlor opened up on the other. The bed-and-breakfast was cheerfully decorated in a 1980s-style interpretation of Victorian splendor.

"Hi, it's Allie McMurphy," I called. Agnes came out of the parlor with a smile on her face. She was a small woman with pale blue eyes and hair dyed a deep black. The color was a bit startling—she was nearly ninety, after all. She wore a pair of polyester slacks and a pressed tee shirt.

"Oh, Allie, so nice to see you again. When was it we met?"

"A few months ago," I said. "Sorry that it's taken me this long to come visit."

"Nonsense," she said, waving me into the parlor. "I know you've been extraordinarily busy. What with taking on the McMurphy and solving all those crimes. I don't know how you do it. Frankly, just the thought of all you do exhausts me." She sat down in a side chair and left the couch to me. I tried to keep Mal from hopping up on her furniture, but she gestured that I shouldn't worry about it, and Mal eagerly cuddled up to me. "Can I get you something to drink? Maybe water for the dog?"

"Thank you, that would be lovely."

"I'll be right back." She got up and disappeared behind me. "This is a good time for a visit. No guests until tomorrow."

I held Mal in my lap and petted her. The parlor was quite pleasant, not what I had expected from a bed-and-breakfast operated by a woman in her late eighties. The gentle sound of spa-like music came from speakers tucked away in the corners, encouraging me to relax.

She came back into the parlor with a tray. It contained a hot pot of water, two mugs, a wooden box holding a variety of teas, and a small silver bowl filled with fresh water. "Here's a secret. I had them add a hot water spigot next to my kitchen tap. That way, I can entertain guests at a moment's notice and not have to wait for a kettle to boil. Isn't that wonderful?" She set the tray down on the end table and placed the silver bowl for Mal just off the blue and white rug that anchored the couch and chairs.

I let Mal down to get a drink and sniff around. "That is a great idea," I said. "I put in a coffee bar, and I leave out one pot with hot water on demand for the same reason."

She offered me the selection of teas, and I chose a green tea with honey and lemon. "Good choice," she said. "It is a bit nippy outside. I hope a hot beverage takes some of the chill off."

"Thanks," I said, waiting as she poured the water into my cup and added the tea bag before handing it to me. I settled back into the couch with my mug and saucer, and she got right to the heart of my visit. "My guess is you want to ask if I know anything about the senior center explosion."

I felt the heat of a blush rush up my cheeks. "Yes," I said. "And to visit with you. You weren't at the card tournament, but I've seen you at the center before."

"I had a doctor's appointment that day. Sad to say, I missed all the excitement. I did have a structural engineer come out and check the Dragonfly for any damages. Have to think about these things when you're a property owner."

"I didn't even think about how the blast might affect surrounding structures into this morning."

"I don't think our culprit thought about it, either," she said, pausing to take a sip of her Earl Grey tea. "You were thinking he might have been inside one of the surrounding buildings when he detonated the explosives."

"Yes," I said. "He had to be nearby to see that we had all left the building before he blew it up. There would only be a small window of opportunity from the time we cleared the building to the time the bomb squad came out. Whoever did this had to have been nearby. And they weren't on the street—we would have seen them."

"So you think they had to be inside a nearby business."

"It does seem logical."

"Well, not mine, dear. If anyone was here, they would have been knocked off their feet. The explosion moved my place half an inch off of its foundation, believe it or not. The engineer said that it was fine for now, but I should keep an eye on any further settling. If I see any cracks, I'm to call right away."

"Can they move it back a half an inch?"

She laughed. "They probably could, but I'm sure

they would prefer to simply shore it up. Either way, it will cost me and my insurance company plenty of money. I'd like to get my hands on the culprit, that's for sure."

"I was wondering if perhaps you might recognize someone in a picture." I put down my mug and pulled out my phone, thumbing through the pictures until I got to one I've been showing around to everyone. I handed her my phone. "This man was dressed exactly like Anthony Vanderbilt. I think Anthony was killed by mistake."

"Oh dear. That would be terrible." She put on reading glasses and had a long look. "I mean, it is terrible about Anthony, but it would be even worse if the killer murdered the wrong person. I don't think I recognize him, though." Handing my phone back to me, she asked, "Do you think the killer was the person who blew up the senior center?"

"I don't know." I put my phone back in my pocket. "In a way, I hope so. That way, we're only looking for one person. But in another way, I hope not."

"Because that means that you might be responsible."

"Yes. If I thought for one minute that my asking the seniors to help solve cases had anything to do with the bombing . . ."

"Well, there is no way you are responsible, dear," she patted my knee. "Drink your tea."

I took a sip. "Do you know anyone who wears a silver wedding band with a blue stripe and a diamond?"

"Sounds pretty distinctive." She finished off her tea, putting down her mug and tapping her chin. "It also sounds familiar. I would try Benson's Jewelry. I think they had a set like that in their window a few years back. They might know who bought the set."

"Oh my goodness, that's brilliant. Thank you!" I put my mug on the tray, got up, hugged Agnes.

"My pleasure," she laughed. Mal ran over to get in on the excitement of the hug, so Agnes patted Mal on the head.

"I really shouldn't take up any more of your time. Thank you so much for the tea and the talk." I grabbed Mal's leash. "One last thing."

"Yes, dear?"

"You didn't happen to see a calico cat around, did you? I let my cat, Carmella, out for her nightly rounds last night, and she hasn't returned yet."

"No, I haven't, but I'll keep any eye out for her. Don't worry, dear. Cats have a tendency to come back."

PUMPKIN SPICE FUDGE

3 cups white chocolate chips
1 (14-ounce) can sweetened condensed milk
3 tablespoons pumpkin puree
2 teaspoons pumpkin pie spice
¼ cup powdered sugar

Prepare an 8-inch-square pan by lining with parchment and buttering. In a microwave-safe bowl, combine chips and sweetened condensed milk. Microwave on high for one minute. Stir. It may need 30 more seconds to be completely smooth. Add pumpkin puree and pumpkin pie spice. Stir until combined. If the fudge is soupy, add sifted powdered sugar slowly until thickened to your taste. Pour into a pan and refrigerate until firm. Cut into pieces and enjoy!

Makes about 64 1-inch pieces of fudge.

Chapter 12

Mal and I stopped at Benson's Jewelry. The store was bustling, considering that it was off-season and a Friday. Four people stood around looking at the designs. It was a testament to Benson's reputation for quality and unique designs.

"How can I help you?" said a young woman in a shift dress. Her hair was up in a messy bun on the top of her head. "Cute pup."

"Thanks. I'm Allie McMurphy, and this is Mal."

"I'm Gail Anderson," she said.

"That's a beautiful name. I was wondering if you could tell me who this is." I pulled up the picture of the zombie on the phone.

"Oh no, sorry. I have no idea."

"I came because I thought maybe someone here would know who bought this ring." I stretched the photo to zoom into the ring on the zombie's finger.

"Oh, that was a design from about five years ago. I'll go ask my manager." She turned and left Mal and me to peruse the glass cabinets and imagine buying some jewelry for myself. It wasn't practical when I had my hands in sugar all day, but it was still nice to think about.

"Hello, I'm Henry Benson." A man in a blue suit coat, white shirt, and blue-striped tie walked up to me.

"Allie McMurphy." I shook his hand.

"Ah, the famous fudge maker turned sleuth."

"I would argue against the famous and the sleuth parts. I'm just a fudge maker."

"Sleuth or not, you do have a question for me. Why don't you and your pup come back to my office where we can speak in private?"

"Okay." I followed him to an office at the back of the building. The building was on the side of Main Street with a beachfront view, and the office had two large windows that looked out onto the lake. Two chairs with an end table between them sat near the window, and a big desk was placed in the opposite corner of the room. I looked from the desk to the windows, noting the distance.

"Surprised that my desk isn't in front of the windows?" he asked me, waving me toward a seat by the window. I didn't immediately move to the chair.

"Is it because it's too cold in the winter?"

He laughed. "It's a reminder that my desk is not the main focus of my business. The customer is."

"Ah," I said, smiling and taking my seat by the window. "So you bring customers in and let them enjoy the view."

"Usually just the paying ones," he said. He tilted his head and studied me. "I've seen you at the town hall meetings. You are quite outspoken."

"Thanks," I said. "I'll take that as a compliment."

"Compliment noted," he said. "You remind me of your grandmother, Alice."

"Thanks," I said again.

"She was a feisty thing. Beautiful woman, too, in her day. So. What would you like to know?"

"Well, I was wondering if you remember who you sold a ring to." I pulled out my phone and showed him the zoomed-in picture of the zombie's hand. "It's quite distinctive, and Mrs. James pointed me to you."

He looked at the photo. "Yes, I recognize it. It was a lovely set for husband and wife."

"Can you tell me who you sold it to?"

"Why?"

I took my phone back and unzoomed to show the back of the zombie's head. "Because whoever is wearing this ring was also wearing the same costume as Anthony Vanderbilt the night he died." I showed him the zoomed-out photo. "I'm afraid he might be in danger."

"Seriously?"

"As serious as I get."

"Fine, I might as well tell you. You would find out from someone, sooner or later. It's Joshua Spalding. He and his fiancée came in and bought the rings about five years ago. What do you think Joshua did to merit someone trying to kill him?"

"I have no idea," I said, standing. Finally, I had the confirmation I needed that the other zombie was Josh Spalding. Now I could confidently act on that information. "But I'm going to find out."

"Are you?" He crossed his arms and leaned back in his chair. "Because what you should do is take this information to the police. In fact, I'm going to call them right now."

"Great," I said. "Call Rex Manning—he's the lead on the case. Have him get down to Josh's place before anything happens to him. Thank you for your time."

Mal and I left the jewelry shop. I texted Liz. *The other zombie is Josh Spalding. Do you know him?*

Is that confirmed? she texted back.

Yes. I went to Benson's Jewelry, where the ring was purchased.

Old man Benson gave you his name? Is that legal?

I said Josh's life was in danger. He's going to call the police.

Where are you now? she texted back.

On Main, near the McMurphy.

I'll meet you there in fifteen minutes.

Ten minutes later, I was in the lobby of the McMurphy, filling Frances in on our new information. Mal was off her leash and happily chewing a rawhide bone in her dog bed.

"Oh my. That's quite a find," Frances said.

The doorbells rang, and Liz walked in. She had a look in her eye that suggested, as my Papa Liam would say, that she was "loaded for bear." Without any preamble, she asked, "What do we know for sure?"

I recounted my story yet again: my visit with Agnes James, her suggestion of where to ask about the ring, and Mr. Benson's grumpiness. "But he told me it was Joshua Spalding. Do you know him?"

"I went to school with his wife, Becky," Liz said. "Becky's packing up to go to her mom's for the month.

She's pregnant and due in just over a month, so for safety's sake she wants to be closer to her doctor."

"Then let's go. Frances, do you want to come?"

"I'll be fine here. I look forward to hearing what you find out."

I grabbed my jacket, and we both stepped out into the crisp air. The street was almost deserted this close to dinnertime. "Should we call before showing up at their door?"

"I texted Becky on my way here, and she said she doesn't mind us stopping in. It's how I knew she was packing."

"Oh, right. What do we do if Rex is there?"

"I asked her to text me if Rex got there first. She asked why, and I told her we would tell her when we got there. But let's hurry—we shouldn't keep a pregnant woman in suspense." We power walked past the marina and the fort to the homes built behind the churches. The Spaldings lived in a little worker's bungalow. It was quite lovely, with white shiplap siding and pale blue shutters. There were empty flower boxes under the front windows, and a lit jack-o'-lantern on the porch. It was clear they took good care of the little house.

"Nice place."

"I know, right? Josh is a blacksmith during the week and a bartender on the weekends. He creates metal artwork, too, and sells that in the art shop downtown."

"Wow. I didn't know anyone was a blacksmith anymore."

"Someone has to shoe all the horses that work on the island."

"Makes sense."

We climbed the three steps to the small porch and knocked on the door. A peek through the window showed a cozy inside that was well lit by a warm fire in the fireplace. Music played softly. Becky opened the door after we knocked a second time. She was a tiny girl, and very pregnant. Her hair was pulled back into a low pony tail with bangs cut straight across her forehead.

"Hi, ladies, come on in. Sorry if the place is a mess. Like I said, I'm packing."

Packing or not, the place was perfect. It looked ready for a *Good Housekeeping* photoshoot. There was the soft scent of pumpkin spice from an orange candle on the coffee table. On the mantle above the fire, wedding and other couple pictures were interspersed with more Halloween decorations.

"What is this all about, and why do you think the police are going to come see me??"

"I'm sorry, we don't mean to scare you, but did Josh go to the zombie walk?" Liz asked without taking the time to sit.

"Yes, I made our costumes myself. He was a zombie professor, and I was a pregnant zombie." She waved her hand over her belly. "Kind of hard to be anything else at this point."

"Where is Josh?"

"He's at work. With the horses mostly gone, he's been picking up more shifts at the Nag's Head. Is everything all right?"

I pulled out my phone and once again pulled up the pictures from that night. "Is this him?"

"Yes," she confirmed. "Why?"

"Because he could be a twin to this guy." I showed her the pictures of Anthony.

"Is that Anthony Vanderbilt?"

"Yes."

She sat down hard on the couch. "The dead guy?"

"He's dressed just like your husband. Where did you get the suit coat? Maggs said that Anthony wore his favorite one because it was getting old."

"I bought it at a used clothing shop." She looked at me. "Did I do this?"

"Oh, honey. No, you didn't," Liz said sat down and grabbed her hands. "This isn't your fault. If anything, you might have saved your husband's life that night."

"Do you know who might want to kill your husband?" I asked.

"No," she shook her head. Her large eyes began to tear up. "No, Josh is a really nice guy. Everyone loves him."

"Maybe that's the problem. Maybe someone else didn't like that everyone loves him," Liz said.

"That sounds weird. Why kill a guy because everyone loves him?" I asked.

"We might be looking for a loner or someone who wants to be loved by everyone but isn't." Liz shrugged and pursed her lips. "Who would that be?"

"Do you think Joshua is still in danger?" Becky asked.

"You said he was at work? He should be fine, as long as he's in public view."

"Wasn't Anthony?"

"No, he was alone in the alley on the way to meet his mom."

"Still, I'm going to text him," Becky said.

"That's probably a good idea," Liz said.

There was a knock on the door. We all looked at each other for a moment. Then Becky got up slowly. Her belly was so large she had to scooch to the edge of the couch and rock herself up. Liz gave her a hand. I saw why it had taken two knocks for her to get to us.

The person outside knocked again before Becky could get to the door. "Hi, Becky," I heard Rex say. "Is Joshua at home?"

"No," she said. "You might as well come in. These girls were just telling me that he might have been who the killer wanted to murder that night. Is that true?"

Rex stepped in and took off his hat. His blue gaze paused on me for a moment, warming my skin. Then he turned to Becky. "Where's Joshua now?"

"He's at the Nag's Head, pulling a shift," she said. "He volunteered for extra duty to try and save up enough money that he could take the first six weeks off of work when the baby came." Becky rubbed her belly. "He doesn't want to miss a moment."

"Brown and Lasko," Rex said into his walkie-talkie. "Go pickup Joshua Spalding from the Nag's Head." He turned his attention back to Becky. "They'll make sure he's all right."

"She was packing to go to stay with her Mom in the Lower Peninsula for the last few weeks of her pregnancy."

"My mom was a flipper," she said.

"A what?" Rex asked.

"A flipper. When she was pregnant, one moment she wasn't dilated, and then the next she was at a full ten. It goes quick in my family, so I want to be near the hospital."

"Why don't you keep packing? I'll stay here to make sure you're safe. And these ladies are going to leave and go to their homes as well. Right?"

"Yes, sir," Liz said, sending him a mini salute. "Come on, Allie, let's go."

"Thank you for seeing us, Becky. I hope you have a safe trip, and I can't wait to meet the new baby." Liz pulled me out of the house. Rex closed the door on us quickly.

"Okay, so maybe you two aren't as close as I thought," Liz said, putting put her arm through mine and walking me toward Main Street. "That was kind of mean."

"He's just mad because we beat him to the clue. It's not like we weren't going to tell him."

"I know," Liz said. "I mean, he'd read it in the morning paper anyway."

We both laughed, but then I sobered. "You aren't going to put that in the newspaper, are you? Don't you think the killer will still try to go after Josh?"

"On the contrary, this is a small community," Liz said. "Once I put in the paper that the killer might have actually wanted to kill Josh, then the whole town is going to keep its eye on him. It's the best safety net there is."

"Wow, it's so kind how people look out for each other here."

"It's not kind," she said. "It's because they want to be the next person to find a dead body. Ever since you started this thing, all the seniors have been dying to get into your shoes. No pun intended."

"Huh. Well, maybe Rex will be able to talk Josh into going with Becky to her mother's."

"Do you think that will keep him safe? Frankly, I'm not so sure," Liz stated. "The killer might just follow him to Saginaw and pick him off where no one's watching."

Chapter 13

Liz left me at the McMurphy. I went inside and gave Frances a hug goodnight as she and Douglas went home for the day. Even though Mal had gotten plenty of exercise today with all our walking around, I took her out again for a short night walk to look for Mella.

It was quiet. The sun went down and the stars popped out early in the autumn and winter. Even though I should have been enjoying such a nice night during one of my favorite times of the year, I couldn't stop worrying about my kitty. It would be difficult for her to get run over, since there were no motor vehicles on the island and very few horse-drawn carriages right now. Most people walked or road bicycles. It wasn't until after the snow fell and people got out their snowmobiles that things would be dangerous for a cat. So what was keeping Mella from coming home?

"Allie, are you alright?" It was Mr. Beecher again. It was just like old times, running into him twice a day while walking Mal. I was glad to see him back to his old routine.

"Still looking for my cat."

"I still haven't seen a calico on my wanderings. Doesn't mean she won't turn up, though."

"Do you think someone would take her or hurt her?" I asked.

"I think you are letting your experience of finding dead bodies color your thoughts. If I remember correctly, she was a stray who adopted you, right?"

"Yes."

"Then she's simply off on a mission."

"I hope so," I said with a shake of my head. "I hope this isn't connected to the murder. She's the one who found the body, you know."

"No, I didn't know. Seems she's a smart cookie. I'm sure she can take care of herself." He reached down and slipped Mal a dog treat, then straightened slowly. "Still trying to get used to long walks with a cane."

"How's your girlfriend?" I teased. "Is she taking good care of you?"

"As good as she can," he said. "She's the best."

"And you don't marry her because . . . ?"

"She won't have it. She's independent and enjoys her time alone."

I turned to walk back toward the McMurphy, and he turned with me. "I understand that, but even us independent types get lonely sometimes."

"Are you thinking about getting married?"

I slipped my arm through his. "Maybe someday. Are you asking?"

His laughter filled the air, warming me. Mal pranced beside us. "Oh, if only I were a young man again." He patted my hand. "I'm sure you want children."

"I do, yes," I said. "I can imagine them playing in the McMurphy. Frances would have to babysit while I made fudge—can't have them behind the counter with the hot sugar. But I'd teach them to make fudge and keep the tradition."

"You are a traditional girl, aren't you?"

"I know some people think it's old fashioned, but for me there is nothing better than walking in the same places your ancestors walked, and where your descendants will walk. There's a nice continuity about it."

We walked in silence down the back alley. He stopped in front of my steps behind the McMurphy. "I'm glad you've come to stay on the island. You give us all hope for the next generation."

"Oh, thank you." I blushed and gave him a quick hug. "You take care."

Mal and I climbed the stairs to my back door. I took a moment to look out beyond the alley to the rolling hills behind me. "Mella, wherever you are, please come home. We miss you."

I glanced down to see Mal looking out to the horizon as well.

"What are you looking at, Juliet?"

Startled I looked down to see Trent standing in the alley beneath my stairs. "What are you doing here?"

"Well, that's a fine way to greet me," he said. Mal slipped out of my grasp and raced down to welcome Trent. He picked her up and carried her back up to me like a small child. "Is this all the welcome I get?"

"Welcome," I said, giving him a hug. "Come on in. I want to know how you and Paige are doing. How's your mom? When did you get here? What are you doing on the island?"

"Slipped that question in a second time," he said as he stepped into my tiny galley kitchen, taking up all the space.

"Why don't you come have a seat in the living room, and I'll get you something to drink. I have some wine and a few beers."

"A beer would be fine," he said, sitting on the couch. Mal jumped right up into his lap as if she owned the area. He chuckled and rubbed her back and ears. "At least someone is excited to see me."

I pulled two beers from the fridge and twisted off the tops, then brought them into the living room and handed him one. "I don't like to be surprised. Lately, surprises have been a bad thing."

He tapped his bottle to mine. "Cheers." He took a swig, and I sat down across from him. Trent was gorgeous. He had that all-American look: wide shoulders, clean-cut hair that always fell perfectly back into place, suit jacket over a polo and slacks.

It didn't hurt that he and his family owned half of the businesses on Mackinac Island. They were legacy residents. Trent's family had moved back and forth between Chicago and Mackinac Island for over a century. He had a yacht, for goodness sakes, and a business empire headquartered in Chicago.

"For you, surprises mean dead bodies," he said. "I heard you found Anthony."

"I did." Sitting back, I took another sip of beer. "Maggs was not far behind. Seeing her pain was worse than finding Anthony dead."

"I understand. She's like family to me. Are you investigating?"

"Yes," I said. "Someone blew up the senior center, too."

"I heard about that. I also heard you were there, and you helped the seniors get out before it blew."

"I helped."

"I miss you. I'm worried about you."

"Trent, we're not a couple anymore. Your mom made it clear that she didn't want her children living on the island year-round."

"So come to Chicago with me."

"What? No!"

He sat up and leaned toward me, resting his elbows on his knees. "You don't have to stay here to prove you aren't a fudgie. Everyone knows you belong here, and they all love you."

"I'm not staying through the winter just to prove I'm not a fudgie."

"No?" He raised an eyebrow. My heartbeat picked up. "Your grandfather closed the McMurphy for the winter. Not because he wanted to leave, but because so few people visit in the winter. It's cold and dark and—"

"Magical, with snowmobiles and ice bridges lined by Christmas trees and Santa runs and sleigh bells."

"There's no reason to stay. The weather will prevent flights. How will you get your fudge out for the online shipments? Come to Chicago. I have a professional kitchen where you can make your fudge by hand and get it out in time for your clients."

"O'Hare in Chicago closes during bad weather, too," I pointed out.

"Not as often," he said. "Bring Mal. She'll enjoy the city, and so will you. If you're worried about where you'll stay, there's a loft over the kitchen—"

"I'm not going to live off the Jessops' generosity for the winter."

"Let me finish. You can rent it from me. Your friend Jenn is there. I'm there. Paige is there. Once the ice forms and the airport gets socked in, there won't be anyone coming in or out. Please think about it." He put his hand over mine. It was warm and comforting, and he smelled so nice. He always smelled nice. In this moment, all I wanted to do was bury my nose in the crook of his neck and smell his skin.

I stood. "I'm staying. My lifelong dream has been to be a year-round resident of Mackinac Island. I need you to understand that."

He stood, too, crowding me a little bringing up memories of our history. "Promise me you'll think it over," he said. His voice was soft and low near my ear, sending chills down my spine. Then he turned to Mal and gave her a pat on the head before setting his beer bottle on the counter and opening the door. "I want you to be with me, Allie McMurphy. Think about it."

The door shut behind him, and I hugged myself. Mal jumped on me to see if I was all right. I picked up my pup. "It's okay, Mal," I said. "We don't want to move again . . . right?"

The next morning, I got up at 5 A.M., as usual, and stuck my head out of the door to see if Mella had come home yet. She was nowhere in sight. The air was sharp, and a heavy frost covered the ground—the first frost of the season. I couldn't wait for the first snow.

I pulled back inside and grabbed my warm coat, hat, and gloves to take Mal out for her morning walk. She was happy to run down the stairs and sniff her favorite spot of grass before using it.

The alley was dark except for the pools of lights from the lamps I'd installed on the McMurphy. I seemed to be the only person up and around. It wasn't hunting season yet, and the other fudge shops nearby had closed up, opting to make and ship their fudge from Mackinaw City.

There was always something about walking alone in the wee hours of the morning that made me want to hold my breath. It was a special kind of quiet. I could hear my footsteps crunch on frosted gravel and see my breath condensing in the air.

Mal seemed to know where she was going, so I let her take the lead. My thoughts were on Trent. I should tell him about Rex, and I should tell Rex what Trent offered. They knew each other well. If I didn't tell them, they would find out anyway. Mal pulled, tugging and dragging me into the wooded area off Market Street. "What is it, girl?" I asked.

She glanced up at me, then nosed off into the trees. I grabbed my phone and turned on the flashlight. It was dark under the trees. Mal took me straight to a pile of leaves and sat down. "What is it?" I asked, curious. I kicked up the leaves and found some kind of sailcloth sack. I was careful to only dig around the mouth of the sack. I'd spent enough time investigating with Mal to know that it was best not to touch things that she'd sniffed out until I knew exactly what it was. I opened the mouth of the sack and peered inside. It was stuffed with hymnals. "Well, that's certainly not a dead person."

I took photos with my phone of the area and the bag, then I carefully dug it out of the leaves. It was a large duffle bag. In fact, it was about the size of a human. If I didn't already know that it was filled with books, I night have been worried.

"Who would bury a duffle full of hymnals?" I asked Mal. She just sniffed the duffle again and smiled up at me with that happy doggy look. I tried to lift the bag, but it was too heavy. "Seriously?" I asked Mal as I struggled with the bag. "What else is in here?" I put my phone where it would shine on the contents and dragged the hymnals out, one by one. After I had a small pile, I tried to move the bag again, but it still didn't budge. "This is nuts." I grabbed my phone with the flashlight on and opened the sack mouth wide, peering inside. Something glinted when the light hit it. "What?" I pulled more hymnals out of the sack, reached in once more, and put my hand on something the size of a brick, something made of metal and very heavy. I dragged it out with both hands and stared, dumbfounded, at the gold bullion in my hands.

Chapter 14

"It sure looks like a gold brick," Rex said, studying it in the dawning light. He flashed a light over the gold I had taken out of the bag, and it gleamed. "How many are in the bag?"

"At least five. It's hard to tell," I said. "They're too heavy to move around much. Thanks for coming so quickly."

"You know my place is just up the road." Rex had come in a pair of sweats, gym shoes, and a thick sweatshirt. He wore a baseball hat with a police emblem. "I've called Brown and Lasko to help guard the site until Shane gets here."

"Oh, we should probably stop touching stuff," I said, putting my hands in the air.

Rex shook his head at me. "It's not a crime scene."

"Yet," I said. "We don't know this hasn't been stolen from a bank or something. Do banks even have gold bullions anymore?"

"Central banks do," he said.

"But there's no central bank on the island."

"Gold is a great investment, often handed down in

families. There are a lot of historically wealthy families with homes on the island."

"It's probably stolen, then," I surmised. "So we really shouldn't touch it."

"If it's real, then yes, it is probably stolen. Anyone who might have wanted to hide gold would have dug a lot deeper. Not just cover it in leaves."

"I don't expect they thought anyone would come back in the scrub trees," I said.

Rex frowned and studied the surrounding area. "Stay here."

"If you're going to look around, you might want to take Mal. She finds things."

He glanced over his shoulder. "She needs to stay and protect you."

"Right."

I watched as he carefully searched the area using his phone's flashlight.

Two police officers pulled up on bikes. I recognized the stocky figure of Officer Brown immediately. The other one was Officer Lasko. She didn't like me much. Frances had suggested once that it was because she had a thing for Rex. Unfortunately for her, Rex had a thing for me. And there was definitely something going on between Rex and me.

"What's up with the bag?" Lasko asked.

"You'll have to come see," I said, waving them over. Mal jumped up on Officer Brown, looking for pets. He scratched her behind the ear as Officer Lasko squatted down and used her flashlight to look inside the bag.

"Is that what I think it is?"

"Yes," I said. "Rex believes it's real."

Officer Brown whistled. "That's a big haul. How did you find it?"

"Mal," I said simply.

Rex stepped out of the scrub. "Lasko, stay with Allie. Brown, you're with me."

"Did you find something?" I asked.

He didn't answer me. The two men disappeared into the woods.

"Well, this sucks," Lasko said in a loud whisper.

"You don't need to babysit me," I said. I picked up Mal and hugged her. "It's what's in the bag that has him worried."

"I know," she said with a stubborn set to her chin.

That was enough for me. I stepped closer to her with Mal in my arms. "Why don't you like me? What did I ever do to you?"

"Who said I didn't like you?" she asked, her expression stormy.

"Ever since I've moved back to Mackinac, whenever you get near me, you send me dirty looks and say sharp things. People have begun to notice."

"What do you care what other people notice?"

"I care if it's going to make our living together on this island hard. Let me know what it is. If I'm doing something that annoys you, then I can stop. Or at least we can agree to dislike each other."

She looked for a moment as if she had tasted something bad, then she turned her face away from me. "If you must know, it's because it's difficult being around a person I like when I know they're not interested."

"So Frances was right. You do like Rex."

She sighed and her shoulders dropped. "No," she murmured. Then she turned to me. "I like you."

"But if you like me, then why treat me like . . . Oh,"

I said, blushing. "So all this time, you've been short with me because you have a crush on me?"

"Yes," she said, "and I know you don't reciprocate it. I've seen the way you look at Rex. So better to try to dislike you than to get my heart broken. There, I said it. Are you happy now?"

I hugged Mal and thought for a moment. "Well, sort of. I'm glad to know the truth. Thank you for being brave and telling me."

"You're welcome. So." She cleared her throat, seemingly eager to change the subject. She kicked the leaves onto the bag and brushed them off with her foot. "Where did all the hymnals come from?"

"They were inside the bag," I said. "On top of the gold."

"So whoever left the bag filled it with hymnals? Do you think they did it to keep people from stealing it?"

"Could be," I said. "I mean, who would want a bag of hymnals? Besides a preacher, I mean."

"Good point, but a do-gooder might pick up the bag to take it to a preacher to find out who the hymnals belong to."

"Like I did," I said. "I easily found the gold."

"So perhaps they weren't using it to hide the gold." She paused thoughtfully. "Maybe it does belong to a preacher."

"Oh," I said. "Do you think the money belongs to a church?"

"I don't think so," Rex said with a hard edge to his voice. "We've got another dead body."

An ambulance siren sounded in the distance. Shane bicycled in just as George Marron and the other EMT pulled up and opened the back of the ambulance.

"What? Who?" I asked. "Where? Does the bag belong to them?"

"Those are all questions I can't answer right now," Rex said. He put his hand on my shoulder. "Let's just say Mal is a very good dog, once again." He reached down to pat my pup, who was just happy to see so many people coming. "What brought you out this way, anyway? I know this isn't on your normal morning walk."

"Are we that predicable? See, I thought that maybe we should vary our walks. I just figured no one was up and about as early as we are. Well, besides other fudge makers."

"Lots of early birds on the island," Rex said. "Beecher is one of them. Several others. Everyone is well aware of where you go. We care about you and want you to be safe."

"That means bad people know my moves, too," I said, frowning.

"What's the scene?" Shane asked as he arrived in his CSU outfit carrying his kit.

"We have two," Rex said. "Allie found this bag first, then I found a body through here. Let's start with the body." He waved George and his fellow EMT over to follow him and Shane.

I knew better than to ask to come see, although my curiosity was killing me. I craned my neck to see if I could catch a glimpse.

Officer Lasko put her hand on my shoulder. "Let me take your statement. Then you and Mal can go home and go about your day."

I recounted again exactly how we had found the bag. "Do you think this is related to Anthony's death?" I asked.

She shook her head. "There's no proof of a link at this time."

I glanced back over to where the guys were working. "I hope it's not anyone I know."

"Rex will be in touch," Officer Lasko said.

"Right," I felt disappointed. Then I shook it off. "Come on, Mal," I said. "We have fudge to make."

"Allie," Officer Lasko said.

"Yes?"

"Be careful."

"I will." I took a step, then turned back to her. "Another thing. My cat, Mella, is missing. I was out this way looking for her. Have you seen her?"

"The calico?"

"Yes."

"I thought I saw Mrs. Flores feeding a calico yesterday. You might want to check with her."

"Thanks." Mal and I went back to the McMurphy. I glanced at the time on my phone. It was nearly 8 A.M., and Frances and Douglas would be getting the McMurphy ready for the seniors to come. I took a deep breath of the crisp morning air and studied the quiet blue sky. Someone else was dead. It tore at my heart.

"Where have you been?" Frances asked as we entered the back door of the McMurphy. I unhooked Mal from her halter and leash, and she went running for water and her treats.

"I thought I'd go looking for Mella. Then Mal pulled me off the road and into some scrub."

"I heard sirens this morning," Douglas said from the lobby where he was setting up tables.

"Oh no, not another dead body." Frances covered her mouth when I nodded. "Who?"

"I don't know, I didn't find them," I said, pulling off my jacket and hanging it on the coat rack by her desk. "Mal and I found something else. I don't think I should tell you about it yet, but I called Rex. Rex canvased the area and discovered the body. He wouldn't let me see it, so that's all I know."

The doorbells jangled and Liz came strolling in. "Tell me everything."

"Hi, Liz," I said. "What can I do for you?"

"Oh, come on. Word travels fast. Something happened this morning that involved the EMTs and Shane. That means a crime scene, and someone was hurt. I know you're involved, Allie."

"How do you know that?" I asked, crossing my arms over my chest.

She mirrored my stance and frowned at me. "You are always involved. Besides, you weren't answering your phone."

"Allie, we need your help setting up for the seniors," Frances said.

"Oh, come on, guys," Liz looked from me to Frances to Douglas. "I know you know something."

"Didn't you follow the ambulance?" I asked. "Those guys know what's going on."

"I went, but they wouldn't let me near the area. They actually have it blocked off." She grabbed the end of a table and helped me unfold its legs. "Lasko wouldn't even let me snoop around."

"When's the official announcement?" Douglas asked.

"Rex said they would update everyone later this

evening, but I can't wait until this evening. I have readers expecting to come to the newspaper's website to find out what's going on. I've got to get under this story before the senior grapevine knows all about it already. It's why I came to you, Allie. I know you know something."

"The seniors are coming here for lunch today," I said. "We're going to be glazing our glass-bottom pinch pots. You can do a story on that."

"Not the same," she said with a shake of her head. She went over and peered into the fudge shop. "I don't see any fudge made this morning." She turned and pointed at me accusingly. "That means you were there."

"No comment," I said. I added tablecloths to the tables and tried to replicate our setup from the other day.

The doorbells rang. It was Tara Reeves, the caterer, with soups and sandwiches for the buffet lunch. Dessert would be brownies and cupcakes—plus fudge, if I finished making it in time.

"Thanks for catering," I said as I walked Tara out.

"I love to do it," she said. "I'm going to start catering full time next season, actually, so if you have any events, please think of me first."

"Will do."

I turned back around to see Liz glaring at me. "Come on, Allie, give me something."

"I don't know anything," I said. "Rex found the body and wouldn't let me near it."

"What were you and Rex doing out this morning?" Her eyebrows rose up, and she gave me a sly look.

I rolled my eyes. "I went for a walk and found a bag of . . . stuff. So I called Rex. He came out and looked through the area, which is when he found the body. Okay? End of story."

"So you were there, and you do know what happened." She grinned at me.

"I can't tell you anything."

The doorbells jangled again. This time it was Haley. She had her big box and her wagon full of supplies. I grabbed the door and held it for her. "Hi, Allie. All the pots made it through the first firing."

"Awesome. I'm excited to learn how to use the glass," I said.

Liz went out through the door once Haley's wagon had cleared it. "Thanks, Allie."

"I didn't tell you anything," I shouted after her as she walked away. She gave me a wave, and I noticed people were staring. Frowning, I went back into the McMurphy. There wasn't anything I could do. I hadn't told her anything she probably didn't already know. Maybe if I didn't read her story, I wouldn't have to know how she spun it.

Chapter 15

Mrs. Tunisian arrived early again with Mrs. Anderson in tow. "Allie, I hear they found another body this morning. Can you tell us anything?"

Mrs. Anderson looked at me expectantly. Oh boy, was this what my morning was going to be like?

"Sorry, ladies, I don't know anything."

"That she can tell us," Mrs. Tunisian said to Mrs. Anderson. "Come on, Rosey, let's go help Haley unload the pottery."

I made a beeline to Frances. "I think I'm going to have to put you and Douglas in charge of today's senior event. I've got about four hours of fudge making I have to get caught up on."

"Not to mention hiding from questions," Frances said in a low tone.

"I'll be in the fudge shop. People can see me, and I'll wave. It might even be a good time for them to watch me make fudge, if they want." I grabbed my apron and tossed it over my head, tying it around my waist.

"Before you disappear," Frances said. "I wanted to let you know that the roofing crew arrived this morning. I let them into your apartment to get to the attic. It was the only way, since you blocked off the utility closet entrance."

"No problem," I said. "I guess I should go check on them."

"It might not hurt."

I took my apron back off, left it on Frances's desk, and took the stairs two at a time to the top floor and my apartment. There was a lot of noise up here. The McMurphy must have been built very well because you couldn't hear the construction in the lobby at all, and it sounded like there were twenty guys up there.

Then I winced. Twenty guys who had tromped through my apartment. I hope it was clean. The door to my place was wide open. I stepped in and did a quick look around. Whew. No dirty dishes on the counter or unmentionables on the floor. "Hello?"

There was no answer—only more hammering and the sound of a wood saw. But the wood saw sound wasn't coming from the attic. I glanced to my left and saw my back door was propped open. Someone was out on my landing with a sawhorse cutting two-by-fours. "Hello?" I said again. I stuck my head out.

The man measuring and cutting the wood stopped and pulled earplugs out. "Hi, Allie." That's when I recognized him. He was Rick Manx, Haley's husband.

"Hi, Rick, good to see you. Where's Elmer?"

"He's in the attic," Rick said and grinned at me. "You've got a lot of structural work that needs doing. Nice apartment, though." He pointed to my open door.

"Thanks," I said. "But I generally don't keep the place this wide open."

"Don't worry. We've got ten guys coming and

going. No one would try to steal anything with all that going on."

"Are you sure? I walked in unnoticed."

"It's safe. We do it all the time."

"Except I also have pets who might come out while you have the door open."

"If you can't tell, it's a little cramped here. There's nothing going in or out on this side that I don't see."

I glanced down to see a large pile of wood stacked up near the bottom of the stairs. "Who brings the wood up, and who takes it down? Or are you doing all three things?"

"I haul the wood up, cut it, and lean it against the side of the building." He pointed to the door that was held open by several fresh-cut two-by-fours. "One of the other guys comes down, grabs what he needs, and hauls it upstairs. Nice and easy. Like I said, no one gets in or out this way without my noticing. What kind of pets do you have?"

"I have a little white pup, who can be incredibly sly about sneaking away, and I have a calico cat. This is usually her space." I waved at the landing area around us. "She hasn't been home in a few days, and with all this going on, I'm not sure she'll ever come back."

"It'll be fine. Cats are resilient," he said. "Trust me."

"I'm not sure I do," I frowned.

"Come on, you like Haley. You should like me." He patted his chest.

I felt put on the spot. "It's not that I don't like you . . ."

"Trust me, I'm bonded and insured. Really, ask Elmer. He's the one who put me to work here."

"You're right," I said with a nod. "Of course."

"See."

"Thanks, Rick. By the way Haley's in the lobby right now setting up for the seniors' 'lunch and glaze.'"

"She was pretty excited when you asked her to do this. She thinks having more people take lessons in the off-season will help supplement what we don't make."

"I'm glad to help." I turned and ran into Elmer.

"Allie, good, you're here," he said. He waved at Rick to continue his work. "I want to tell you about what we're doing right now."

He took me by the elbow and told me the details of the structural work. "Come on up and you can see what's going on." He handed me a hard hat.

I put the hat on and went up the steps that folded down from the attic opening and up into the attic itself. The front two thirds of the attic had floorboards. Papa Liam had installed them because he came up here to work on patching the roof all the time, and he worried about losing his balance and falling through the ceiling. The attic was only about seven feet high, and since the roof was flat, there wasn't any peak to it. That meant it would be ideal for a deck, but it also meant that it leaked a lot. I was glad the crew was working on it. When it was done, Elmer had promised that it would never leak again. He followed me up the stairs.

The attic was filled with men working. They laughed and joked with each other as they put up a giant center beam. Elmer pointed out where they would reinforce beams and joists to support a crowd on my roof.

"The men are working on the center beam first. It

will hold most of the load and help distribute the weight down the sides of the building."

I noticed the guys were sweating. It might be crisp outside, but in the attic with so many men, it had grown warm. "Do you want me to bring up something to drink?"

"No, it's okay. We've got our own water." He pointed to a case of water bottles sitting on the floor.

"But it's warm," I said.

"It's still refreshing. We don't want to drink too much and have to take bathroom breaks. By the way, is it okay if we use yours?"

"Sure." I would have to go tidy it up quickly before heading back down to make fudge. "Okay, things look good. How long do you think it will take you to get this done?"

"A couple of days," he said. "Give or take."

"Great. Well, I've got senior citizens gathering in my lobby and fudge to make. I'll leave it to you."

"Sounds good," he said, then turned to the guys to shout out an order. I made my way down the stairs into my apartment. The temperature difference was amazing. I bet Rick was happy he was working on the landing. I put the hard hat on the kitchen counter, straightened my bathroom, and went back downstairs.

The lobby was bustling. It was nearly eleven, and everyone was there. They took their same seats at the tables, and Haley and her helpers were distributing the little pots.

"Hey, Allie, are you going to work on your pot?" Mr. Worther asked me.

I grabbed my apron. "I'll do mine later. I'm behind on making fudge," I said, hurrying through the crowded lobby.

"Allie, I heard there was another body found," Mr. Redfin said. "Were you involved in that?"

Suddenly the entire lobby went quiet. I felt all eyes on me. I swallowed and turned to the crowd. "I didn't find the body this time. I think it was Rex—Officer Manning, I mean—who found it."

"But you were there, right?" he pressed. "Is it why you haven't made your fudge yet?"

"Well, if you want fudge after lunch, you'll need to let me get in there and make it," I said, sidestepping the question and sending them a weak smile. "I'll just go now. Thanks."

I went into the glass fudge shop and closed the door with a sigh of relief. I had to be careful. They could still see me, but at least I could pretend like I didn't hear them in there. But, in fact, I heard every word as they discussed what had happened this morning. I listened as I started gathering ingredients and dumping them in my big copper kettle. Stirring and boiling the basic fudge ingredients was a time-consuming yet calming part of fudge making.

I placed sugar, cocoa, and butter into the kettle and slowly heated it to boil. The whole thing needed to boil for over seven minutes to reach softball stage. In the meantime, I listened to see if anyone knew about the gold that I had found. No one mentioned gold or hymnals or even a bag. So that part, at least, was a secret.

Once the fudge hit softball stage, I added vanilla and rum extract. Then I poured it onto the cooling slab. When had I a full crew and was making fudge for demonstrations, I used a larger pot. The one that took two people to muscle over to the table. While making fudge alone, though, I used a smaller kettle—

one that a single person could lift to easily maneuver the hot sugar substance.

After the liquid was poured onto the cooling surface, it needed to be stirred. I took the long-handled metal spatula and lifted and flipped the mixture until it started to thicken. Then I traded the long spatula for the short and began to make fast flips and form the long loaf. This was a simple dark chocolate fudge with no extras. Some of the seniors might be disappointed it didn't have nuts, but others would rejoice. I didn't want to exclude anyone who might have an allergy, especially now that I knew Mrs. Addison was allergic. I cut the loaf into the standard one-pound slices, then chopped three of those slices into smaller, more manageable pieces and brought them out to the seniors. They were almost finished glazing their pinch pots and putting them up on the table to be packed up. Some of the seniors had already gotten their lunches and gathered in small groups to eat and gossip.

I put the tray out on the buffet table with the other desserts.

"Allie, you should glaze your pot," Haley said, pointing to my lonely little pot on the table.

"Would you do it for me?" I asked. "I've really got to make more fudge. I'm way behind today. Oh, I just saw your husband, Rick, upstairs as part of the crew working on my roof."

"He did mention it," she said. She picked up my pot, selecting the glaze color without meeting my eye.

I caught that she didn't seem too happy that I mentioned him. I stepped closer and leaned toward her to keep the seniors from hearing. "What's going on? It may be none of my business, but are you two okay?"

Haley's face turned bright red. "Was I that obvious?"

"No," I reassured her and touched her shoulder. "I'm a bit intuitive, that's all." I had expected her to glow at her husband's name, not turn away. "Is there anything I can do?"

"No," she said, her shoulders drooping. "It's just one of those slumps you go through. We've been married seven years now, and I think it's that seven-year itch thing they talk about."

Without thinking, I blurted out, "Oh no, is he cheating on you?"

"What?" She turned to me, her eyes big. "No, I don't think so. I don't think Rick would do that."

"Then what is it?"

"Are you married, Allie?"

"No."

"Then you really wouldn't understand." She shrugged and started to glaze my pot. "Things were said, things not done, just . . . life."

"I'm here if you ever need a friend."

"Thanks," she said. "I'm making your pot blue. I hope that's okay."

"Blue is great." She clearly didn't want to talk about it further, so I left her alone and hurried back to my fudge shop before the seniors could start asking more questions about what happened this morning.

By the time I finished making and packing my last batch of fudge for the day, the seniors had all left. Frances and Douglas were taking down the tables and putting the McMurphy back to its normal state. Haley packed up and left giving me a small wave on her way out.

I called the delivery guy to come get the fudge for shipping, washed the dishes, and cleaned the shop. I'd never been this late before. It was nearly 2 P.M., and I was famished.

The doorbells rang, and Trent walked in. He looked like he stepped straight out of *GQ* magazine. His hair was perfect, his clothes expensive and tailored. Just the sight of him brought up memories of the smell of his cologne. I stepped out of the fudge shop, smelling of sugar and chocolate. My apron was sticky, and the hairnet I wore really completed my look.

"Allie, I'm glad I caught you. I heard about this morning. Are you okay?" The last part of *okay* came out with a grunt as Mal ran and slid into him with her exuberant puppy joy. "Well, hello, Mal." He patted her on the head, and she was in heaven.

"I'm fine," I said. "You caught me just finishing up the fudge for the day. I got a bit behind. What brings you here?"

"Again, the dog is happier to see me than you are. Where's the hug and kiss and 'so glad to see you'?"

"Trent," I touched his arm. "I am glad to see you. I'm always glad to see you. You look great."

"Thanks," he said and thumbed some sugar off my cheek and licked his thumb. "You look amazing as well."

"Right," I felt the heat of a blush rush up my cheeks.

"You have to be starving. I bet you didn't eat breakfast and worked right through lunch."

"Am I that obvious?"

"It's obvious you're a busy woman. Let me take you

to lunch. I know you have guys working on your roof. So let's get out of here and enjoy a nice, leisurely meal."

"I have to shower first," I said. "I'm not going anywhere smelling like a fudge shop."

"I kind of like the smell."

"Give me fifteen minutes. Where shall I meet you?"

"I can wait," he said. "It'll be good to visit with Frances and Douglas, and catch up on all the island gossip."

"Right. Okay." I hurried up the stairs and entered my apartment only to realize I had ten or more men going in and out and using my bathroom. Frowning I grabbed clean underwear, a sweater and jeans and went down to a room on the third floor to use the shower. You could hear the noise a bit on the third floor, but I felt safe in room 317. I showered quickly, keeping my hair up. It would still smell of fudge, but I didn't have time to wash it. I ran some dry shampoo through it and combed it out. Then I pulled it back into a bun at the top of my head, got dressed, and headed out. This quick visit to room 317 told me that I would have to plan for the third-floor remodel during the fall of next year. I sighed. Maintenance and upkeep were the biggest expenses in running a hotel. But the McMurphy was mine, and I had promised my Papa Liam long ago that I would keep it going and see it thrive.

He had said to me, "Do you know how to make a little money in the hotel business?"

"No," I had said. "How?"

"Spend a lot of money." He had laughed in that wonderful, Papa Liam way, and it had warmed my heart. I was a bit naïve then. I had no idea how the bills got paid, or how to grow the business. I was still learning. It wasn't that I was in dire straits. This summer had been the best season in years, and my online sales were flourishing thanks to the reality television show. But I was not rich by any means. I thought of the gold bars in the bag. Someone of lesser character may have kept them, and maybe sold them somewhere in the Lower Peninsula.

It made me wonder who on the island might feel that way. Could they have stolen the money and then realized how heavy gold was? But why leave it in the woods, and why the hymnals? Was the poor soul Rex found killed over the money? And most importantly, was this tied to the bombing of the senior center or Anthony's murder?

Chapter 16

"The yacht club is kind of fancy for a late afternoon lunch," I said as Trent put his hand on the small of my back and guided me up the steps to the club. The yacht club was located in an old cottage across from the marina. Only members got through the door usually. It was so exclusive, my family had only ever been inside for island fundraisers. Trent could just walk in and ask them to serve us lunch in the sunroom.

"I know the chef," he said with a raise of the corners of his mouth. "I've asked for steak salads. I hope that's okay."

I gave him a sideways glance. "Why steak salads?"

"I recently heard you liked them."

"I do, but I didn't know that was general knowledge."

"I have my spies."

We were seated in an empty dining space near the window. The waiter came out, poured us fresh sparkling water, and then disappeared. A second waiter came out with a lovely zinfandel.

"To us and our friendship," Trent said, raising his glass.

I raised mine as well and touched it to his. "To our friendship." I took a sip of the excellent wine.

He sipped as well, then covered my hand with his. "Allie, I want it to be more than a friendship. Have you thought about my proposal? You could have the best of both worlds. Mackinac in the summers, and Chicago in the winters. You can grow your online fudge sales and get them shipped out quickly and reliably."

"It does sound nice."

"You know you don't have to live on the island year-round to be a native. Most people don't. If I remember right, your grandfather told mine that he had been planning on winters in Florida starting this year."

"It's because I was going to take over."

"And because there isn't enough business during the winter months to warrant keeping the McMurphy open."

"But there's Christmas, and the first snow, and the ice bridge."

"All wonderful, but January through May, there's no reason for anyone to be here. Plus, Jenn is in Chicago. You could bring Mal and Mella. They would like a change of scenery."

"Who would take care of the McMurphy over the winter? Don't pipes need care?"

"You can have someone check on the ol' girl. Trust me, it's cheaper to hire someone to check on the building than to keep it going all winter with no guests."

"Trent—"

The waiter brought out the salads and placed them in front of us. Mine looked wonderful, and I was hungry, but I couldn't start eating until I got something off my chest.

"Trent, I have to tell you—I'm sort of seeing someone else."

"I know Rex is in the mix still," he said casually, cutting a bite for himself. "I don't want to see you get hurt."

"I'm a big girl, and I can take care of myself."

"Fine," he said without blinking an eye. "Come to Chicago as my friend. I've got the kitchen and the apartment above it empty. I need someone to house-sit it for me until April. You can wait until January if you want. The offer still stands."

"Even though I'm seeing Rex."

"This is about helping my friend," he insisted. "Now, enough of the hard sell. How are you? What's the news? I heard that Sandy is moving to the Grander Hotel."

"She got an offer, yes," I said. "I assume she took it, but it's not until next season. So for now, she's still running her chocolate shop out of my fudge shop."

"I didn't realize there'd be much call for chocolate sculptures in the off-season."

"She's got her own website and has been selling things online. She has to pack them extra carefully, and she's even been known to fly to help set them up, if need be. She's a real talent. I was lucky to have her for one season."

"She should have her own shop."

"Working at the Grander will pay her enough to save for her own shop."

"She's smart. Have you put out an ad for a new assistant fudge maker for next season?"

"Not yet," I said. "Are other places hiring for next season already?"

"Most other places use college students to work the summers. But for specialties like fudge makers or chocolatiers, you should be looking right now. Better to have someone lined up now than to miss out on an opportunity."

"That's smart," I said. I finished my meal. Even with our history, it was not awkward to be with Trent. We still had a good relationship whenever I saw him. It was all the time he wasn't here that had broken down our path to a more serious relationship. That's one thing I had to say about Rex—he was always here.

I relaxed as we finished the dinner. Another glass of wine had me smiling and chatting with Trent as if we were still a couple. I missed him. But there was a part of me that worried that for him, I was merely a challenge. Merely a woman who had said no. Trent Jessop wasn't used to people saying no to him. If I did give in, would he lose interest? Was that why he was gone so much this summer?

We stepped out and I drew my navy wool peacoat closer around me. The wind had picked up from the north, blowing cold across the island. It whipped across my face, stinging my cheeks.

"Thanks for lunch," I said.

"I'm afraid I'm going to be relentless about you coming to Chicago," Trent said. He gave me a hug. "It really would be a good thing. You could see Jenn. I could see you. You'd be able to grow your business. It's a win-win."

I laughed and looked up at him. "You sound like you're brokering a deal."

"I am," he said. "You'll find I'm a shrewd negotiator. Look, like I said, we don't have to date if you don't want to. We can just be friends. Paige would love to spend time with you, and I'm sure Jenn would be thrilled to see you."

"I'll think about it."

"It's all I ask."

We walked to the street and ran into Rex. He looked from me to Trent and back to me. "Jessop. What brings you back to the island? I thought you were gone for the season."

"Yes, well, I had some business to take care of," Trent said, then he put his hand on my back. "I enjoyed our lunch. Would you like me to walk you home?"

"I'm good," I said. "Thanks."

I pushed passed Rex, turned up my collar and shoved my hands in my pockets. I had a feeling they both watched me walk away. I was kind of glad I didn't have to hear what words went on between them. I didn't want to feel like a bone being fought over by two alpha dogs. Maybe I should just go back to Detroit for the season. Sometimes space helped put things into better perspective.

Shane was at the McMurphy when I got back. "Hello," I said as I unbuttoned my coat. "You haven't stopped by since Jenn left. Are you doing all right?"

"I'm as good as can be expected." He shrugged and pushed the glasses up on his thin nose. "Have you heard from Jenn recently? She's been busy."

"Yes. But she still seems excited about the work she's doing." I hung up my coat. "You look cold. Can I get you a coffee?"

"That would be great," he said, blowing on his hands. "It's cold working a crime scene."

I poured him a coffee with cream and sugar, heavy on the sugar. He sat down by the fireplace and held out his hands. "Was this a tough scene?" I asked. "I mean, I know it was in the scrub patch, but did you know the person?"

He took the coffee from me and took a sip. "The body was at least a month old."

"Oh," I said. "Was there much left of the remains? Anything to identify the person?"

"They were still dressed, so maybe we can go on that. I'm going to have a forensic artist create what the person might have looked like." He sipped more coffee.

"If it was a local, someone would have reported them missing, wouldn't they?"

"Not necessarily," he said. "September is about the time people start leaving for their winter roosts."

"Huh," I sat back. "What about the bag? Do you think the two are connected?"

"We'll have to see. The canvas was pretty good cover for the hymnals, so it's possible they were there this entire time."

"But not likely."

"No, not likely. We've had some good storms this last month. The books at the front should have gotten wet."

"The bag was closed tight when I found it," I admitted. "I didn't think it was part of a crime scene, and my curiosity got the best of me."

"So you opened it."

"I did."

Just then, Elmer Faber came tromping down the stairs with two men on his crew trailing behind him. "We're done for today," he said. "I've left the pile of two-by-fours at the bottom of your steps. I figure with all the cameras you have, it will be safe." He paused and nodded at Shane, then turned back to me. "We've locked your place up tight. Frances has the dog, but we haven't seen the cat."

"Thanks for checking," I said, getting up.

"We'll be in at eight tomorrow. Any guests we need to worry about?"

"No guests."

"I'll have my interior crew here as well finishing up the second-floor remodel. I figure one more day of that and we'll be done, at least with our part. You'll still have to do all the decorating and stuff. We just do the heavy lifting."

"Thanks," I said. I waved to the other guys as they left through the front door.

"I didn't know you were remodeling. Your apartment too?"

"No, actually they're working on the roof deck supports," I said. "I've had men in and out of my attic all day."

"Ah, Jenn's idea."

"Yes," I said. I sat back down and curled my legs underneath me. "She will be super proud when she comes back."

"I'm going to see her next weekend," Shane said. "So don't you be getting into any trouble between now and then."

"Oh no," I said. "Who will be our CSU when you're out of town?"

"Hey, a guy's got to have a vacation, you know."

"You have to admit I've been keeping you employed."

He frowned. "The lab is so backed up now, I could not have another scene to investigate until the end of May and still not get through all the tests. It's just me and one lab tech, you know."

"Who's the lab tech? Do I know him?"

"Her," he said. "Kendra Zeller. She got out of Northwestern a year ago with her MS in forensic science. Best scientist I've ever met, even though she's young."

"Is she living in St. Ignace?"

"Yes."

"Why?" I asked, then smiled. "I mean, if she's the best, then she would want the best equipment and opportunity to grow in her profession, right?"

"She's been on a mission to help clear backlog at county labs. It's like this thing. She figures if she can clear backlog, then she can move to another lab in need about every two years. It's brilliant, actually. She will get to work cases all across the United States while helping others. I almost wish I could join her."

"Almost?"

His features softened. "I don't really want to go anywhere and leave my girl back home—well, in Chicago."

I sat back and studied the flames. "Trent is back on the island."

"Huh."

"He asked me to move to Chicago after Christmas. He's got this idea that it will be hard to ship my fudge once deep winter hits."

Shane nodded his head. "He's right. Gets real cold, real fast, and the flights coming in and out are scarce."

"I was afraid of that," I said, tightening my lips. "He's got a commercial kitchen for rent with an apartment over it."

"Is it furnished?"

"I didn't ask. Why?"

"One bedroom or two?"

"Also didn't ask . . ."

He winked at me. "I'm looking for a place to crash when I go to Chicago."

I frowned. "You're not staying with Jenn?"

"She has a roommate. She's trying to save money to start her own business for real."

"She'll get it done." I paused. "If I spent the deep winter in Chicago, I could see Jenn every night for wine, if I wanted."

"Not every night if I'm in town."

"Okay, not every night. But I miss her. It would be nice to have a friend nearby."

"You have friends here."

"Yes, I do, but they're all starting to pack up and leave for the winter. I don't want to be alone. What if I end up being a body decomposing in a wood somewhere until someone notices I'm gone or stumbles across me?"

"Now you're being morbid."

"Yeah, maybe." I sipped my coffee. "I want to experience a full year on Mackinac island. I've dreamt of it my whole life."

"Don't go, then. Rex will be here, and Brown and Lasko. They're your friends."

"Yes, true. And I know Liz said she's not going south this winter. I never asked Sophie, though."

"Who do you think pilots here a couple of times a

week?" he asked. "But she has family in Green Bay so she usually doesn't stay."

"Not because she doesn't want to," Frances said from halfway down the stairs. Mal ran from her heels to me and hopped up on my lap before I even knew what hit me.

I petted my dog and laughed at her antics. "Why doesn't she stay?"

"No place to get a room. Everyone closes down," Frances said. She pulled up a chair. "Are you thinking about closing?"

"Trent's offered her a commercial kitchen and an apartment to rent for the dead of winter."

"Really?" Frances said, studying me. "I suppose you would be able to see Jenn."

"He said that I'll find it hard to ship from the island after Christmas. I could keep the online fudge business going more easily if I went back to Chicago for the winter."

"Or Detroit, I suppose," Douglas said as he came into the lobby from the backdoor area. "I'm sure your parents would love to see you."

"What about you two?" I asked, craning my neck to see them both. "What would you do if I left?"

Douglas looked at Frances.

"We were talking it over after you asked last time," Frances said. "We decided if you did end up closing, we wouldn't stay. Our honeymoon in Hawaii was so much fun, we thought maybe we would try out some other islands for a few weeks." She smiled warmly at her husband.

Great. My entire little family that I thought I was

building wanted to go separate ways. What was I going to do now?

————————

BUTTERSCOTCH FUDGE

2 cups butterscotch chips
1 (14-ounce) can sweetened condensed milk
2 tablespoons butter
1 teaspoon vanilla

Prepare an 8-inch pan by lining with parchment and greasing with butter. In a microwave-safe bowl, combine butterscotch chips with sweetened condensed milk and butter. Microwave on high for one minute, then stir. It may need 30 more seconds in the microwave. Stir and repeat as needed until all chips are melted. Add vanilla and stir until combined. Pour into pan and refrigerate until firm. Take out of pan and remove parchment. Slice and enjoy!

Makes about 64 1-inch pieces of fudge.

Chapter 17

Mella still hadn't come home by Saturday morning. I finished making the fudge, hung up my apron, and went to check on the progress of the remodelers on the second floor. In one week, they had pulled up and disposed of all the carpeting on this floor along with the mattresses on the beds. The hallway and all the rooms had received a fresh coat of paint. The floors had been sanded and stained, and today the workers were pouring the urethane to protect the wood. To do that Douglas had helped move the furniture out of the rooms, into the elevator, and up to the third-floor hallway.

The workers moved swiftly. The smell of the urethane was pretty thick, so all the windows were opened. I wore a jacket because I'd turned off the heat in the building. No sense in heating the entire island, especially when there was a chill October wind blowing in from the lake.

"Winter's coming," Elmer said. He blew on his hands, but otherwise showed no sign of being cold.

I held Mal to keep her off the floor, and we both shivered. "Can't wait."

"I hear you're thinking of going to Chicago after the Christmas season."

"Who told you that?"

"A little birdie," he said. "If I were you, I'd consider it. It gets hard living on the island in the dark months. It can be a rough place. Not so nice for a woman alone."

"Well, I didn't think I'd be alone," I said.

"Suit yourself," he shrugged. "Most of my crew and I will be under the bridge with the trolls during those months. Work is hard to come by in construction once the snow flies. My family and I have a lake house in Branson, Missouri."

"What about your kids?"

"One's married and living in Denver. The other's in college."

I sighed and looked at the floors. "We have to stay off the floors for twenty-four hours, right?"

"Yes. It's why I do them on Saturdays. Gives the guys Sunday off, and then we'll check the floors on Monday. If all goes well, we'll be moving the furniture back on Monday and putting final touchups. The new mattresses will arrive Tuesday. We'll get them on the beds, and then get back to the roof work."

"Great," I said. "It's gone by pretty fast."

"Well, lots of guys are looking for work right now, so I was able to pull together a large crew," Elmer said.

"I would have thought other hotels would remodel after the season was over."

"Most close for the winter and start booking their maintenance and remodel work in the spring. That's our busy time. You were smart to do it now. Got my best crew and thirty percent off the price."

"Yes, well, I learned during the remodel I did this

past spring just how pricey it can get. Thanks for the tip on doing it in the fall."

"My pleasure. Let's go up to the attic and look at the work we've been doing there."

We went up to my apartment. The apartment was also freezing, as the back door stood wide open for the guys to easily cut wood and move it up. I glanced out and noticed that Rick Manx wasn't working the saw today.

That morning, I'd tidied up my apartment and cleaned the bathroom for the guys. Silly, I knew, but my mother had taught me to be hospitable.

"As you can see," Elmer started as we walked into the attic, "the beams are all being reinforced. What we're going to do next is lay new decking right over the top of your existing roof."

"Won't the nails put like a million holes in the roof?" I asked

"Well, first we're going to lay down this new product that will make sure we have a water-tight seal. Then we'll install flat two-by-sixes about every sixteen feet on the roof surface. The decking will attach to that. So no holes in your roof."

"Sounds great," I said

"Hi, Allie." Rick looked down from a ladder, where he was nailing in a roof support. "Haley's firing those pinch pots today."

"Thanks for the update," I said to him, then turned back to Elmer. "You guys have done some great work. You deserve tomorrow off. Thanks."

"Hear that, crew? Sunday's your day off."

The guys cheered.

"I'm going to take Mal for a walk now. Thanks,

Elmer. Oh, and Frances and Douglas are still here if you need anything."

Mal and I went out, this time with a heavy heart as I once again scanned the sidewalks and back alleys for Mella. Mal was enjoying how much these searches let her explore new places, at least.

We were in a back alley between residential homes when I saw two people kissing. It was a deep embrace and I tried to look away, but there was no way out of the alley without either turning around or passing them. By that point I was pretty far from the opposite entrance, so I figured I'd just pass quickly. The hard part was keeping Mal from nosing at them. She liked to do that—poke people with her nose as they walked by. Not a single bark or growl, just silently walk up and touch them with her nose.

I wrapped her leash up so that she had to stay close to me. "Excuse me," I said as I passed them.

"Oh, sorry," the guy said.

I glanced at the couple quickly, then did a double take. The woman was Haley Manx. Haley was wrapped up in some strange man's embrace in the middle of the afternoon in a back alley beside a dumpster. "Oh!" I said. "I'm so sorry." I tried to hurry by, but Haley called out to me.

"Allie! Allie, slow down. I want to explain."

"No need to explain," I said. I kept walking away, not wanting to look at her. I was embarrassed to have seen her, and I figured she was just as mortified.

"Please, don't tell anyone." She grabbed my arm and stopped me. "Please."

"Haley, I'm sorry to have seen that."

"Just promise me you won't tell."

"Tell who? Rick? The seniors?" I shook my head and looked at her sadly.

"We didn't think anyone would be in this area. The season is over, and the island is basically deserted except for Main and Market streets."

"I'm looking for my cat, Mella. She went missing."

"The pretty calico?"

"Yes."

"I haven't seen her, but if I do, I'll let you know. Please, don't tell anyone what you saw."

"I've got to go." I walked on, letting Mal lead me. So Haley and Rick's marriage wasn't solid, but it wasn't Rick's fault, like I'd assumed. The man she had been kissing seemed familiar, but I was far too distracted by the sight of Haley to pay much attention to him. I sighed. Sometimes relationships were hard, and things had to fall apart before they got better. Maybe Haley would think about what she was doing before someone else saw her in an alley with a man who wasn't her husband.

Which brought me to my own dilemma. I hadn't heard from either Trent or Rex today. I was sort of glad that I hadn't heard from Trent because I didn't need to be pushed to move to Chicago again. The thing is that while it all sounded wonderful, something in my gut told me that I would regret not spending the entire year on the island.

"I guess if it's going to be hard, then I need to know how hard it is," I said to Mal, who looked up at me with a happy face. "You won't abandon me, will you?" She barked her response. We reached Mrs. Flores's house, and I stopped and knocked on the door. The house was another bungalow built for the servants who had worked at the cottages and hotels during the 1940s. It was painted a cheery yellow with green shutters. Three pumpkins of various sizes sat on the front porch, and a witch on a broom adorned the door in place of a wreath.

"I'll be right there," I heard an older woman's voice call. Mal jumped up on me asking to be picked up.

"No," I said. "We're here to talk to Mrs. Flores, not to play the 'pick up Mal' game." I knew Mal liked to meet people face to face and kiss their cheeks. It's why she asked to be picked up so often.

The door cracked open, and a tiny woman with a very thin face peered out. She had white hair that was cut short and stuck up in strange places. Her eyes were spring green. She wore a housecoat and slippers. "Hello?"

"Hi, Mrs. Flores? I'm Allie McMurphy. This is Mal. She won't bite."

The door opened wide and she bent to pet Mal. "Of course, she won't bite," the old woman crooned. "She's a good girl, aren't you?" She petted Mal, and my pup was in seventh heaven. "Well, don't stand out there in the cold. You'll catch your death. Come on in."

I followed her in and took my shoes off at the door. Her place was warm and cozy and neat as a pin, as my grandmother used to say. I looked at Mal, and she looked at me. I picked her up so that if she had dirt on her feet she wouldn't track it in.

"Sit while I make us some coffee." Mrs. Flores didn't even look to see if I complied. She bustled off to the kitchen.

I dutifully sat on the old but immaculate couch. By the style and color, I thought it might have been purchased in the 1970s. But there wasn't a worn mark on it.

"Kept it covered in plastic when my kids were younger," she said when she saw me looking at the couch closely as she walked in carrying a tray with two cups, a coffee pot, small containers of cream and sugar, and a plate of cookies.

Standing, I asked if I could help take the tray.

"Nonsense," she said. "I'm old, not crippled. I've handled many a tray of cookies and coffee. Now, I don't get many visitors, but I've been following the stories about you in the *Town Crier*. What a mind you have for figuring things out! It's like our own personal soap opera. So tell me, who are you dating now?" She leaned forward.

I felt heat rush up my cheeks. "I was wondering if you've seen my cat, Mella. She's a calico and has been missing for days. Someone said I should check with you."

"I see," she said. She reached for a cookie, took a bite, and sat back. "You're not ready to talk about your love life."

The blush crept over my face again. I tried to remain calm. "Fine. Trent Jessop wants me to go to Chicago after Christmas to run my fudge shop out of a commercial kitchen there."

"Are you going to go? Or are you going to stay here with Rex?"

"Goodness. Does everyone know everything about my life?"

She shrugged. "It's a small island."

"Then how come we can't find out who killed Anthony Vanderbilt?"

"Ah, that's a mystery, isn't it?" She mused "Or is it?"

"Do you know who would do this?"

"I have no clue. Anthony Vanderbilt was a great kid. He volunteered at the church as choirmaster."

"The church? Which church?"

"St. John's," she said. "You know. The church all the seniors went to when the center blew up."

"Huh," I said, thinking about those hymnals.

"Why?" She narrowed her eyes. "What do you know about the church? Do you think there's a connection?"

"I don't know," I said, then shook my head. "There can't be. What churchgoer would hurt a choir director?"

"Now that's the question, isn't it?"

I frowned. "Do you know Haley and Rick Manx?"

"Cute couple. She makes that glass-bottomed pottery. He works in construction." She leaned closer with a glint of glee in her eye. "I hear Haley is having an affair with that Joshua Spalding—even with him having a wife ready to pop out their first kid!"

"Wait, Josh Spalding? I thought he was off the island with his wife for her last few weeks."

"So you know them?"

"Yes, we went to see Becky the other day. She was packing to leave. I thought Josh went with her."

"You never know about some people," she said, sitting back. "I'd have never thought anyone would blow up the senior center, but there you have it. It was done. And they still don't know who did it. Someone with an ax to grind, I think."

"Or someone with something to hide," I said. "Thank you for the coffee and the talk." I stood and picked up Mal. "I've got to go."

"Anytime, young lady. Come back and see me sometime. I don't get out much, you know. It's nice to see a friendly young face and such a sweet puppy. If you find your cat, you can bring her by anytime. I'm not allergic."

"Thank you," I said. I left Mrs. Flores's house and put Mal down, and we hurried back to the McMurphy. Mrs. Flores might be right. The man I saw with Haley could be Josh Spalding. My heart sank for Becky. But infidelity was also a motive for murder. And if Anthony was killed mistakenly, then Rick Manx was suspect number one.

Chapter 18

Rex walked into my apartment that night looking very much the action hero. He wiped his feet on my kitchen mat and removed his hat. Mal greeted Rex warmly. "I wasn't expecting you to call," he said, his voice vibrating through me.

"I hope it wasn't a bad surprise," I said. "Come in, I fixed us a cocktail. I've got a couple of steaks, too, if you haven't eaten."

He tilted his head and studied me. "Is this the 'thanks for the good time, but I'm moving to Chicago' talk?"

"What? No!"

"You sure?"

I rolled my eyes and handed him a gin and tonic. "Please, come in. Have a drink, sit down, and take your shoes off."

"Fine." He took his shoes off at the door. They were spit-shined service shoes. He was still in his uniform, neatly pressed as usual. It's like the man was never ruffled. He moved around the kitchen bar to the living area. I picked up my cocktail and followed. Mal kept jumping on him. There was a part of me that wanted to jump on him, too, but I was keeping my cool. "What do you want to talk about?" he asked.

"Have you seen Mella anywhere? She loves you. I think if anyone would see her, it's you."

"How long has she been missing?"

"A couple of days. The thing is, ever since she appeared, she's never been gone more than a few hours. Then I was told maybe Mrs. Flores had her."

"Who told you that?"

"Officer Lasko."

"Why did she think she had Mella?"

"I don't remember. I just remember that she said to check with Mrs. Flores. I assumed she was a cat lover."

He lifted the corner of his mouth. "She's not." He sipped his drink.

I sat next to him. "Yeah, I kind of figured that out after I went to see her. Her place was far too neat for pets. She did like Mal, though. So I thought maybe she might like cats, but wasn't crazy about them."

"But she didn't know anything about Mella."

"Not a thing," I said, shaking my head. "But she did have some interesting information."

"Like what?"

"Well, when I was out looking for Mella, I ran across a couple making out in a secluded alley."

"That must have been interesting."

"It was embarrassing. Even more so when I realized the woman was Haley Manx, and the man she was with was *not* Rick Manx."

"And why exactly is that interesting? I would have thought that you were above spreading gossip."

I frowned at him. "This isn't about gossip. When I went to see Mrs. Flores, we talked about how small the island was. She knew a lot of things about me that

I thought were personal. She said that she knew things about everyone . . . like that Joshua Spalding is having an affair with Haley Manx while his wife is pregnant."

"I know you have a point in there somewhere."

"Josh Spalding was the guy wearing the same zombie costume as Anthony. If the whole island knows about Joshua and Haley . . ."

"Then so does her husband Rick," he said.

"It gives him a motive for murder."

"Spalding is still in danger."

"Yes. He was alone with Haley in a back alley. I don't think he's taking this seriously."

"I'll have my men go talk to Rick Manx."

"Thanks," I said. "While you call it in, I'll cook our steaks."

"Panfry in butter?"

"The only way to eat a steak."

After dinner, Rex helped me wash the dishes. "Can you tell me who the person was that you found dead in the brush?"

"The medical examiner hasn't made a positive identification yet," he said.

"But you didn't let me see them . . ."

"You have enough death in your life. You didn't need to see that. The body had been there long enough to decompose down to just clothes, bones, and a little skin."

I winced. "Was it foul play?"

"Again, the medical examiner will determine that."

"Do you think they were connected to the bag with the hymnals and the gold?"

"Maybe," he hedged.

"I'd say most likely," I said. We finished the dishes and took cups of coffee back to the living room. "What did you do with all that gold?"

"It's in an evidence locker," he said. "No one is going to touch it."

"I'm surprised that no one came forward about the missing money, or even the missing hymnals. Do you know which church the hymnals might have come from?"

"There are only a handful of churches on the island. I took one of the books and visited all the pastors this afternoon. None recognized the hymnals."

"What was the publish date on the books? Maybe they're old."

"They weren't out there that long," he said. "If they had gotten through a winter, they would have been a mess."

I finished the dishes and let out the water. "It doesn't mean they aren't old. They might have been stored with the gold in someone's attic, or even a church's attic."

"Now that makes sense," he said. "Some of the pastors are relatively new to the island. Maybe I should be talking to the older parishioners."

I smiled. "I've got the seniors coming back for lunches three days this week. Why don't you stop by and have a chat with them? I'm betting someone has seen those hymnals before."

"They probably know the deceased as well. As Mrs. Flores said, it's a small community."

"Speaking of Mrs. Flores, did you know that Anthony was a choir director at St. John's? Mrs. Flores told me. Do you think that has any connection?"

"It seems weak," he said, then glanced at his phone. "What is it?"

"I had the guys go talk to Spalding and Manx. Pulaski just texted to follow up. He says Manx didn't act as if he knew anything about Haley having an affair. Trust me. If the guy knew about it, he would have said something to my men."

"What about Josh?"

"Josh admitted to the affair. My guys asked if he thought anyone knew. He was pretty sure only you."

"Well, he's wrong. If Mrs. Flores knows, then the other seniors know. I'm surprised they didn't say anything to Haley when she was teaching us how to make pinch pots."

"Knowing this island, they've all got some kind of skeletons in their closets."

"So they're afraid to confront her in case their own skeletons show?"

"That would be my guess," he said. He finished his coffee. "Thanks for dinner and the info from Mrs. Flores."

"Yes, well, I feel sorry for Becky Spalding. I don't think it's my place to tell her, but someone should."

Rex's mouth became a thin line. "Josh should be the one to tell her. I'm going to meet with him tonight and highly suggest he make things right."

"It's probably for the best," I said. "If Anthony was killed by mistake, the killer might still be after Josh."

He stood. "I'm going to have to go."

I followed him to the back door. "Thanks for coming by. It's been a heck of a day."

He had his hand on the doorknob when he turned and studied me with his gorgeous blue eyes. "Are you going to go to Chicago after Christmas?" he asked softly.

I hesitated. "Everyone is leaving after Christmas. Jenn has already left. Sandy is going to the Grander Hotel. Frances and Douglas might be going to the Caribbean. Are you going to be here after Christmas? I mean, with so few people left, I can see them cutting down on the police presence. Do you go somewhere for a month or so?"

He watched me carefully. "I don't go on vacation. It's why my second marriage broke up. She couldn't take the year-round Mackinac experience."

"If I stay, will it be just you and me?"

"Lasko is here year-round as well," he said. "We need to keep an eye on the drunks and make sure no one goes snow crazy."

"Snow crazy?"

"Yeah, sort of like cabin fever, only it's from being stuck on the island. I'm not going to lie. It's isolating, and it can break people." His gaze hardened for a moment. "I know firsthand how it changes people. I don't want you to change like that just because you want to prove something to yourself or this island."

I drew my eyebrows together. "Are you telling me to go?"

He reached behind my head, gently drew my forehead to his lips, and kissed it. "I'm telling you to do what is best for you. I care about you, Allie. You've been working so hard to fit in, but you don't need to work so hard. You do fit in. I'm not the only one who has full confidence in you." He studied me, his hands on my shoulder. "I wish you had as much confidence in yourself as we all do. Every single person on this island believes in you. That's a thing very, very few people earn in a season. I'm letting you know that no matter what you decide, I'm here for you. And that's an always thing." He put his hat on his head and stepped out into the night.

I watched him walk down the stairs and down the alley. He didn't look back. I think it made his words even more powerful. I went inside with Mal, not knowing what I was going to do after Christmas. But maybe right now that was okay, after all.

Chapter 19

Sunday morning, and still no Mella. It had been over a week since she found Anthony Vanderbilt's body. At least today there was no construction activity. I finished my fudge for shipping in silence. The plane left every day, even Sundays. I finished in time to take a shower and get dressed for church. I left Mal in her crate with a treat and a toy and went to St. John's 10 A.M. service.

Pastor Henry gave a sermon on gratitude, specifically for everyone being protected from the explosion. I noticed there were several of the seniors at the service, but the church was far from full. Most of the island residents went to St. Anne's or Trinity, I think mostly out of tradition. Plus, the service at St. John's tended to drone on a bit, I thought. The music was lovely, though. The choir was small—twelve people— but mighty. I could see someone young like Anthony working with them. Right now, Haley led the choir. She looked natural up there. If Mrs. Flores hadn't told me that Anthony was the director, I wouldn't have known Haley was new to the position. She had a beautiful voice. It floated above the rest and lifted the harmonies.

After the service, I stopped and shook Pastor Henry's hand.

"Thank you for helping the seniors the other day, Allie," he said. "I'm so glad you came to services today. You should attend more often."

"I usually go to St. Anne's. It's where my grandparents went. But Mrs. Flores told me that Anthony Vanderbilt used to lead your choir. Is that true?"

"Ah, yes, Anthony did. In fact, when they finally release his body, his mother has a service planned here. Haley has had the choir practicing the most beautiful songs for his send-off. The whole church will be filled with tears." His eyes grew damp. "I miss the boy. I can't understand why anyone would want to hurt him. But I'm certain he is with the Lord now—hopefully, looking down on us and helping to protect us from further harm."

"Mrs. James told me that she had to have her house looked at for structural damage because of the blast from the senior center. The church is even closer." I glanced at the building. "Is it okay? Was it damaged?"

Pastor Henry frowned. "It was. I didn't mention it in today's service because I wanted the service to be about the joy God brought us by ensuring everyone was safely out of the senior center and protected by the church. But the church itself was pushed nearly two inches off of its foundation. We have a church council meeting this week to address what happens next."

"It sounds like it's going to be an expensive repair."

"We have insurance," he said. "But we're not sure it covers acts of terrorism."

"Is that what they're calling the bombing?"

"Isn't that what it was?"

"Yes," I said. "I guess it was."

"Well, in any case, our annual garage sale is scheduled for the upcoming weekend, but I'm pretty certain it won't cover what we need to repair the building."

I looked at the crowd of parishioners. It was small, but some of the families were wealthy. "Maybe you can find a patron."

"It's my sincerest hope."

I shook his hand and moved down the front stairs to leave. It was the warmest day so far this month, and I took my jacket off. The sleeves of my dress ballooned in the breeze.

"Allie," Haley called to me.

I waited for her to catch up. "Nice service. I didn't know you could sing."

"At one time, I thought I would be a singer-songwriter," she said as we walked down the street toward the McMurphy. "It's actually how I met Rick. I was singing in a local bar. He asked me out, and we were both immediately smitten. Once I got married, I settled down and no longer toured." She shrugged. "I took up pottery and being a wife."

"And now?"

"I told Rick about Josh last night," she said, blowing out a long breath. "It was time."

I stopped in my tracks. "Are you okay?"

"No, I'm a cheater. Josh and I—well, we just sort of fell into things. I was unhappy, he was unhappy, and together we found a sort of happiness. I'd forgotten what it felt like to have that spark again."

"I'm glad you told the truth. How did Rick take it?"

She winced. "He threw some things and stormed out. I haven't seen him since. My marriage is over. I guess it's been over for some time, really."

"What about Josh?"

"He broke up with me over a text," she lifted her phone to illustrate. "I guess I deserve that. He said he was going to stay with Becky. He wants to make it work, especially with the baby on the way."

"Didn't you feel the least bit guilty having an affair with a man whose wife was pregnant?"

She blushed hard. "I didn't know Becky when this started, and Josh didn't tell me. I found out last week when I saw her at the art fair. I confronted Josh, and he told me it didn't matter to him. But I guess it really did."

"He's going to be a father really soon. Maybe Becky moving off the island to prepare for delivery made it more real."

"Maybe," she said, and sighed. "Josh told me that you and Liz went to his house because you thought that Anthony's killer might have killed him by mistake?"

"Yes. Anthony and Josh were wearing very similar zombie costumes. It's why the cops called your house last night. You see, once I found out you were having an affair with Josh, it made your husband a prime suspect in Anthony's murder."

"Rick wouldn't hurt a flea."

"You never know what a man would do for love."

She crossed her arms over her chest. "Rick wouldn't hurt Anthony. They were good friends. Besides, the cops called after I told Rick. I told them I didn't know where he was, but it was probably a good bet he was at the Nag's Head. Rick drinks when he's hurt."

"So Rick knew about your affair before he talked to Officer Pulaski last night?"

"Yes, of course," she said. "After you discovered Josh and me in the alley, I knew I had to tell Rick right away. If you knew, others would know soon."

"Are you saying I'm a gossip?" I felt insulted. "The only person I told was Rex, and that's only because your affair gave Rick a motive for Anthony's murder."

"No, no," she said, putting her hand on my arm. "No, I certainly didn't think you would gossip about what you saw. I mean, I asked you not to, and I think you're a good person. But I knew that if you knew, then others probably did as well. You seeing us was my wake-up call."

"I'm glad you told Rick," I said. "It would have been hard to see him tomorrow when he comes over to work on my roof. I hate lying to people. And you were right. Others do know. I went to see Mrs. Flores because someone said she might know where my cat was. She didn't know about Mella, but she certainly knew about you and Josh."

Haley had the grace to blush. "Mrs. Flores is the old lady who lives near the alley where you found us?"

"Yes."

"She rarely gets out. In fact, Pastor Henry brings her groceries and takes care of her yardwork and her house."

"Pastor Henry?"

"He said it was his mission to see that no one in need goes without. Plus, he's young and handsome.

The old ladies like it when he comes over and does handyman jobs for them."

"Huh." I glanced back, but the church was out of view by now. I hadn't gotten the impression that Pastor Henry was particularly young or handsome, or even a handyman type. Strange. I was usually a good judge of those things.

"I've got to go home now," she said. "I've got some pots coming out of the kiln today. They need to be cooled and inspected before they're packed and shipped tomorrow. And Allie . . . I hope we're still friends."

"Of course," I said. I gave her a quick hug. "The seniors are coming back to the McMurphy for lunch on Tuesday. You can bring the pinch pots and hand them out then, if you want."

"Oh, no," she said, shaking her head. "I'm sure it's already all over the island that I've cheated on Rick. I couldn't face them."

"I can come get the pinch pots and distribute them for you, if that's better."

"Would you do that for me?" She looked relieved. "That would be great. I didn't know what was going to happen. I really can't face anyone right now. It was so hard to come to church this morning, but I'd had a long talk with Pastor Henry and he encouraged me to be a part of the service. He said forgiveness starts with telling the truth and owning your foibles."

"Yeah," I said. "I think he's right."

"I will come back to the seniors. I just need a little time first."

"I understand. I'll come by your place tomorrow and pick up the pots."

"You're a doll. Thanks." She turned and walked in the opposite direction from me toward her house.

I wondered where Rick was staying. What he thought about Haley and Josh. Mostly, I felt sorry for Becky. Relationships were hard. You could only do your best and trust your partner to do the same.

Frances and Douglas had this Sunday off since we didn't have any guests, so it was just Mal and me knocking around in the McMurphy. I admired the work on the second floor and went from room to room, putting together a list of things that I would need to finish the redecorating once furniture was put back in and the new mattresses were on the beds. Right now, my third floor looked like a warehouse. If Mella were here, she'd have had a heyday playing in all the boxes and crevices made by the stacked furniture.

My heart squeezed at losing Mella. I decided to print out pictures and post flyers. It was a small island—someone had to know something.

I took my stack of flyers and a staple gun, and Mal and I went out to start posting them. After posting one on each corner, I went into Doud's. Mary Emry was behind the counter, flipping through a weekly gossip tabloid. "Hi, Mary. You haven't happened to see my calico cat, Mella, have you?"

"Nope." She didn't even look up.

"Can I put a flyer in the window?"

"Can't promise it'll stay."

"Okay, well, a few hours are good enough." I taped the flyer to the glass and left. Mary wasn't much of a talker anyway. I crossed the street and entered the Nag's Head Bar and Grill.

"Allie!" Liz waved me down almost immediately after I walked in. She was at a table with Rick Manx. She had her phone out as if recording something. "What are you doing here? Hi, Mal." She patted my dog.

"I'm putting up signs to see if anyone has seen Mella."

"Who's Mella?" Rick asked.

"My cat," I replied, handing him a flyer.

"Oh, this is the cat you were worried that I would let out when I was cutting wood."

"Yes," I said. "Have you seen her? I'm posting a small reward."

"No, but I'll keep an eye out," Rick said. His eyes were bloodshot, and he didn't look happy as he folded the flyer and put it in his pocket.

"Have a seat," Liz said, patting the seat next to her.

"I wish I could, but Mal and I are on a mission to distribute flyers to all four corners of the island. Aren't we, Mal?" She wagged her stumpy tail.

"Allie, were you the one who called the cops on me?" Rick asked flat out.

"I'm sorry?" I hedged. I could feel heat rising in my cheeks.

"Someone told the police that Rick's wife Haley was having an affair with Josh Spalding."

"Why would they do that?" Okay, so I was a bad liar. They both gave me the side-eye. I sighed and sat down. "Look, I'm trying to figure out who killed Anthony. It's eating Maggs alive. And Josh Spalding and Anthony were wearing very similar zombie costumes."

"And you think I might have flown off in a jealous

rage and killed Anthony by mistake," he said in a gravelly tone. He rubbed his hands over his face. "Well, the answer is no, I didn't kill anyone. I would never kill anyone. I didn't even know until Haley told me yesterday." He looked straight into my eyes. "Our marriage has had its ups and downs. I haven't exactly been a saint, either."

"Haley told me you threw things and stormed out."

"Heck, yeah, I did. She asked for a divorce."

"I see."

"Unless you've been married, you have no idea," he said. He looked at Liz and me. "Have either of you ever been married?"

"No."

"For a short time," Liz replied. That surprised me, and I looked at her sharply. She shrugged. "I was nineteen. It lasted three months. I'm not sure it counts."

"You are going to give me details later," I said.

"Beside the point, ladies," Rick said. He waved at the bartender for another beer. "Neither of you have any idea what it's like to be in a relationship for a long time."

"My mom said it's hard, but worth it."

"Worth it if you can work things out," Rick said as the bartender put a fresh glass of foamy tap beer in front of him and took away his empty one. "We could never quite get into the habit of working things out."

"I'm sorry," I said.

"Do you want a drink?" the bartender asked me.

"No. Actually, I just came in to see if I could put this flyer up in your window."

"Sure," she said. "Good luck finding your cat.

She can't have gone far. It's not likely she swam off the island."

"Okay, thanks," I said. I stood up. "Liz, call me later?"

"Sure thing," she said.

I taped the poster up in the window and went to the next shop. It took me nearly an hour to cover the entire island with flyers. It seemed no one had seen my Mella, but they would let me know if they did.

Mal and I went home, exhausted from the search. Trent was waiting by the door. "Closed?" he asked, rattling the locked door.

"Yeah, we didn't have any guests booked, so I gave Frances and Douglas the day off." I unlocked the front door, and Trent held it open for Mal and me to walk through. The McMurphy always smelled like fudge, coffee, and that faint scent of age that comes from years of wood being waxed or oiled to keep its beauty.

"I saw you put up some flyers for Mella," he said. "She really can't have gone far."

I tucked the hotel keycard into my purse and took Mal off her leash. "I know—everyone keeps telling me that. It's just weird that I can't find her."

"Someone has to have her." He put his hands in the front pockets of his Dockers.

"I'm starting to worry that whoever killed Anthony might have her."

"Why?" He tilted his head.

"Mella was the one who found Anthony in the alley that night. If she hadn't found him and had blood on her feet, I wouldn't have gone looking, and Sophie might not have stumbled on Anthony."

"I doubt a killer would hurt a cat for having bloody paws. It's not like the cat can tell you who the killer is."

"Maybe not," I said, walking upstairs. Trent studied the new floors and paint.

"Great job on the remodel. Who did the work?"

"Elmer Faber is my foreman. He also has a crew working on my roof. We're putting in a rooftop deck."

"Smart."

"It was Jenn's idea. The views from up there are awesome."

"Mind if I look?"

"No, not at all. But you have to take the stairs from the outside. I don't have any on the inside yet."

We passed the packed third floor and entered the hall that led to my office and apartment. "I assume you're going to put the stairway in this hall?"

"Not the stairs," I said. "A doorway to a landing, and then outside stairs from there to the roof. I had this fun idea."

"What?"

"We're going to make it a secret doorway. The rooftop will seem very exclusive. Only those who know will have access."

"How are you going to do that?"

"Well, there won't be any access to the lower floors on this side due to the building attached next door, so the stairway will have be narrow. And the historical society won't let us change the exterior of the house that is in sight of Main Street, so we got a permit to create an enclosed, winding staircase in the narrow space."

"Sounds like a fire hazard."

"It's not. There's also access from the stairs at the

back of my apartment. We can safely move fifty or so people off the top of the roof very quickly should anything happen. And that's beside the point." I felt my enthusiasm rise. "To access the stairs from this hallway, we're going to install an old-fashioned phone booth. A person goes inside and dials the number seven, and then the back of the booth opens up to let them onto the roof. Isn't that cool?"

"So before you had a secret tunnel in your basement for bootlegging, and now you'll have a secret phone booth for the roof?"

"It's something people will remember." I tilted my head. "Come on. It's kind of cool, isn't it?"

"Yeah. Who thought of it?"

"Me," I said. "But truthfully? I read an article about a bar in New York that did something like that for people to gain access. I thought that would be fun for the fudgies."

"Will they be able to get back in through the door?"

"They'll have to swipe a keycard. Or they can go down my back staircase to the ground. I plan on putting a security camera over the door."

"Smart."

I took him outside and up to the roof. The men had only just finished reinforcing underneath. The deck itself hadn't been started yet. "They'll put down waterproof webbing first, then float the deck over the top."

"Really nice," Trent said, studying the view of the straits and the fort. "Will you have handrails?"

"I didn't think they would be necessary."

"Unless you have kids at a rooftop event."

I made a face. "I'll order handrails tomorrow."

"Smart. How about a hot tub?" His grin widened. "I can imagine how great it would be to sit up here at night in a hot tub with a glass of wine and a view of the night sky."

"Maybe next year," I said. "Right now, money's tight. This project is pretty expensive. I'm hoping I'll earn back its worth within two years."

"Again, smart," he said. He put his arms around me, resting his chin on the top of my head. "This view is dynamite."

For a brief moment, I allowed myself to relax into him. He smelled so good. Then I straightened and pulled away. "Mackinac is a small island. And you know I'm sort of seeing Rex."

"So?" he said. "You aren't exclusive, are you?"

"No, I don't think so." I shook my head. "We haven't talked about that."

"Then there's nothing to worry about. Have you given my invitation any further thought?"

"I talked to Frances and Douglas. You're right—everyone wants to leave after the Christmas season. Even Rex told me I should go." I hugged myself.

"So come," he said. "I'll send you the details on the kitchen and the apartment. It's just for three or four months. It will do you good to get off the island."

"I'm fine with the island."

He rubbed my forearms. "I know you're fine with it. But this place can narrow your view. Come on, you're young. You need to live a little."

"Trent, we've broken up."

"This isn't about us," he said. "This is about you, and what's best for you. Listen, I'll send you the information. Think about it. It won't be expensive. You can make up the cost of rent by selling and shipping more fudge online." His phone rang, and he pulled it out of his pocket and read the number. "I've got to take this. I'll be back next month. See you then."

Mal and I stood on the top of the McMurphy and watched the sun go down over the lake. I tried to picture fairy lights and a hot tub gazebo up here. Yes, I think the new rooftop deck was going to be a wonderful place for families to celebrate.

Chapter 20

"I don't think Rick Manx is our killer," Liz said later that night. She sat on my couch, and I sat in Papa Liam's favorite chair. We had wine and a snack tray. "He was too shaken up over Haley telling him about the affair. If he knew about it in advance, that wouldn't have happened."

"Yeah, I agree. Have you heard who the dead body was that Rex found?"

"Yes, there was a press announcement. I put it on my blog."

"Oh, sorry. I was busy and didn't get to read it."

"It was Ralph Jorgensen. They identified him by the clothes and ring he wore. It took them a while to notify the family."

"Why? Are they out of state, or downstate?"

"Well, according to Rex, Ralph left after Labor Day to visit his sister in Ann Arbor. There was just one catch."

"Go on . . ."

"When the cops went to the Ann Arbor police to

help notify the family, there was no sister in Ann Arbor. Seems she died two years ago."

"Maybe he was going to return to close up her estate."

"Except that he wasn't the executor."

"Who was?"

"Haley Manx."

"What? How is Haley related?"

"Ralph's other sister was Haley's mom."

"So the dead guy is Haley's uncle? Does Haley know that he's dead?"

"Rex went down and informed her the moment he found out. She was devastated, to say the least. He was her last living relative."

"And now she's even splitting up with her husband. I'll go visit her tomorrow and ask her if there's anything I can do."

"I'm sure she'll appreciate that."

"What about the bag of hymnals?"

"The bag of what?"

"Wow, they really aren't telling you everything."

"What do you mean?" She leaned forward. "You know something? Spill."

"Well, run this by Rex before you publish it, but the only reason we found Ralph's body is because Mal dug up an old bag of hymnals."

"That's why Rex was going from church to church asking if anyone was missing a hymnal or knew who it might belong to?"

"But there was more than hymnals in the bag," I said, leaning forward.

"Okay, now you are literally killing me. What else was in the bag?"

"I don't think I can say. It sounds like Rex may be hoping someone could tell him what all was in the bag so that they can prove it belongs to them."

"What is it? A diamond ring? Tennis bracelet? Was someone robbed? Do you think Ralph was the robb*er* or the robb*ee*? I have so many questions." She sipped her wine and sat back.

"I think you should ask Rex," I said.

"Oh, come on. We're friends. What good is my sharing news with you if you don't share what you know with me?"

I changed the subject. "Some people think that Pastor Henry is good-looking. Do you?"

"Who? What? Me? No!"

"That sounded guilty," I said with a grin. "Do you have a crush on the good pastor? I didn't see you at church, so how else would you know him?"

"It's all innocent," she protested. She sat up and put her wineglass on the coffee table. "Gramps made me do a story on him when he first arrived."

"When was that?"

"About two years ago," she said. "St. John's was really nothing but a shell. Pastor Henry showed up one day and moved into the rectory. Before you know it, he had all kinds of people helping out. They restored the church. It's been a small but vibrant community ever since."

"But you don't go."

"I like Trinity myself."

"Pastor Henry said they're having their annual garage sale this weekend to try to raise money. But they're going to need more than a garage sale to pay for the church to be put back on its foundation."

"On its foundation?"

"The blast knocked it off the foundation a bit."

"Huh, that's going to be expensive. I suppose he could get the yacht club involved."

"I was thinking something more fun."

"Like?"

"Like a bachelor and bachelorette auction. You know. We could get some cool celebrities to come and auction off a date night with them. Dinner and drinks only, of course."

"Of course," Liz said. "That sounds like fun. But do you think that's appropriate for a church event?"

"I can ask Pastor Henry. It's only Sunday. The garage sale isn't until Saturday. We could put something together by then, I'm sure."

"Well, I don't think you'll get any big celebrities to come with only a week's notice."

"Probably not, but it might be worth a try to get some local celebrities. Like maybe that newscaster in Sheboygan. I'll go visit Pastor Henry tomorrow and see what he thinks of the idea. If he likes it, then I'll solicit volunteers. You'll do it, right?"

"What?" Liz straightened. "Me? That would be horrible. What If I only raise a dollar?"

"Oh, I have an idea! We can pick four people—two guys and two girls—and we can ask the town to help choose which of the two girls and which of the two guys will draw the most attention. The participants could have to go around doing good deeds to win the popular vote and a spot on the final auction block."

"That's crazy." She sat back and sipped her wine. "It just might work."

"I bet it will. Remember when the island was divided

between Trent and me? We can try to recreate that with little pins and different colored ribbons. The participant will do something good, and if the recipient likes it, they'll wear that person's ribbon for the auction. Then Saturday night will be the final, where the one with the highest bid wins."

"You may have something."

"Think of all the seniors who may need help winterizing their places, or packing and moving, or general around the house work."

"I think you should volunteer to be one of the people," Liz said. "I happen to know two men who would bid pretty high for a date night with you."

I felt the heat of a blush rush up my cheeks. "No, I'll be the emcee."

"Oh no." Liz put down her wine and picked up her phone to text someone. "I think you would be the best one to compete, and I bet Frances will agree with me."

"What are you doing?"

"Contacting Pastor Henry to let him know about the idea, and how you volunteered to be one of the girls."

"No, don't," I said, trying to swipe her phone, but she stood and held it out of my reach as she continued texting. "If I'm a participant, then Trent and Rex won't volunteer for the male part."

Liz paused for a moment and thought about it. Then she shrugged. "There's nothing that says participants can't bid."

"There could be a rule," I said and grabbed for her phone again. "We're making this up right now. I say there's a rule."

Her phone dinged. "Oh, look, Pastor Henry thinks it's a fabulous idea." She flashed her phone at me, and my heart sank. "He wants to thank you for the idea and for volunteering."

"Give me that," I said. "It's nearly nine at night. What pastor answers a text this late? For that matter, why do you have Pastor Henry's phone number?" I grabbed the phone.

She shrugged slyly. "Everyone likes you. People would bid a lot to go on a date with you."

"I heard about poor Ralph," Frances said as she and Douglas came to work the next morning. "Here we all thought he went off to stay with his sister."

"But his sister died," I pointed out. "Someone on the island should have known that."

"We didn't know her well," Douglas said. He took off his coat, then helped Frances with hers and hung them both up on the pegs in the small hall under the staircase. "She lived alone in Ann Arbor, and no one here knew that she died."

"Do we know how Ralph was killed?" Frances asked.

"I haven't heard anything." The doorbells rang, and the construction crew piled into the lobby. Most of them were laughing and joking, but I noticed that Rick was quiet. I went over to him. "I'm sorry about Haley."

He shrugged. "I should have known. She's been distant lately."

"Alright, men. You know what to do," Elmer called out. "Allie, I've got four guys finishing up down here. The rest of us will be on your rooftop laying down the waterproofing and sealing it."

I watched them all climb the stairs to their relative spaces. Mal sat beside me watching as well. She'd raced to get pets from each one before they went upstairs, but by this week, their presence was old news. She'd rather stay down in the lobby with Frances and me. That's where the treats were.

"I saw that you put up flyers for Mella," Frances said. "Did you hear anything from anyone?"

"Not a soul," I said. "I'm worried."

"Cats have nine lives." She patted my shoulder. "Mella will show up."

I took off my baker's coat and hat. "I've got a meeting this morning with Pastor Henry."

"Oh, I heard about that too," Frances said with a smile. "That was a very good idea, and kind of you to volunteer."

"How could you have heard?" I asked, putting my hands on my hips. "Liz and I came up with the idea last night. I haven't told a soul."

"No, but Liz has been busy. Did you see this morning's *Town Crier*?"

"Darn," I said, making a face. "Now I guess I really have to do it."

The doorbells jangled again, and Mary Emry came in with a small box. "I'm supposed to deliver this to you."

"What is it?" I asked as I took it.

"Not my business," she said, and walked out.

I opened the box. Inside was a roll of yellow ribbon and a packet of safety pins, along with a note. "Make up your ribbons and start recruiting people to your team. I'm your competition, and I have the inside track." It was signed by Mrs. Tunisian.

Great. I was competing with a senior citizen. If I didn't win this, I would never live it down.

CANDY CORN FUDGE

1 (8-ounce) package cream cheese
12 ounces white chocolate chips
4 cups confectioner's sugar
1 teaspoon vanilla extract
Red and yellow food coloring

Prepare an 8-inch pan by lining it with parchment paper and coating with butter.Put cream cheese in a microwave-safe bowl and microwave on high for 30 seconds, then stir until smooth. (This might take a little more time, depending on your microwave.) Use a double boiler to slowly melt white chocolate chips. Once melted and smooth, add the cream cheese, confectioner's sugar, and vanilla. Beat until smooth. Divide into three bowls. Leave one bowl as is. Mix 2–3 drops of yellow food coloring (more or less depending on your preference) into the second bowl and stir until combined. In the third bowl, mix equal drops of red and yellow food coloring to make a bright orange and mix thoroughly. Layer sections in pan: first white, then orange, and finally yellow. Chill until firm. Remove from pan and slice into small rectangles or triangles. Serve.

Makes about 32 ½-inch squares or 1-inch triangles of fudge.

Chapter 21

"Welcome to the first meeting regarding our new bachelor/bachelorette auction fundraiser," Pastor Henry said. "First of all, I want to thank Allie and Liz for coming up with this fun idea. Second, thank you to our four volunteers: Allie, Mrs. Tunisian, Trent, and Shane."

"Please, call me Louise," Mrs. Tunisian said. "I want to fit in with the kids—and besides, who would want to have a dinner date with a 'Mrs.'?"

"Wait, is your first name Louise?" Liz asked.

"Louise is my middle name," she said with a head-shake. "I feel like Louise is young and hip and dateable. And not at all connected to my dear husband, God rest his soul."

"You are young and hip and datable," I said. "I love that you're so involved."

"The best part about this event is that each of you four volunteers need to do good works for someone in order for them to wear your pin. This reinforces that idea of community," Pastor Henry said. He pushed his wire-rimmed glasses up on his nose. "You have the rest of this week and until noon on Saturday to get as many people as possible to wear your pin. Then they must come to the auction and support you. The competition will be scored on the number of pins worn at the auction, as well as the amount in dollars you can bring in—both through bidders and donations."

"Since Allie is in the competition, Sophie and I will be planning this event," Liz said. "Part of your work is to get sponsorship from a local restaurant to create a romantic night on the town for your date. Meanwhile, we'll be publicizing the event and preparing for the auction. Are there any questions?"

Trent raised his hand. "Can we bid for each other?"

Liz grinned and looked to the pastor. "It's up to Pastor Henry."

"I'm going to have to say no," he said. "It takes focus away from your bidders if you're bidding on someone else."

"Got it," Trent said.

"Can we fly our bidders in for the weekend?" Shane asked.

"If you can get someone to sponsor that, yes," Pastor Henry said. "Now, Mary Emry has delivered to each of you the ribbons and pins. Go out and enjoy helping others, and spread the word about the fundraiser."

We stood and shuffled out of the church.

"May the best woman win," Louise said, holding out her hand. I shook it. She hurried off to start knocking on doors.

"You have a real challenge there," Trent said. "That woman has more energy than most twenty-year-olds."

"And there are a lot of older guys on the island to bid on her," I said.

"Oh, come on now," Shane teased. "Who's to say only older guys will bid on her? Have you ever had one of her shortcakes? All she would have to do is offer that as dessert, and half the men on the island will be fighting over her."

"Great," I muttered. "I guess I need to get to work doing good deeds."

"Want to act as a team?" Trent suggested.

"What do you mean?"

"We can go house to house and do good deeds together."

"But then whose pin will they wear? It is a competition," I pointed out.

"And not fair if you two team up," Shane said.

"Right," Trent said. "Well, then, may the best person win."

The first thing I did was make a casserole and bring it to Haley's house.

"What is this?" she asked when she opened her door to find me standing on her porch.

"I understand that your Uncle Ralph's remains have been identified. My mother always said take food to the family. You can freeze it for later, if you want."

"Oh my gosh," Haley said. She hugged me. "Thank you. Please come in. You're the only one who said anything."

Pastor Henry was inside. "Hello, Allie," he said, standing to shake my hand.

Haley took the casserole dish and went into the kitchen. "Coffee?" she called from the other room.

"Yes, please," I said and sat down. "How is Haley holding up?" I asked the pastor.

"She's trying to be strong. Ralph was her last remaining relative. She's losing her husband and her family all in the space of a day or two."

"I don't understand how she didn't know her aunt was dead. I mean, everyone thought he went to visit her, but she's been dead for two years. It doesn't make sense. Wouldn't Haley have known?"

"Haley's aunt, Ruth, was estranged from the two of them," Pastor Henry said. "The news of her passing only came out on Mackinac when the police tried to contact Ruth after finding Ralph. And Haley only found out a few weeks ago."

"So it must feel like a lot of family death all at once," I said.

"I wasn't close to Aunt Ruth," Haley said. She came out of the kitchen with a tray and a fresh pot of coffee and a cup for me. She and Pastor Henry had their own cups on the coffee table already, along with cream, sugar, and a plate of cookies. "She disappeared from the family ten years ago. I was quite young. Then when my mother passed a few years ago, Uncle Ralph sort of took me under his wing."

"When was the last time you saw your uncle?" I asked.

"The middle of August," she said. "I'm embarrassed to say that we had a bit of a fight." Her eyes welled, and she grabbed a tissue. "He had been looking for Ruth. He said he thought he might have found where she lived in Ann Arbor, and he was going to go visit. I told him I needed him here. He insisted that he had to find Ruth. He had a bad feeling, he said."

"How did you learn of Ruth's passing?"

She got up, went to the desk in the corner, and pulled out an envelope. "I got this in the mail last month."

I took the envelope and opened it to find a newspaper clipping. It was a death notice for a Ruth Jordan. No obituary—just a notice. "I'm sorry." I handed the note back to her.

"I thought it was Uncle Ralph who sent me the notice, but Rex told me that Ralph has been dead for almost two months. So I have no idea who sent this, or why."

I hugged her. "I'm sure they wanted you to have closure. Did your aunt have any children? A husband?"

"No children that I know of," Haley said. "But her last name is different, so she must have married. Or changed it for some reason."

"Are you certain this person was your aunt?"

"Yes," she said. "I contacted the county police when I got the notice, and they sent me a copy of her driver's license. She looked exactly like my mother."

"I'm so sorry you have had to deal with so much loss recently."

"Pastor Henry thinks dealing with Ruth's loss without any family support might be what led me to having an affair." She patted his hand. "Grief can make you act in strange ways."

"We're talking to Rick about coming back and working on the relationship," Pastor Henry said. "Haley needs her friends and family now more than ever."

"I understand. Again, I'm so sorry for your loss. I hope you enjoy the casserole. But now I've got to go. I've got some good deeds to do." I hugged Haley, and she walked me to the door. Before I left, though, she stopped me.

"Wait. Don't you want to give me a pin?"

"What do you mean?" I asked.

"Pastor Henry told me about the fundraiser competition. Isn't that why you brought the casserole?"

I felt the heat of a blush rush up my cheeks. "Maybe a little, but I would have brought it anyway. With all your loss, I just couldn't ask you to be a part of my team."

"You are such a doll," Haley said. She hugged me again. "Please, leave me a pin. I'll wear it proudly for you."

"Thank you," I said, giving her the pin.

"I'll wear one, too," Pastor Henry said. "For your compassion." I handed him the pin and left.

Next, I went to check in with Maggs. It had been a while since I'd seen her, even though her home was only a few blocks from the McMurphy. I knocked on the door.

"Come in, it's not locked," she called out.

"Hi, Maggs," I said as I entered. "I came to check on you."

She was tucked into her couch with an afghan covering her. A pot of tea and a cup rested on the coffee table, and handfuls of used tissues were scattered across the floor. "Hi, Allie. I'm not sure if you want to come in. I might still be contagious."

"What happened?" I fearlessly went over and gave her a hug.

"The doctor at the clinic said it's flu brought on by stress."

"Can I get you anything?"

"I'm fine. Please, sit, and tell me what's going on in

the world. I don't have a television, and people have been avoiding talking to me about anything news-worthy since Anthony's death."

I sat down. "They probably don't know what to say. I'm sure Frances has been by."

"Every single day, bless her," Maggs said. "Tell me, have you come any closer to finding my Anthony's killer?"

"No," I said, shaking my head. "I did find out that Anthony was dressed very similarly to Josh Spalding. We worried that Josh was the intended victim—especially since we discovered he was having an affair with Haley Manx."

"But Rick Manx wasn't the killer, was he." It wasn't a question.

"No." I drew my eyebrows together. "How did you know that?"

"I saw him going into the Nag's Head just before I went to meet Anthony that night." She grabbed a tissue and sneezed, blowing her nose. "Sorry."

"No, don't worry," I said. "Can I get you some soup or something?"

"I'm good." She leaned back and momentarily closed her eyes. "I'm kind of tired of soup. All I can do now is wait it out." She peeked at me from under her lashes. "I heard that you found a second body."

"I guess I'm making that a habit," I said. "I don't like finding one body, let alone two. But Mal and I were out looking for Mella."

"Your cat?"

"Yes, she's still missing. Have you seen her?"

"No, dear, I've been housebound for a few days now. How did you come across the second body?"

"Mal pulled me into a patch of scrub on the corner. I found a canvas bag filled with hymnals, so I called Rex. He scanned the area and found the body. Apparently, it was Ralph Jorgensen, and he'd been dead a couple of months."

"I'm surprised no one reported the smell. Death has a smell, you know."

"Well, that scrubby patch wasn't exactly on the tourist part of town."

"Do they know how he died?"

"I haven't heard," I said. "I just went to Haley's house to bring her a casserole."

"We celebrate the dead in October, but this is too much dead," Maggs said, pinching the bridge of her nose.

"I didn't want to upset Haley by asking probing questions, but I was wondering . . . do you know if the hymnals could be connected to Ralph in some way? I mean, if I hadn't found them, Rex wouldn't have found Ralph. But Rex said he took the hymnals around to all the churches and no one recognized them. I think they were old ones. Did you know Ralph? Do you think he'd be carrying a bag of old hymnals?"

"I only knew Ralph through church," she said. "He'd come sometimes when we had our ladies' auxiliary meeting. He was the janitor at St. John's, you know. But before he worked there, he puttered around St. Anne's."

"Why did he switch churches?"

"Well, St. John's didn't have a pastor for decades. So a group of us got together a few years ago and petitioned the main church to assign us a pastor. They pulled Pastor Henry from missionary work two years ago. First thing he did was gather the congregation and other volunteers to clean and repair the church building. It was in disarray after all those years of neglect. Ralph stuck with the place, making it his full-time job. Anthony used to tell me how Ralph was always at the church. He was quite handy. According to Anthony, Ralph replaced drywall and flooring, and he reworked most of the windows."

"Wow, sounds like Ralph was a real handyman. Was Anthony at the church a lot? I mean, besides choir practice . . ."

"Oh, yes, he loved to sing. He wanted to be a famous singer when he was young, but when he decided to go to law school, he put that aside. So he decided to sing for the Lord, and he made it his mission to create the best chorus on the island." She smiled softly. "I've asked the choir to sing at his funeral. But, of course, the police won't release the body until they have everything they need to make an arrest and conviction."

"I wish I had known Anthony better," I said. We sat in silence for a moment, each with our own regrets and sadness. "Is there anything else I can do for you?"

"Thanks, dear, but this was enough. I'm tired."

I stood and gave her another quick hug. "Do you want me to have Frances bring you anything when she stops by this evening? Ice cream, maybe?"

"Rocky road would be nice."

"Rocky road it is," I said.

"Before you go," Maggs stopped me. "Leave me one of your pins."

"How did you know about that?" I drew my eyebrows together, confused.

"Frances calls me on the hour. I promise to wear it at the auction. I can't have 'Louise'"—she used air quotes around the name—"beat you."

"Thank you," I said. "I don't know who will bid on me. Trent can't—he's on the bachelor team—and Rex . . . well, he's working Anthony's case."

"I'm sure it will be someone nice. Have you got your sponsorship yet? You know, for the date night?"

"I was thinking that I would call Tara Reeves. She's been doing the lunches for the seniors at the McMurphy. I could offer a picnic basket at Tranquility Point Overlook."

"Will the Mission Point Resort allow you to bring in catered food?"

"I already checked. They said it was fine because it's off-season and only a party of two."

"Well, then that will be nice."

"Let's hope so. Goodness knows, I'll never live it down if Mrs. Tunisian beats me."

"I'm just glad you're helping the church. Anthony would have loved that."

"It's my pleasure."

Chapter 22

"How's the investigation going?" I asked Rex when he joined Mal and me for our early Tuesday morning walk.

"I'm no closer to finding Anthony's killer." He seemed pensive as he walked beside us.

"Do you ever worry about the forty-eight-hour thing?" I asked as Mal sniffed her way down the alley. I liked to think she was reading her morning news, seeing what happened during the night.

"What?"

"You know, the saying that after the first forty-eight hours, it gets harder to find a killer."

"They say that?"

I frowned and smacked his muscled arm. "They do say that."

"Have I ever worried about that?"

"No."

"And should I tell Ralph's family that it's too late to find his killer?"

"No. But wait, are you saying he *was* killed? You hadn't said before whether he died of natural causes or not." I stopped and turned to him. "Someone killed him? Do you think it was over the gold?" I drew my eyebrows together. "If they killed him for the gold, they would have taken it, right?"

"Unless they couldn't find him."

"What do you mean?"

"I'm going to be blunt. It takes time to die. It's rare for any creature to drop dead in their tracks. Ask any hunter. Most times, you have to track your animal and find them where they finally fall. Adrenaline takes a dying animal far."

"You think he ran and hid, and then died?" I sounded as horrified as I felt.

"It's the only thing that makes sense, if the killer knew that there was more than hymnals in his bag."

"You think the killer knew about the gold."

"Why else would Ralph cover the bag in leaves when he was dying?"

"He was hiding it from his killer."

He was silent, and we walked a bit. "I think the gold came from St. John's."

"Why?"

"The hymnals. They were older, and St. John's was abandoned until two years ago when Pastor Henry took it over."

"But why would someone hide gold in an abandoned church?"

"I don't know."

I shook my head and frowned. None of it made sense. "Maggs told me that Anthony said Ralph was always fixing drywall and floors and rafters and such. If there was gold hidden in the church, maybe he found it and tried to take it."

"Someone caught him, and they fought."

"Yes," I said. "You know, Anthony may have figured it all out, and that was why he was killed."

"Because he figured out a two-month-old murder with no body?"

"He might have figured out that Ralph was looking for something, and looked into it himself," I said. "He might have found more gold. That could be why he was killed."

"No. If he was killed for the gold, why wait and kill him in the alley? Besides, no one reported a break-in at his place."

"I don't know." I felt my shoulders fall in defeat. "I don't have any answers."

We walked in silence while Mal did her thing, then we headed down to the lake shore and back.

"I heard you're up for auction on Saturday," Rex said finally.

"Yes," I said, sending him a sideways look. "St. John's was knocked off its foundation in the senior center explosion. So I thought having a bachelor auction would help raise some money."

"So you volunteered?"

"Liz told Pastor Henry I would do it. Then it was too hard to get out of it. And now I'm in a weird competition with Louise."

"Who's Louise?"

"Mrs. Tunisian."

"Really?" His blue eyes sparkled.

"Yes," I said, "and she's probably going to win. We have to get people to take a ribbon and wear it at the auction. The person with the combination of highest bid and most ribbons wins the overall prize."

"What's that?"

I shrugged. "A trophy, maybe? Really just bragging rights. How will I ever face my friends if Louise beats me?"

"She does have the advantage of about sixty years more than you on the island."

We walked past one of the flyers I'd put out the other day. "You haven't seen Mella, have you?"

"She's still missing?"

"Yes," I said. I reached down and picked Mal up. "At least I still have you, Mal." I gave her a squeeze, and she kissed my cheek and wiggled back down to the ground.

"I'll wear your ribbon," Rex said. "I'll be at the auction."

"Really? I haven't done anything kind for you."

"You're always kind. Besides, it would be my pleasure."

"Thanks," I said. "Come on in, and I'll get you a ribbon."

We were about half a block from the McMurphy when a deafening noise filled the air. Rex sprang into action, grabbing Mal and me as we were thrown to the ground by the shockwave. He shielded us from the debris raining down. I felt it sting the back of my legs as I choked on smoke and dust.

When things settled, we rolled onto our backs and sat up. Mal shook hard, and dust went flying. I wiped the debris from my face. What had just happened?

Rex was on his feet, calling dispatch on his walkie-talkie. It took me a moment to stand up. People started to come out of their nearby homes and apartments to gather in the street.

The top of the McMurphy had just blown off.

My apartment and all my grandparents' things now lay buried in smoking rubble. I sat down on the curb, tears running down my cheeks. I'd been through a lot this year, but I never imagined I would be the one to lose our family business.

Rex studied me grimly. "I hope you have insurance."

I sat in Frances's kitchen with my hands wrapped around a hot cup of tea. Mal was in a doggy bed, chewing on a bone at my feet. "I keep thinking that I've got fudge to make. I should be getting it to the delivery guy right now if I'm going to make my shipment."

"It's shock," Frances said. She put her hand over mine and squeezed it.

"Put this blanket around your shoulders," Douglas said, draping a wool blanket over me.

"I'm not cold," I said as my teeth started to chatter. "Do they know what happened yet?"

"The fire chief is investigating right now."

"I just replaced the boiler last spring." I looked at Frances. "You don't think it was a gas leak, do you?"

"I doubt it," she said. "Douglas keeps his eye on maintenance."

"I would have noticed anything amiss," Douglas said. "I'm just darn glad you and Mal weren't inside at the time."

"I don't understand. Who's doing this? Why are they doing it? Is it because I have offered the McMurphy as a place for the seniors to gather? Was it something that I might have known or uncovered?"

"You can't blame yourself, dear," Frances patted my hand. "Crazy people are just crazy."

"You've said that before," I said.

"And she was right both times," Douglas said.

"Listen. I've made up the spare bedroom. You and Mal can stay here until you decide what you're going to do next."

"Oh no, I couldn't impose . . ." My phone rang. It was my mother. I got up, answered the phone, and stepped into the hallway. "Hi, Mom."

"Allie, what happened? We heard that the McMurphy blew up. Is it true? Are you okay?"

I spent the next half an hour pacing in the living room and trying to convince my mom that I was fine. She spent the same amount of time insisting that I move back home to Detroit. My mom was never a fan of Mackinac Island, I think because she felt like my father's family tradition might have stifled him. Fortunately, Papa Liam had allowed my father to step out of the family obligation and pursue his dream of studying architecture.

I sort of wished my mother had the same respect for my dream of continuing the family tradition of hotel and fudge shop.

"I've got to go, Mom," I said.

"I'm flying up there tomorrow."

"Please, Mom. I'm fine. There's no place for you to stay. I promise to call every day."

Frances opened the front door, and Liz and Sophie walked in.

"Are you okay?" they asked at the same time.

"I'm fine," I said after hanging up my phone. Both

girls hugged me hard. Mal greeted them, and they reached down to pet her.

"I'll get some tea," Frances said, slipping into the kitchen.

"Who did this?" Sophie asked as she straightened up.

"Any idea how?" Liz asked.

"I don't know," I said with a shrug. I sat on the sofa. "Mal and I took our usual early morning walk, and when we were on our way back—*bam!*"

"You have cameras everywhere, right?" Liz asked, sitting on a wingback chair. "Surely they caught someone on them. You can't just put explosives in a building as locked down as the McMurphy. Someone had to see you do it."

"Do you think it's the same person who blew up the senior center?" Sophie asked, crossing her arms.

"Is it because you're having the seniors at your place for lunch?" Liz pondered.

"Why would someone not want the seniors together?" Sophie asked. "I mean, the bomber is always careful that no one is in the building, right? So why?"

"I wish I knew," I said. "As soon as they release the building, I'm going to go back and see how bad it is."

"Honey, you shouldn't," Liz said. "Not after all the money you've put into the renovations."

"Look at the bright side," Sophie said. "Now you can start from scratch and rebuild it fresh."

"She won't have to," Rex said as he entered from the kitchen. Douglas and Frances were behind him, so they must have let him in. Mal leapt up and bounded on him for pets.

"Are you okay?" I asked. I stood to touch the stitches on his cheek.

"Nothing some whiskey can't cure." He touched my hair. "There's a knot on your forehead the size of a goose egg."

"Yeah, I went down hard. I think Mal was the only one unscathed. I really doubt I'll win the bachelorette auction now."

"You're gorgeous no matter what," he said, his voice low.

I tried not to blush. "You said I won't have to rebuild the McMurphy from scratch?"

"No," he said, gesturing for me to sit back down. He sat beside me on the couch. "The fire chief looked it over. It appears that only the roof imploded. I'm afraid that your apartment and office will need to be redone along with the roof, but it appears the foundation is good, and the second and third floors have held their own. He thinks that you should hire a structural engineer, but once they give the okay, it won't take long to raise the roof again."

"Oh my gosh, that's so wonderful!" I hugged Rex maybe a tad too tight.

A throat cleared, and we broke apart. It was Trent. Douglas had let him in. "Are you okay?"

"Yes," I said. "Just a bump on the head. Rex told me that the McMurphy might be salvageable."

"That's great news." He gave me a quick hug. "So the Chicago move might be necessary sooner than we thought."

"No, it seems like there is even more to do here now," I said, turning to Rex. "Can I go see it?"

"It's probably best that you wait until the inspector is finished."

I slumped down in my chair. "I have fudge to make,

and the auction to fight for, and the seniors were coming for lunch."

"Honey," Frances put her arm around me. "None of that matters. What matters is that you and Mal are okay, and so is Rex."

"I'll call the security service," Douglas said. "Maybe they have film of who did this."

"That might be a good idea," Rex said. "But right now, we're not sure it wasn't simply structural."

"What do you mean?"

"There doesn't seem to be any evidence of explosives," he said. "You've had a crew working on your roof, right?"

"Yes, but they were reinforcing it, not weakening it."

"Well, that's for the engineers and inspectors to figure out."

"If it wasn't an explosion, then the roof could have collapsed on us at any moment." That thought horrified me. I felt my skin go cold.

"Put your head between your knees," Douglas ordered.

I did what he said and tried to breathe.

"Get her some water," Trent said.

Someone handed me a glass of water. I raised my head enough to take a sip.

"We should let the seniors know there won't be lunch at the McMurphy today," I said.

"Honey, they know. It was a large explosion right in the middle of Main Street," Liz said. "The police and newspaper's phones were ringing off the hook."

"It shook things up all right," Sophie said. "We felt it at the airport."

"How could a simple roof collapse have done that? Especially if it *was* just structural?" I asked.

"We'll figure it out," Rex said.

It hit me that everything was working against my staying on the island. All my hard work and success from the season was disappearing under my feet. Maybe I should give up and go with Trent to Chicago. It was what any sane person would do, wasn't it?

Chapter 23

"Are you okay?" Pastor Henry had come to Frances's house to check on me. I was tucked up on the couch with Mal. Frances and Douglas refused to let me do anything other than rest.

"I'm fine, really," I said. "I'm sorry that I won't be able to really help with the fundraising." I touched my throbbing head. "The doctor at the clinic told me I was going to have quite a shiner. Not exactly something you want to look at when you're out on a romantic date. I'm going to have to step down from the auction."

"It's okay," he said, patting my hand. "We can find another volunteer. The fact that you thought up the auction and got it going is enough." He paused. "Do you have any idea what happened? Is it tied to the senior center explosion?"

"They don't think so," I said. "Rex said it might be structural. There was a crew working on my roof. That may have stressed it and caused it to collapse."

"Hopefully it didn't knock your building off its foundation."

"Well, unlike the church, the McMurphy shares

walls with the two buildings beside it. That might have saved it from being a total loss." I closed my eyes. "I just had the second floor remodeled, too."

"Maybe the fundraiser should be for you," he suggested. His eyes were kind. It struck me that he really was a very handsome man, and kind of young for a pastor, after all.

"No, I have insurance. It'll be fine. That's what Frances keeps reminding me, anyway."

"Well, there you have it. It's great to have good friends like Frances and Douglas."

"Didn't the church have insurance for the building?" I asked.

"We've been busy revitalizing the congregation," he said. "Every penny has gone into shoring up the building, utilities, and such. It's tough to be a nonprofit."

"And to lose members of your congregation," I said, touching his hand. "I understand Ralph worked for the church as a handyman."

"Yes, his loss is going to be felt deeply. Ralph volunteered much of his time. He was always knocking on the walls, looking for wood rot and other damage. Did a lot of good work for us."

"I understand there were some old hymnals near where his body was found. You didn't recognize them?"

"No," he said, sitting back with a shrug. "But I've not been here long. They could have been old books he found in the church attic. I haven't spent any time digging around up there. I asked him to clean it up, and he brought down some boxes for the garage sale before he left. Well, we thought he left."

"What kind of things can be found in a church attic?" I asked, curious.

"Over time, parishioners leave things to the church.

Some families just clean out the cottages and give it to the church to sell at our fundraisers."

"Any treasures up there?"

He laughed. "Now that would be something, right? Maybe a painting? I should go check. It's not like Ralph was an art or antique expert."

"How did you hire Ralph?"

"I didn't have to," he said. "When I arrived, he came over and offered his services for a minimal charge. The church was poor, and it needed work. It worked out great."

"Why would he work for so little?"

"I figured he was retired."

"Probably," I said. "How nice of him to offer so much time."

"Indeed."

I was interested in learning more about Ralph, but I couldn't help but still be agitated about the McMurphy. "With the McMurphy out of commission, where will the seniors meet?"

"It's probably best that they don't meet," Pastor Henry said. "I would offer my church, but it needs to be shored up until we can put it back on its foundation."

"There must be somewhere else. Maybe city hall?"

"You don't worry about that," he said. "I'll look into it. Mrs. Tunisian is still campaigning to win the auction competition. I'll work with her on that."

"You're very kind." Mal jumped up into my lap, and I hugged her.

"Well, you take care of yourself, and don't worry about Saturday."

He left, and I sat with Mal. The sun was starting to

go down. I threw off the afghan and got up, put my shoes on, and hooked Mal's leash to her harness. I had to see the McMurphy. I had to know how bad it was.

I walked down the street and onto Main. People still moved from shops to bars. The ferries weren't running this time of year, but that didn't keep people from flying onto the island or taking chartered boats.

I could smell the dust before I saw the damage. A portion of the roof of the Old Tyme Photo Shop had been torn off, and the street in front of the shop was littered with debris. I blinked back tears as I approached the McMurphy. It looked like a pile of rubble. The entire fourth floor was exposed to the cool fall air. The front door was covered with debris, and the windows on the front were shattered. My expensive cameras hung by their cords on the sides of my family's legacy.

I began moving debris from the front of the door. There was a lot to sift through. Splintered wood, shards of glass, pieces of the new waterproofing they had just put on the roof. I tried not to think too hard about all the money I'd lost. Or how winter was coming, and the McMurphy had no roof.

But I just thought of it more, and it hit me hard. I'd pushed for a new rooftop deck, and by doing that, I'd lost the entire top part of the McMurphy. Tears welled up in my eyes, and my stomach felt sick.

Mal barked and jumped on me. I wiped away the tears and shivered. The sun had gone down, and I wore only one of Douglas's sweatshirts over a light top and pants. Mal barked again and dug at the door. "Stop, baby," I said. "You'll get hurt."

Then I heard it. A meow. I dropped Mal's leash,

grabbed my phone, and turned on the flashlight. There was a shine from a pair of yellow eyes and another meow.

"Mella?" I dug in earnest. Mal barked. Suddenly, someone reached over me and lifted a heavy board. I looked over my shoulder to see Rex. Mella meowed and squeezed out of the lobby and into my arms. "Mella, my girl. How are you? Are you okay?"

I stood and held her. I couldn't stop petting her.

"Is she okay?" Rex asked.

"I don't see any blood. Do you think she was in the McMurphy the entire time?"

"Maybe," he said. "It's a big place."

"If she's been inside this whole time, she hasn't eaten in days," I said. "Her food dishes weren't touched."

"Dishes?"

"I keep one in the apartment, and one downstairs. She likes to roam, and sometimes she gets caught downstairs, so I set up an extra litterbox, food, and water dishes."

Mella wiggled out of my arms and leapt to the street.

"Hey!" Mal took off after her. We followed close behind. Mella turned a corner, went under a fence, and through a cat door.

We stopped, and Mal went through the cat door, too, right into the house. "Oh no!" I looked at Rex. "Did that just happen?"

He knocked on the door. I could hear Mal barking with joy and Mella meowing. I winced at the sound of breaking glass. My pets were having a field day in a stranger's home.

The door flew open to reveal a lovely older woman

looking slightly frazzled. She held two kittens. "This is not a good time to be selling something," she said.

"I'm sorry, but that's my dog and cat," I said. I rushed into the living room of the tiny bungalow and grabbed Mal by the leash.

"Your cat?"

"Yes, Mella, she's my calico. Sorry, I'm Allie McMurphy." I picked up Mal, and Mella rubbed up against my legs.

"Oh, dear girl. I heard about your hotel. Please, sit down. Hello, Rex."

"Hi, Sheila," he said, giving her a kiss on the cheek. "Two new kittens?"

"They belong to this cat, actually," she said. She put the kittens down, and they went over to Mella. Shocked, I watched her lie down and let them nurse. "Can I make us all some coffee?"

"That would be great," Rex said. He sat down on the chair opposite me.

"Sheila?" I asked him as she left for the kitchen.

"Sheila Vissor," he said.

"Where have I heard that name before?"

"She and Mr. Beecher are a couple."

"Oh!" My eyes grew round. "*That* Sheila."

"Yes, I'm that Sheila," she said as she wheeled in a tray with coffee cups, cream, sugar, a thermal carafe of coffee, and a plate of cookies. "I'm sorry that we haven't met before, Allie. I've been housebound with a bad ankle."

That's when I noticed the wrap on her ankle. "I'm sorry. What happened?"

"Well, I stepped off a curb and broke it in three places. It's been quite impossible to heal, I'm afraid." She put the tray down, and Rex took over pouring the coffee. "It happened in June, actually, but it wasn't healing right, so they surgically broke it and added some pins and plates and nonsense. I'm just now getting around more. Mr. Beecher has been taking good care of me. Now, tell me why you call my cat Mella."

"*Your* cat?" Mella had shown up at my door in July, and no one claimed her when I asked around, so I had taken her in. Now I was attached, and I didn't want to give her up.

"Oh yes. Angel has been with me five years now," Sheila said.

"Oh." My heart sank. "She has been with me for a few months. I thought she had adopted the McMurphy as her home."

"She must have been looking for attention while I was injured." The kittens had finished, so Mella jumped up and curled up in Sheila's lap. "She's my special girl."

"But wouldn't Mr. Beecher have known that?" I asked. "He knows Mella. He never said she was yours."

"Well, it is true that I never officially adopted her. She comes and goes as she pleases, as do most of the cats on the island, and he never pays much notice to which cat is visiting me at any given time. I'm a bit of a cat lover. My cat door is always open."

"That's nice." I said. I tried not to be too disappointed. "We dug Mella out of the debris at the McMurphy just now. Has she been here today? Or was she in there the entire time?"

"Oh goodness, I haven't paid too much attention to her over the past few days," Sheila said. "With my ankle still being iffy, and now the new kittens, I guess I've been distracted. How bad is the McMurphy?"

"The roof collapsed," Rex said.

"Oh my goodness, that's terrible."

"Yes, it is," I said.

"Are you alright?" She blinked at me and Rex. "Well, it looks like perhaps not. I'm sorry." She sat back. "I should have noticed right off. My goodness, is this somehow connected to the senior center bombing?"

"That's not clear," Rex said.

"We don't think so—" I started at the same time, and then looked at Rex.

"It looks like the roof joists were cut, and there is evidence of explosives."

"But you said—"

"It was early on," he said, his mouth a thin line.

"Why would anyone want to hurt the McMurphy?" Sheila asked.

"I don't know," I said. "But perhaps because we've been hosting the seniors' lunches since the center was bombed."

"Someone doesn't want the seniors together."

"Maybe they know something about Anthony Vanderbilt's death, or Ralph Jorgensen's," I suggested. "At first we thought that Anthony was killed by mistake, but now I'm not so sure."

"We have no proof that any of this is connected," Rex said with caution.

I frowned. "Sheila, do you know anything about St. John's?"

"Sure," she said. "I grew up in that church. It was quite a shame when it went dormant for so many years."

"Do you know why?"

"Oh, well, the old pastor died, and with most people

on Mackinac being snowbirds, the church couldn't afford to bring in a new pastor."

"Then why did they bring in Pastor Henry?"

"They didn't," she said. "He showed up one day and set out on a mission to revitalize the congregation."

"He showed up?" I asked. "Isn't that odd? I thought that the community worked to have a new pastor brought in."

"Well, some of us thought so, but he had a letter from the bishop, so we were happy to let him into the community either way. He's been a blessing, slowly restoring the church." She smiled. "Back in the day, before my time, the church had patrons who left parts of their estates to the church. But then the Great Depression hit, and many of the stock portfolios and estates were depleted. For a while, the church ran on funds earned by selling property or items given to them. But even that eventually gave out. The last pastor basically lived off of people bringing him food and donating money to pay the electric bill. Couldn't even afford gas in the winter."

"That's sad."

"You know, there was a rumor that during the Depression, one of the congregation members invested wisely in gold and gave it to the church, but it's never been found. It's sort of like those rumors of family burying money in the backyard or basement. The secret dies with the elderly. Some think that the secret of the gold died with the last pastor back in the seventies."

"I don't understand," I said. "If he had gold, why live so poorly?"

"Pastor Umbra had dementia. Couldn't remember

things. The congregation took good care of him. Well, as best as we could."

I looked at Rex. "Ralph found the gold."

"And someone killed him for it."

"What?" Sheila asked.

"Mal and I found a bag of hymnals, and at the bottom of the bag were several gold bars. I called Rex, and he came and found Ralph's body. "

"Ralph died with a bag of hymnals and gold bars?" Sheila looked astonished. "And you think he was killed for the gold?"

"Yes—but if he was, why didn't the killer take the gold?" I asked.

"I'm still thinking that he got away before the killer could take the bars," Rex said.

"That means the killer is still out there, and most likely still looking for the bars," Sheila said. "Do you think that Anthony might have known who killed Ralph and been killed before he could tell?"

"I don't know," I said. "We don't know if there's a connection at all."

"Except for the church," Rex said. "It all comes back to St. John's."

"Which is also the church across the street from the senior center," Sheila pointed out. "You two should go talk to Pastor Henry."

"I talked to him just this morning," I said. "He stopped by Frances and Douglas's place to check on me."

"Does he know about the gold?"

"No, I don't think so," I said. "I never mentioned to anyone that there was gold in Ralph's bag. Did you?" I asked Rex.

"No," he said. "But it's a small island. I'm sure word got out. The gold is in the evidence locker. My crew has been trying to trace its origins, but so far, no luck."

"Check the old congregation of St. John's," Sheila suggested. "One of the seniors would know. It's probably why the bomber is trying to keep us all apart."

"Thanks." I stood, letting Mal down but holding firmly to her leash. "Is it okay if Mella—I mean Angel—comes and visits me?"

"Of course," Sheila said. She stood, too, after giving the two kittens a pet. "Share the wealth, I say. Besides, I'm not going to be around forever, you know."

"Don't say that," I chided, giving her a quick hug goodbye. "You've got years."

"I've got something, all right," she said. "Now, don't you two be strangers."

We left and walked quietly toward Frances's home. "Ralph must have been looking for the gold all along," I said. "That's why he was checking the walls and the floors of the church."

"I'll do some digging into who else might have been looking for the gold," Rex said. "And Pastor Henry. It's a small island, but it might be more than a coincidence that both Anthony and Ralph belonged to the same church."

"A church with hidden assets."

"Exactly," Rex said. He walked me to the door. "Go inside and stay safe. There's a killer out there, and you have a target on your back."

I gave him a quick hug and kiss on the cheek. "You do the same." I went inside, wondering what tomorrow was going to bring.

CHOCOLATE-COATED TRUFFLES

½ cup milk chocolate chips
3 (14-ounce) bags dark chocolate chips
    (roughly 5 cups), divided
2 tablespoons butter (coconut oil can be
    substituted)
100 milliliters cream
100 milliliters chocolate liqueur of your choice
    (I used chocolate red wine that I found at
    the grocery store)

You will need a pastry bag to create a drizzle design
and a silicone mini muffin pan or silicone ice trays
(the silicon makes it easy to pop the truffles out and
gives them a nice sheen).

Melt the milk chocolate carefully in a microwave-
safe bowl—I set it for 20 seconds, stir, and then put
it back in for another 10, if needed. The milk
chocolate should be runny enough to drizzle. Cool
slightly before handling to avoid burning your
fingers. Pour chocolate into pastry bag and create
squiggles or diagonal lines of milk chocolate inside
the muffin pan or ice cube tray. You only want
lines—don't coat. Chill until firm.

Once the squiggles are chilled, take two cups of dark
chocolate chips and two tablespoons of butter and
microwave for one minute. Let sit for 30 seconds,
then mix. You should get a nice shiny, runny glaze.

Take a spoon and pour a teaspoon into each cavity over the hardened drizzle and swirl to just coat each tin. The drizzle may melt a bit into the chocolate. Chill until firm.

Once the chocolate coating is firm, pour 100 milliliters of cream into a 2-cup glass measuring cup, then add the 100 milliliters of liqueur. Mix and microwave on high for one minute (I had to add an additional 20 seconds—you want it to just start steaming). Place two cups of dark chocolate chips in a bowl. Pour the warmed liquid on top, and stir until the chocolate is melted and it's all combined. Spoon into the center of each cavity. Smooth the tops with a butter knife or spatula.

Next, take the last cup of dark chocolate chips and place them in a microwave-safe bowl. Microwave on high for thirty seconds. Stir until melted and smooth. Frost the tops of the muffin pan or tray to seal in the center of the truffles.

Chill for 2–3 hours. Then remove from fridge and pop the truffles out of the muffin pan by pushing the silicon inside out. They will be gorgeous, shiny truffles. Serve, or give as a gift.

Makes about 4 dozen truffles.

Chapter 24

"This all sounded familiar, so I did some research." Frances pointed to her computer. "They have all of the old newspapers online at the library. Anyway, it seems that the story of gold and St. John's goes back a long, long time," she said. "I found a news article that says a couple of boxes were left on the church's doorstep as a donation. The pastor at the time found the gold, but banks were dying left and right due to the Depression, so he hid it for later when the church needed it."

"Then what happened?" I asked. "After the government fixed the banks, why didn't he put the gold in an account?"

"Things got busy, and he forgot where he put it," Frances suggested.

"Like that's possible," I said with a shake of my head.

"Oh no, I don't think he forgot. He was a wily one. It was the lure of buried treasure that had people attending St. John's church functions," Douglas said. "Pastor Umbra understood that if he put it in the bank, people would lose interest."

"So he kept it hidden, eventually got dementia, and

then forgot where he put it," Frances said. "Apparently, after his death people went into the church and searched everywhere, but they never found it. The place was boarded up, and the whole thing forgotten."

"Do you think Pastor Henry knew about the legend?"

"If so, he didn't mention it," Douglas said. "Surely he would have, though, since it was such a big deal."

"Maybe he was treasure hunting himself and didn't want anyone else to know he was looking," I suggested. "I mean, someone was. Someone figured out that Ralph found it and tried to kill him over it."

"You think Pastor Henry killed Ralph? That sounds absurd," Frances said. "The man has done nothing but good since he's been here."

I frowned. "You're right. Do you think Anthony might have figured out who killed Ralph?"

"If he had, he would have gone straight to Rex about it," Frances said. "He was a good boy."

"Unless he knew the killer and went to them asking for a confession first," I said.

"And then the killer lashed out and killed Anthony," Douglas deduced. "Yes, that sounds plausible. But who? And how did Anthony know about the gold when we didn't find Ralph's body until after Anthony died?"

"I'm getting a headache," I said.

"Oh dear," Frances said. "Is it a concussion? Watch my finger." She waved a single finger in front of my face, side to side and up and down. "You're following it all right. I'm sorry we have to keep you up, but it's part of the doctor's orders. We need to keep an eye on you and make sure nothing goes wrong."

"You mean nothing gets loose in my head," I chuckled. "You two need to sleep. I'll be fine."

Frances shook her head. "We need to check on you hourly."

"Don't be ridiculous," I said. "But if you're going to stay up anyway, let's at least try to figure out what's going on. Who do you think the bomber is? Or the killer? It seems like an extreme response to the small possibility of the seniors remembering about the gold. After all, the bombing happened before anyone knew about the gold."

"But the bombing also knocked St. John's off its foundation, which meant the church would have to be reset," Douglas said. "If you think about it, it's quite clever. A construction crew would have to come in and rework the building."

"So what, you think the bomber is part of a construction crew?" I asked.

"Could be."

"That makes sense," I said, sitting up straight. "The only people in or out of the McMurphy that had access to my attic were part of the construction crew. And they were there every time the seniors came for lunch. They must have heard someone say something that made them nervous."

"They showed their hand," Douglas said. "I'm calling Rex."

Douglas went into the other room to make the call. Mal and I rested on Frances's couch. She had made up the guest room for me, but then the doctor had advised that tonight I sleep on the couch where they could keep an eye on me. So far, so good.

"Here I thought Anthony was killed because of his costume. That doesn't seem to be the case at all," I mused. "As for the construction crew . . . I really doubt

Elmer would do something like that. It would ruin his business."

"I bet he didn't know about it," Frances said. "It's someone on the crew."

"Did the senior center have any work done on it the day before it blew up? Some winterizing, maybe?"

"Come to think of it, yes," Frances said. "A crew came out to clean the gutters, caulk the windows, and add insulation to the attic."

"Who was on the crew?"

"Oh gosh, I forget. But Douglas would know," Frances said.

The doorbell rang, and Mal dashed off, barking. Frances answered it to find Haley Manx standing there with a casserole dish in her hands. "Hi, how's Allie doing?" she asked. "I brought her a casserole. I know no one died, but I figured with her apartment gone, she might need some extra food."

"Thanks," Frances said. She took the dish.

"Hi, Haley," I said, starting to stand.

"Don't get up," she said. "I'll come to you. My goodness, look at the bump on your head. Does it hurt?" She gave me a quick hug and took the chair across from me.

"A bit," I said. I couldn't help touching the goose egg-sized contusion. "I'm supposed to put ice on it, but it hurts."

"I would have come sooner, but I had an appointment with a funeral home in Mackinaw City and was gone all day. I was horrified when I heard."

"Thanks for coming," I said. "I know you're busy."

"They haven't released my uncle's body yet, but I have to get plans together for when they do."

"I'm so sorry for your loss."

"I know," she said. "It's okay. You said you found a bag of hymnals with him?"

"Yes," I said. "We've been trying to figure out where he got them. We're guessing out of St. John's."

"Yeah, he was obsessed with the place," she said. Then she leaned into me. "He told me once the church had a buried treasure from the 1920s, left from when the banks went under. But there's no way anyone could keep a buried treasure on this island. Everyone knows everything."

"I heard the story about the treasure just today."

"Well, my uncle told me about it almost two years ago. He was drinking, and I thought he was making up stories. He was that kind of storyteller, you know? Always embellishing things. Then, when Pastor Henry came, my uncle started spending a lot of time volunteering. I figured he was trying to keep the old legend alive."

"You're part of the choir. Did you know Anthony Vanderbilt well?"

She smiled softly. "Anthony was a friend. He was a very straight-and-narrow kind of guy. 'Get plenty of sleep before church. Drink lemon water. Gargle with salt water. Save your voice.' Real standup sort."

"Did you ever see anyone fight with him?"

"Anthony? No. Well, mostly no. Like I said, he was a standup guy. But he used to get mad if my uncle was at the church with a whiff of alcohol on him." She paused and frowned. "You don't think Anthony killed my uncle, do you? I mean, that doesn't make any sense . . ."

"No, I don't think Anthony did that. I think your uncle found the treasure, and someone killed him for it."

"My uncle found the treasure?" She laughed. "If he found that treasure, he would have come straight to me first to brag about it."

"He didn't?"

"No," she sat back. "Trust me. If he found the treasure, everyone on the island would have known."

"The treasure belonged to the church," I said "If he told anyone, then he couldn't have done anything more than brag he found it."

"He wasn't looking for the money. I think my uncle wanted everyone to remember his name."

"Do you have any idea why he might have taken hymnals? I mean, it seems strange to take a bag of old books."

"I have no idea," she said. "You found the bag, right?"

"Yes," I said. "It was buried in a shallow grave with leaves covering it. Not far from the church, actually, in a scrub area. I'm sure someone would have found it in the spring when everyone came back on the island to spruce up for the season. Mal and I were out looking for my cat when Mal found the bag. Rex found your uncle right after."

"I see," she said. "Listen, I have your pinch pot and the rest of the things for the seniors. Would you do me a favor and come by my house tomorrow? We can load up the pots and visit the seniors."

"It would be my pleasure," I said.

"Great. I'm going to take off. I don't want to tire you out."

"I'll walk you out," Frances said as she came back into the room.

I lay my head down on the couch. Mal jumped up and circled at my feet making her bed. I closed my eyes for the night—or at least until Frances had to check on me in an hour.

The next morning, I was awake early. The night had been a bit rocky with Frances and Douglas waking me every hour to look at my pupils. But it seems I've survived the incident with little more than a knot on my forehead and the blossoming of a deep bruise starting around my eyes. The bruise was going to be ugly. But not as ugly as the McMurphy.

There was little I could do to make fudge right now. Unless I went to Chicago. It felt like the universe was telling me to go, at least until after winter. I took Mal out for her early walk and walked by my poor hotel. Someone had thrown a large blue tarp over it. I made a note to remember to get ahold of Elmer and see what he could do to save what was left of the building.

"Allie?"

I turned to find Haley on the street. "Haley. What are you doing up this early?"

"I like to walk just before dawn," she said. "Sometimes I get inspired by the colors of the early morning. I like the silence, too. It's like no one exists but you."

"Mal likes this time of day, too. Usually, we walk now, and then I start the fudge. But there's a lot of debris between me and my fudge table."

"It must be hard seeing a dream die."

"It's not dead yet," I said.

"I heard through the grapevine that your little dog Mal is good at finding things," Haley said.

"She is," I said. I glanced down at my pup fondly.

"She could be a hound with her nose. Or with all these mysteries, maybe she's more like Scooby-Doo."

I looked up to see that Haley was pointing a gun at me. "What are you doing?" I asked, shocked.

"Come with me," she said. "Don't scream, don't do anything to draw attention to yourself, or I will shoot your dog first." The gun went to Mal.

"Okay," I said. I put up my hands, my heart racing. "Where are we going?"

"You're going to take me to the gold."

"What?"

"You found my uncle's gold. You're going to take me to it."

"I can't—it's in evidence lockup," I said. "You didn't need to pull a gun on me. I would have told you that."

"Keep walking," she said. "Show me where you found my uncle's bag."

Mal and I took her to the spot in the scrub. It wasn't far from St. John's. "Mal found it in the bushes here." I pointed to the spot a few yards off the road. "Rex found the body a little farther in there. But again, you didn't have to pull a gun on me. I would have told you."

She walked over to the spot where the bag had been and kicked at the leaves. "You wouldn't have told me about the gold."

"But you could have asked me or Rex about the bag, or where your uncle died."

"You were about to figure it out," she said with a frown.

"Figure what out?"

She rolled her eyes. "My husband worked on your

roof. He cleaned the gutters and fixed the insulation at the senior center."

"Rick is the bomber," I said. "Did he kill Anthony because he thought Anthony was Josh Spalding?"

"No," she said with disgust. "You really aren't as good at this as I was told. Maybe you weren't going to figure it out, after all."

"I never claimed to be good at anything. It's my pets who find the bodies and help solve the murders."

"Well, I've got you and one of your pets here, and that's good enough for me. At this time of day, there isn't anyone who will come and save you." she said. "And with your hotel caved in, no one will miss you. I'll tell them you decided to leave the island for the winter. They won't find you until at least next spring."

"Your husband killed Anthony, and then blew up the senior center and the roof of the McMurphy?" I asked. "Why? Was it because he thought you were having an affair with Josh?"

"There was no way he would have thought that. I wasn't having an affair with Josh—not until you told everyone that Anthony had a twin at the zombie walk, that is. You gave me the idea, really. It was priceless. I made a play for Josh, and he fell for it. I was sure to do it right where you would be."

"Wait, the alley? But I didn't usually go down that alley. I was looking for—"

"Your cat?" She smiled. "I love that cat. Drew her out myself. She stayed with me until you came looking and found what I wanted you to find. Then I let her go back to Sheila Vissor. The cat started there, you know."

"I know now," I said. "So you *wanted* me to think

your husband killed Anthony? Why? And now you want to kill me because I might figure out your husband blew up the senior center and my place? I don't understand. Are you incriminating him or not?"

"You are very bad at this," she said. Then she glanced around. "The sun is coming up, but we're in the brush. Start digging."

"With what?"

"Your hands," she said. "Do you think I'm going to give you a shovel?"

"What am I digging for?"

"You're digging your own grave. Make it long and wide. Shallow or not is up to you."

"The dirt is pretty hard packed."

"No, it's not," she said. "It's mostly sand. So get down on your knees and dig."

Chapter 25

I knelt and pushed the leaves and debris away, revealing sand and rocks. I grabbed a bigger rock and used it as a scoop to push the dirt away. Mal thought it was a great game and started digging beside me.

"Can you at least tell me who killed Anthony?"

"I thought you knew," she said.

"Was it Rick?"

"No, silly. Rick wouldn't hurt a fly."

I looked over my shoulder at her. "You killed Anthony? Why?"

"Why would I get my hands dirty doing that? I thought you determined it was a crime of passion."

"You didn't kill Anthony, but your real boyfriend did," I said slowly. I finally understood what she was trying to tell me.

"Now you're getting there," she said. "Dig faster. The sun's coming up, and some of those pesky senior citizens will start walking around soon."

"How long have you been having an affair with Pastor Henry?" I asked as I continued to scrape out a shallow grave.

"You're a good guesser," she said.

"He's not a real pastor, is he?" I said to the ground. "He came here looking for treasure. The treasure your uncle found."

"The treasure my uncle was obsessed with," she said. "Nearly two years we hunted for that gold. Then when we actually find it, my stupid uncle can't wait to tell everyone about it. Stupid man. He was going to run straight to the senior center and blab the whole tale."

"So you killed him."

She shrugged. "We argued, and things got heated. That's it."

I sat back and looked up at her. "You argued with your uncle, but Pastor Henry killed him."

"I told you it got heated. My uncle attacked me. Henry knocked him down. End of story."

"Someone bashed your uncle in the head. It killed him, just not right away. He got away and took the gold with him."

"When he didn't come back, Henry told me he must have left the island."

"And the gold?"

"We thought it was still in the church. We didn't know it was in that bag of stupid hymnals he had taken. And I suspected Henry might have it, of course. Kept my eye on him. What's that old saying? Keep your friends close and your enemies closer."

"That's why you made friends with me. But really, why did Anthony have to die?"

"He knew something was up. He kept asking about Ralph. Then he caught me with Henry and figured it out pretty quick. Henry had to silence him."

"Because you hadn't found the gold yet, and your uncle wasn't anywhere to be found, either."

"We were sure it was in the church. I told Henry to shake the place to the rafters."

"So he came up with the idea of exploding the senior center. How did you talk Rick into bombing it?"

"I told him about the gold. He came up with the idea of the fake bomb to get everyone out. No one was going to get hurt, but the bombs were set with enough impact to shake the church off its foundation. It gave us a chance to go back through the church and all the spots my uncle had dug around in without anyone thinking anything of it."

"Until we found your uncle."

"I knew there was more than hymnals in the bag when your boyfriend started going around asking about what was in the bag. No one goes to all that trouble to identify a bunch of old church books." She shook her head. "That grave isn't digging itself."

"If you shoot that gun, people will come running."

"She doesn't have to shoot." It was Pastor Henry—or, I supposed, just Henry. He had a baseball bat in his hands. "A club is quieter and deadlier. Just ask Ralph."

My heart skipped a beat. Mal stopped playing in the dirt and leapt up to jump on the priest and ask for pets.

"Hello, pup," he said. He swooped down and grabbed Mal by the scruff, lifting her up to look into her face. "Do you like to play baseball? Huh? Want to be the ball?" He acted as if he was going to toss her when Mella leapt out of the bushes and onto his back with a hiss. She scratched and clawed and bit at him, and he dropped Mal and whirled. I grabbed a handful of dirt and threw it into Haley's eyes, picked up my pup, and sprinted to the street.

A gunshot went off, and I ducked. Mal barked. In the distance, I could hear Mella yowling. I fumbled for my phone and dialed 9-1-1 as I ran, terrified. I felt like I had been running forever and for no time at all when Henry appeared in front of me with the bat in his hands. His face was scratched and bleeding where Mella had done a number on him. "Where do you think you're going?" he asked.

"It's a small island," I said. "People will know what you've done."

"You should have let her be," Henry said to Haley, who came up from behind me.

"She was going to figure it out," Haley said.

"If you had let her be, the money would have come back to the church, and we could have left quietly. Now we have to kill her and make it look like an accident."

I held Mal to my chest. "Pastor Henry, Haley, you should stop now," I said. "I'm certain everyone heard the gunshot."

"The cat attacked me," he said. "I was afraid it was rabid, so I had to kill it."

"Mella! No, no, no!" I put Mal down and rushed him. He must not have expected it because he stepped back. It was enough for me to hook my leg around his and push him backward. The bat came up and whacked me in the face. I barely registered it as I planted my fist in his face over and over.

"Stop!" Large, steady hands pulled me off of the pastor. They belonged to Rex.

"He killed Mella!" I struggled against Rex. Mal barked beside me.

Officer Brown had Henry up and was handcuffing him. Officer Lasko had Haley in handcuffs as well.

"Mella's fine," Rex said. "She's okay. Look." He pointed to the edge of the brush, where my beautiful calico cat sat licking the blood from her paws.

"Oh," I said. "Good." Then everything went black. I woke up to George Marron standing over me, flashing a light in my eyes. "Hello," I said. "You're handsome."

"Hang in there, Allie."

The next thing I knew, I was in a moving vehicle. I felt lighter than air, and there was a cartoon character in the corner smiling at me. "What's going on?"

"It's okay. We've got you," said a female voice.

There was an old slab and grind of a *chunk, chunk, chunk.* I tried to sit up, but I was tied down. The ceiling was too close to my face. I heard a disembodied voice telling me to stay still.

Then I was in a hospital room. The place was dark. There was a window, but it was night out. Rex and Trent were sleeping in chairs opposite each other.

"Hello," said a soft voice.

I turned to see a nurse peering down at me. "Hi." My throat was dry.

"I can get you some ice chips," she said. She disappeared.

I closed my eyes for a moment, and then it was morning. Someone held my hand. I turned my head, and it throbbed. I peered out from under my eyelids to see Trent standing there. He had a five o'clock shadow on his chin and looked decidedly sexy in a rumpled Italian suit. "Hi," I said.

"Hey." He squeezed my hand. "You gave us quite a scare."

"Did they get Pastor Henry?"

"We got him." Rex's voice floated over me. I turned my head to find him on the opposite side of the bed.

He wore a freshly pressed police uniform and held his hat under his arm. His face was cleanshaven.

"Mella?"

"She's alive and well," Rex said. "Sheila is watching over her. Frances is taking care of Mal."

"Okay." I tried to sit up and it hurt so I eased back down. "What happened? Why am I here? I have a vague memory of hitting Pastor Henry." I looked at my right hand. The knuckles were bruised and scraped.

"You were hit in the head with a baseball bat," Rex said.

"Oh, right." I closed my eyes. "Pastor Henry tried to hurt Mella. I sort of flipped out."

"They're calling you a right-handed slugger," Trent said with a short laugh. "Not good for Henry."

"He's not a pastor," Rex said. "His fingerprints were in the system. It seems the real Pastor Henry died in his sleep three years ago. This guy—his name is Fredrick Albert—had heard about the legend of the gold at St. John's. He assumed Pastor Henry's identity and moved into the rectory to look for the treasure."

"My baby's awake!" My mother pushed her way into the room, grabbed me, and gave me a big hug. My head pounded and pain shot through my cheeks.

"Ouch."

"Oh, honey, I'm sorry. I'm just so glad you're awake and okay."

"How are you doing sweetie?" my dad asked and carefully kissed my forehead.

"I'm okay."

"That's my slugger," he said with a half-smile.

"You heard about that?"

"It's all over the news."

"I'm sorry, Dad," I said.

"About what?"

"The McMurphy. I had it less than a year, and it's ruined."

"It's not ruined," he said. "It just needs a new roof, and the apartment could use a remodel. Trust me, I'm an architect. I can draw up some plans to make it even better."

"In the meantime, you'll come home, of course," Mom said.

"Home?" I winced. "Mackinac Island is my home, Mom. You know that. You don't live with your parents."

She sighed. "I was married to your father when I left."

"I don't have to be married to make that decision."

She patted my hand. "No, honey, you don't."

"Where are you going to stay, then?" Dad asked.

"She'll stay in my old place," Frances said as she and Douglas entered the room with flowers in their hands. "It's perfect for a single woman. I haven't had the time to put it up for sale."

"It's only until we get the McMurphy back to livable conditions," I said. "I'll have a team on it right away. I want to save as much of the lower-floor remodeling as I can."

"There's going to be a lot of damage, kiddo," Dad said gently. "The explosion must have set off the sprinkler system."

"I've got the insurance claims adjuster set to come in tomorrow, now that the fire chief is done with the building," Douglas said. "They'll get you the seed money you need to repair it."

"I've got some extra money saved up," Dad said.

"No, Dad. I can figure this out."

"The Jessops would be happy to invest in another Main Street property," Trent said.

"No, thanks," I said firmly. "The hotel has been McMurphy owned since the beginning, and I'm not going to change that now."

"That's ridiculous," Trent said. "When you get married, you'll change your name, and the hotel will change families."

"Who's getting married?" Mom asked. "Allie?"

"I'm not getting married," I said, giving Trent the stink eye.

"Wait, so you're never going to get married?" Mom looked panicked.

"Not yet," I said. "Someday."

"And on that day, the McMurphy will be under a new family name," Trent pointed out with his arms crossed over his chest. "So why not let another family invest in it now?"

"An investor makes sense," Dad said.

"Dad, I thought you of all people would want to keep it in the family. And it doesn't matter if I get married or not—I'll still be a McMurphy."

"Honey—"

"My head hurts," I said, lying back down. I was ready for this conversation to be over.

"Maybe you should let her rest," a nurse said. "Lots of visitors in here." She shepherded them all out.

"Where am I?" I asked her, glancing out the window.

"They air lifted you to Cheboygan Memorial," she said. "I'm Emma. How are you feeling?"

"I'm okay."

"You look pretty beaten up."

"You should see the other guy." I smiled, and it hurt. "Ow."

"Your hands don't show any defensive wounds. Just a lot of dirt and a few broken nails."

"My cat got him," I said.

"Good cat," she said. "The doctor wants to hold you for twenty-four hours. You've had two head injuries in a short time. We need to keep a good eye on you."

I sighed. "Where are my pets again? I can't seem to hold a thought in my head."

"Frances is looking after them both," Rex said from the doorway.

"I thought you all had to leave," I said as the nurse let herself out.

"I'm a cop. I get to ask you questions."

"I know you saved me yet again." Tears welled up in my eyes. "Thank you for coming so quickly."

"You dialed 9-1-1," Rex said, "and left the phone on. We had already heard the shot and were heading in that general direction, and your call allowed us to find you more easily. Good work."

"Mella came out of nowhere and attacked Pastor Henry, or whoever he is."

"We got fingerprints off the portion of your roof where the detonator was. They belonged to Rick Manx. We picked him up early this morning, and he told us everything."

"Everything?"

"Everything," Rex said. "Like I said, Pastor Henry isn't the real Pastor Henry."

"Right. How exactly was he able to assume Pastor Henry's identity?" I asked. "Didn't someone know he wasn't real?"

"The real Pastor Henry died three years ago in Minnesota," Rex said. "Fredrick Albert was the caretaker at his church. He overheard someone tell the story of the treasure of St. John's, so he stole the pastor's identity and forged the letter from the bishop."

"He pretended to be a pastor in order to find hidden gold?" I asked. "That seems like a lot of work."

"Not really," Rex said. "He got free room and board, and a salary. Plus, he was siphoning off church funds."

"But I thought the church didn't have much money," I said, rubbing my forehead. "How can you steal what isn't there?"

"The church had money. Mr. Albert was embezzling half of the donations that came in."

"How do you know?" I asked.

"Rick told us."

"Can you believe him?"

"I think so," Rex said. "I'm having an accountant go over the church books."

"I don't understand," I said. "How is Rick involved?"

Rex sat down. The nurse, who had returned, scowled at him, but we both ignored her. "Let me start at the beginning. Haley's uncle, Ralph, was looking for the gold.

"He had a deal with the pretend pastor, he thought. If Ralph found the treasure, then he would get a finder's fee and the church would keep the gold."

"So Ralph did it?" I asked

"Ralph found it in the bag of hymnals, and he hid it in the woods. Then he told Henry, aka Albert, that he had found it," Rex said. "Ralph didn't know he wasn't dealing with the real Pastor Henry. The pastor wanted Ralph to bring it to him, but Ralph wanted to be the hero. He wanted to tell everyone he had found the gold and to make a big splash about giving it to the church."

"But Henry wanted to keep it himself. The last thing he wanted was for everyone to know the gold was found."

"Exactly," Rex said. "They struggled, and Henry hit Ralph on the head with a two-by-four. Ralph went down, and Henry panicked. Haley came in and saw her uncle unconscious on the church floor."

"Why didn't she go to the police?"

"She and Henry were having an affair. She knew about the gold and was helping Henry embezzle money."

"Did she know he wasn't the real pastor?" I asked.

"I don't think so. But she saw her uncle and figured he was dead, so the two of them went into the back of the church to get something to hide the body in, but Ralph disappeared when they weren't looking. He must have come to and tried to get back to the gold, but then collapsed and died from his injury."

"Wow," I said. "Haley and Pastor Henry must have been really worried Ralph would turn up and let people know about the gold."

"Except months went by," Rex continued. "And that's when Rick got involved. Haley and Fredrick Albert convinced Rick that Ralph had found the gold, but then gone missing. They were pretty sure he hadn't taken it off the island and figured it had to still be in the church. They convinced Rick to bomb the senior center in order to rock the church off its foundation."

"So the congregation would have to hire a construction crew to take the building apart," I said. "Rick was on the construction crew scheduled to do the demolition. He would be poised to find the money."

"Yes."

"How is Anthony's death part of this?" My head hurt.

"Anthony found out that Haley and Pastor Henry were having an affair. He must have done some digging and found out that the man was a fraud. He pulled him aside the night of the zombie walk to confront him, and Henry killed him."

"Why didn't Anthony go to the church council?"

"Rick told us that Anthony thought Pastor Henry was doing such a good job with the church that he wanted to give the guy a chance to explain," Rex said. "But Albert must have panicked and killed him."

"What about Josh? Did Haley really set him up?"

"Yes," Rex said. "You were asking about Josh because he had the same costume as Anthony. Haley saw it as a way to frame Rick. So she lured Josh to kiss her in front of Mrs. Flores, and then again in the alley that day when you saw her."

"She used my investigation to point the finger at her own husband?"

"When she gave Rick an alibi, she then blackmailed him into doing whatever she wanted."

"So she convinced him to sabotage the roof of the McMurphy."

"Haley figured out you found the gold," Rex said. "You got too close to the truth, and she wanted you punished."

"But no one was in the building when the roof collapsed."

"You got very lucky," Rex said.

"She came after me herself," I said. "She's really crazy."

"Yes," he said. We were both silent for a few minutes. Then he interrupted my thoughts. "I hear they're going to keep you overnight."

"Yes."

"Are you coming back to the island after?"

"Yes. It's my home. Frances offered me her old place."

"You could stay with me," he said carefully.

I glanced up at him. "What?"

"I have a two-bedroom place," he said. "Room for a dog and a cat and whoever else shows up."

"That's a nice offer."

"Hey, Allie."

We turned to see Trent walking through the door.

"I thought I wasn't supposed to have any visitors," I said.

"The nurse likes me," Trent shoved his hands in his pockets and gave me his most charming smile. "I have to go fix some business stuff soon, but listen, Allie. I know Frances offered her place, but my offer to stay at my place in Chicago still stands. Now it really is the only way you can continue fudge sales through the winter. No, don't worry about deciding right now. I know you need to recover. You just let me know, and I'll send Sophie's plane to come get you and your pets."

I swallowed hard as Trent walked to my bedside. "So you're leaving today?"

"Yes. Paige called—there's some trouble in Milwaukee, and I have to go and see that it's taken care of." He planted a kiss on my forehead. "I'd kiss your cheek, but it looks like it might hurt."

"I can only imagine how terrible I look right now."

"You're a brave girl. Please, consider my invitation. I'll call you soon." Trent straightened. "Take care of our girl, Rex."

"I will," Rex said. He turned on his heel to follow Trent out.

"Wait," I said.

Rex stopped in the doorframe and looked back at me.

"Are you leaving, too?" I asked.

"Just getting coffee. I'm not going anywhere."

Those words were music to my ears. "I didn't have a chance to answer your question before we were interrupted."

"Okay," he said.

"Um, does your offer still stand?"

"Always," he said. "But I don't have a commercial kitchen . . ."

"That's okay. I'll use what I've got, for now. And we can build one."

"Yes," he said. "We can." Then he gave me a smile and a nod and left the room.

The warmth in his face had my heart racing. I was beaten up. The McMurphy was beaten up. But I still had Rex and Mal and Mella and, most importantly, Mackinac Island. I closed my eyes. All in all, the future looked pretty bright. Time to heal. There was a lot of work to do.

ACKNOWLEDGMENTS

Thank you to the people of Mackinac Island for putting up with my questions and antics. I love your hospitality. Special thanks go out to my family for their love and support. The only way to get a book written is with a lot of help and patience.

Thank you to the team at Kensington, especially my editor, Michaela, for the support of this series and making it a joy to write.

And always, special thanks to my agent, Paige Wheeler.

Exciting news for cozy mystery fans!

Don't miss the first book in NANCY COCO's
Oregon Honeycomb Mystery Series

Death Bee Comes Her

Coming soon from Kensington Publishing Corp.

Keep reading to enjoy a sample excerpt . . .

Chapter 1

The people who lived on the Oregon coast were a bit . . . quirky, shall we say? Here, hippies, grunge, and hipsters melded their colorful and interesting personalities into a community. That's the way I liked to think of us, anyway. When most people thought of the West Coast, they probably thought of sun, surf, and sand, right? That didn't always apply here. We had fog, cool breezes, and rocky shores. Ever see the movie *Twilight*? It was more like that. In fact, parts of it were filmed nearby.

Now, I'd lived here my whole life, and I've never seen a vampire, but I have seen a few sparkly people. One was Mrs. Baily, who owned a gift shop near the beach. And right now, she was out sweeping in front of her shop.

"Glitter is the herpes of the craft world," she'd told me once. "If it gets on you, it will never truly go away. I still find it in the most interesting places."

"Hi, Mrs. Baily," I said. I smiled at the sight of her glittered tee shirt.

"Hello, Wren. How are you and Everett doing today?"

"We're well," I said. Everett, my cat, purred his reply. "Going for a walk on the beach."

"Good day for it," she said, waving her right hand in the air. "I'd stroll with you, but I'm setting up for next week's Halloween extravaganza. Is your shop doing anything?"

"I'm making honey taffy. And we're dressing up, of course."

"Of course," she said. "This year, I'm going as Little Red Riding Hood. What are you going to be?"

"Everett is going as a warlock, and I'm going as his familiar."

Everett meowed his approval.

Mrs. Baily laughed. "I think that's appropriate. See you at the costume parade on Halloween!"

"Bye," I said, waving. We continued toward the beach—which was actually only a block or two from my shop. Most people didn't look twice when they saw me walking my cat on a leash. Everett loved going for walks. He was a social cat with short, slick, chocolate brown hair and bright green eyes. My Aunt Eloise was a cat fancier and bred Havana Browns. Everett was the great-grandson of her best show cat, Elton, and just as handsome, if I say so myself.

"Hi, Wren," Mrs. Miller said as she stepped out of Books and More. "Hello, Everett. Are you two off to the beach?"

"I thought we'd walk the shore for a bit," I said. "I've been making candy all morning, and I needed to stretch my legs."

"Are you making honey taffy for the town's Halloween celebration?"

"It's a favorite for Halloween," I said. "Funny how

people like the honey taffy for Halloween but prefer dark chocolate for the Bigfoot Festival."

"Everything in your shop is wonderful," she said. "In fact, I need a couple of new candles. Is someone minding the store?"

"Porsha is there," I said. "She can help you pick out the best beeswax candles for the season."

"Oh, good," Mrs. Miller said. "I'm on my way over there now. Tootles." I watched her walk off. Mrs. Miller was my grandmother's neighbor. They had grown up together. While Grandma had to use a walker, Mrs. Miller still got out and around quite well in her athletic shoes, jeans, and jacket. Her short hair was gray and white, but it framed her wide face well.

Everett and I headed down the nearly empty street. Since it was October, most of the large crowds of tourists had left the coast, leaving the die-hards and the locals. It was my favorite time of year. I loved the colors of fall, when the ocean was a deep cold blue. The trees had begun to turn red and yellow, while the pines stayed dark green. Orange pumpkins dotted the sidewalks and fall wreaths and Halloween decorations adorned the houses.

Everett was a bit of a talker. He liked to comment on things we came across on our walks. And I had gotten so that I talked with him. "Want to go down to the beach?" I asked him.

"Are you talking to that cat?" Mrs. Woolright said as she passed by.

"Oh, hello," I said. "Yes, I guess I was."

She shook her head at me. "You're a bit too young to be a crazy cat lady."

"I'm not crazy," I said with a smile. "But I'll admit to being a cat lady."

Mrs. Woolright shrugged and went down the street as I winked at Everett. "Shall we go to the beach?" Cats don't usually care too much for water, but Everett had grown up beside the ocean, and as long as we didn't get too close to the water's edge, he didn't mind the sand.

He meowed his agreement, and we left the promenade. There were a few slight dunes where the wind had blown the sand between the promenade and the Pacific Ocean. They rolled gently, no more than a yard high, and were covered with waving beach grass. Everett loved the feel of the grass against his fur.

Bonfires were allowed on the beach, and the evidence of them crunched under our feet. I was enjoying the sound of the ocean and searching the waves for evidence of whales when I felt Everett pull on his leash. "What?" I asked as I looked down. He had discovered a woman sleeping in the sand. "Hello?" I picked the cat up and looked at the woman. She wore nice clothes and didn't have the look of someone who regularly slept on the beach. "Ma'am?" I shook her shoulder, but she was stiff and cold. "Oh boy." I jumped back and wiped my hand on my long skirt.

I grabbed my phone and dialed 9-1-1.

"9-1-1, how can I help you?"

"Josie?" I recognized my friend's voice.

"Wren?" she asked.

"When did you start working as a dispatch operator?" I asked, distracted.

"It's my first day," she said with what sounded like nervous pride. "You're my first call."

"Oh," I said.

"Wait, are you okay? I mean, you called 9-1-1."

"There's a woman on the beach, and she's dead."

"Oh! That's terrible. What are you going to do?"

"Um, call 9-1-1?" I said and bit my lip, hoping my slightly ditzy friend could help.

"Right, hold on." There was the sound of shuffling papers. "Okay, let's see. Are you in danger?" she asked as if reading from a script.

"I don't think so," I said, glancing around. "I seem to be alone on the shore."

"Um, okay, right." She seemed a bit rattled. "Hold on. Okay, I'm going to contact the police."

"Okay, should I stay on the line?" I asked.

"Yes? I mean, yes, of course," she said. "Please, stay on the line. You're sure you're safe?"

"I'm sure," I said. There was a long, awkward pause.

"The police are on their way."

"Great."

"Please stay on the line so that I know you are safe."

"Okay," I said. I waited a couple of long moments of silence.

"Um, so this is awkward. What does she look like?" Josie asked. "Anyone we know?"

I leaned down closer. "She's dressed like a country club type. Nice shoes, expensive dress slacks in a swirl pattern, tunic-style black top, and blond hair," I said. "She might be in her sixties. Strange, though . . ."

"What?"

"The sun is out, but you know the wind off the ocean."

"Brisk, I bet," she said. "Why?"

"She isn't wearing a jacket."

"Weird," Josie said. "Most ladies that age would be wearing a puffy coat."

"Maybe someone killed her and took it," I said, squatting down to take a closer look. "It wasn't robbery. She still has her wedding rings and what looks like diamond earrings. They're large"

"So does she look familiar?"

"There's something familiar, but her face is hidden," I said with some relief.

The woman was on her belly with her face down. There didn't appear to be any wounds, but she did have sand stuck in her hair.

"Any idea how she died?"

"I don't see any obvious signs of trauma," I said. "There's some goop in her hair—you know, sand and beach stuff."

"And no one else is nearby?"

I glanced around. "There are a couple of kids walking down the shore toward me."

"Keep them away," she said.

"Right." I stood and watched them. "If they get too close, I'll wave them off. I'm just afraid that if I wave now, they will come see what's going on."

"Oh, okay," she said. "Can you hear sirens yet?"

I held my breath and listened to my heart beating in my ears. "Not yet," I said.

"Don't worry, they're on the way," she said. "Boy, this job is more stressful than I imagined. I mean, I never imagined anyone dying . . . You know what, I'll check again with dispatch."

I looked down at the dead woman at my feet. Everett was lying nearby, watching everything from a rise in the dunes. The grass sprang up around him, and he looked like a lion on the Serengeti. It struck me that I should keep an eye out for tracks or other evidence and make sure no one stepped in it. I glanced around and saw indentations that might have been the woman's original tracks in the sand. It didn't look like anyone else had been there.

Her hands were curled into fists, drawn against her at the waist. There was a flutter of paper from the edge of one hand, so I took a closer look. She was clutching something. I knew enough to grab a tissue out of the pocket of my skirt before carefully turning her hand to reveal the paper. It started to whip about in the breeze. I wanted to take it, but I didn't want to upset a crime scene. Still, it might just blow away in the wind. Thinking quickly, I grabbed my phone and took a few pictures. Then I used the tissue to pry the paper from her fist.

It was a label. A familiar label.

"What's going on, Wren?"

I turned at the sound of a male voice. It was Jim Hampton. Jim was a beat cop and a regular on the promenade. "Josie, Jim Hampton's here. I'm going to hang up now."

"Okay," she said. "Call me later?"

"I will."

"Wren?" He raised an eyebrow. "What's going on?"

"Everett found her," I said, pointing to the body.

Jim hunkered down and felt for a pulse. "She's dead."

"I know, I called 9-1-1," I said, raising my phone. "Josie said she called the police. I'm glad you're here, but I didn't hear a siren."

It was then that I heard the siren in the distance

coming closer. He looked up at me. "I was walking on
the promenade and saw you. You looked . . . upset."

"I guess I am," I hugged my waist. "It's not every
day you find a dead body."

"Everett seems to be handling it well," he said.
He nodded his head toward my cat, who rolled in
the sand.

"He's used to dead things," I said with a shrug.
"He's a cat."

"What's that in your hand?"

"My phone?"

"No, the paper you were looking at."

"Oh, I found it in her hand," I said. I held it out to
him. "It's the label off one of my lip balms." He took
it from me.

"Your lip balm?"

"From my store." I looked around. "I make it. It's
beeswax, coconut oil, and honey. My recipe. I also
designed the label."

"Yes, well, it's evidence, and you moved it," he said,
standing.

"I have a picture of her holding it," I said, as if to
prove my limited prowess in evidence collection. "I
watch crime shows."

He made a dismissive sound. "I'm not sure that will
hold up in court."

The siren was an ambulance that stopped at the
edge of the promenade. Two EMTs hopped out and
went in the back for their gear. Jim stood. "Better call
the morgue. This woman is long dead."

"That's what I told Josie," I said. Everett took an interest in the flashing lights of the vehicle, so I picked
him up.

"Neither one of you is a doctor," the female EMT said. Her name tag said *Ritter*. She hauled a stretcher out. Her partner was a young guy about my height with bleach-blond hair and a surfer's tan. He winked at me.

"Gotta let Ritter check her out," he said. "We'll call the morgue if she's—"

"Oh, she's dead," Ritter said as she knelt beside the body. "She's stiff. Fender, call Dr. Murphy and let him know that we've got a dead body for him."

"Will do," the younger man said. He grabbed his walkie-talkie and started talking.

Jim Hampton took some pictures with his cell phone, then he and EMT Ritter turned the body. I saw her face and gasped.

It was Agnes Snow.

"You know her?" EMT Ritter looked up at me.

"It's Agnes," I said. Agnes was my aunt's rival at the local craft fair. They had been feuding over who won the grand champion ribbon for decades. It didn't matter which craft my aunt picked up, Agnes was always there with an award-winning entry.

Aunt Eloise had begun to act secretively, hiding her latest craft, certain that Agnes was spying on her. She'd even gone as far as driving all the way to Portland to buy her materials on the off chance that Agnes was somehow keeping track of what my aunt bought at the local craft store.

I should have known Agnes from the way she was dressed. Agnes always wore high-end, boutique clothes. She looked like a woman who came down to spend two weekends a year in her million-dollar beach house. In fact, Agnes had lived in Oceanview her whole life.

She had married into a local family with plenty of political clout. Her husband of thirty-five years had been mayor of Oceanview for over half of those years, although now he was just a regular citizen. They never had children. Instead, Agnes had gotten good, very good, at every craft known to man.

"Wait, is she the ex-mayor's wife?" Ritter asked.

"Yes," Jim said. "Mayor Snow's wife—and Eloise Johnson's biggest rival." He glanced at me, his blue eyes squinting in the bright autumn light. "Might explain the label you found in her hand."

"Label?" Ritter asked.

"One of my lip balms," I said. "I own 'Let It Bee.' The honey store in town. I make handcrafted lip balm, lotion, candles, and—"

"Candy," the surfer dude EMT said. I turned to him.

"Yes, candy."

"The best candy," he said, grinning a toothpaste grin at me and leaning in. "The salted caramel with honey is to die for."

"Let's hope Agnes didn't agree," Jim said.

"I'm sure there's no connection," I said. "Besides, it was a lip balm label, not candy."

"It still doesn't look that good for you," Jim said, his face suddenly sober.

"Wait, you think I had something to do with Agnes's death? That's nuts. Why would I call 9-1-1 if I killed her?"

"You watch crime shows," Jim said. "You know the answer."

"Because I want to involve myself in the investigation?" My voice crept up two octaves. "That's crazy. That doesn't happen in real life. Does it?"

Jim raised an eyebrow. "It happens often enough that they put it in television shows." Jim was a handsome man. He reminded me of that old actor, Paul Newman. My Aunt Eloise raised me on old movies, and I remember he played a cop in one of them. Jim looked especially like him just now.

"Well." I hugged my cat. "It's silly to think I could hurt anyone."

"Any idea how she died?" Fender asked. He leaned over the dead woman and studied her. "I don't see any obvious trauma."

"Cause of death is for the coroner to determine," Ritter said.

"Stand back," said a woman my age as she walked up with a black bag in her hand. She wore a blue shirt that was marked with CSU. "You all are muddying up my crime scene." She put down her bag, opened it, then pulled on a pair of gloves. She glanced at me. "Is that a cat?"

"Everett," I said. "He found the body."

She stepped over to me. "Hello there, handsome," she practically purred and scratched Everett behind the ears. He purred back at her.

"Is he wearing a leash?"

"He loves to go for walks, and the leash keeps him safe," I said, patting his head.

"Okay," she said. Then she turned on her heel. "All of you, do not move! I need to see where you all have come in and messed up the crime scene." She shook her head and took a large camera out of her kit. "Really, Officer Hampton, you know better."

"We moved the body," he said. "Needed to see if she was hurt."

"I have pictures," I said, holding up my phone.

"Someone is smart," she said as she took more pictures. "I'm Alison McGovern."

"Wren Johnson," I said.

"Wren, like the bird?"

"Yes," I said. I was used to the question. "My mom loved them."

"It's cool," Alison said. "Okay, you two can remove the body." I watched in fascination as she continued to work the crime scene and bully the EMTs and Jim. I swear, she bullied the grass into giving up its secrets. But she did it in a slow and methodical way.

After a while, Jim stood beside me and watched her work.

"She's good," I said.

"Thorough," he agreed. "I'm surprised that cat is letting you hold it so long."

"Everett? He loves to be held."

"That is not my experience with cats," he said. "My experience is they lure you in to pet their belly, only to scratch and bite and run to hide under the bed for the next day and a half."

I laughed. "Yes, that also sounds like a cat. They're all different, you know. Just like people."

"So where were you for the last twelve hours?"

I turned to him. "Are you still thinking I'm your number one suspect?"

"Can you answer the question?"

"Can you?" I asked him. "I mean, twelve hours is a lot of time to account for."

"I've been working for the last six," he said.

"That doesn't mean you didn't kill someone," I

countered. "Did anyone see you every minute of the last twelve hours?"

He shook his head at me. "I'm not a person of interest."

"I'm not, either."

"Not yet," he said, taking out his notepad. "That could change any minute." He started writing in his pad. "Let's start from the beginning. You found the body?"

"Yes."

"How?"

I went over how I found Agnes step by step, right up until the time I turned her hand over and pulled the label out of her fist.

"I see," he said as he took notes. "And you know Agnes how?"

"Like I said—and you know—Agnes and my aunt have this informal competition going."

"Can you explain what you mean by informal competition?"

"The two of them have been competing against each other my entire life," I said. "I think it started when they were in elementary school."

"What kind of competition?"

"Everything," I said with a shrug. "Most recently, it's been about crafts."

"Crafts?"

"Quilting, scrapbooking, knitting, crochet, flower arranging, jelly making . . ."

"Right," he said. "And how do you do any of that competitively?"

"Oh, there are all kinds of contests," I said. "Church contests, county fairs, senior center contests . . ."

"I get it," he said. "I think. So they were rivals."

"Yes, everyone knows that. You even said it yourself."

"So I did. Do you think your aunt killed her?"

"What? No, no," I said, hugging Everett just a bit too tight. He squeaked. "She would never. Besides, she was in Portland last night."

"Why was she in Portland?"

"She had a date," I said with a shrug. "I assume she has an alibi for every minute of her night."

"Did you have a date?" he asked.

"Is that relevant to this case?" I replied, raising my eyebrow.

He shrugged. "If it provides you with an alibi."

"No," I said with a sigh, watching the outgoing tide. "I was home alone, making a batch of hand and body scrub."

"Hand and body scrub?"

"Honey is good for the skin," I said. "I make the scrub with sugar and salt. It helps exfoliate and soften."

He grinned. "I can imagine honey is great for the skin."

His look made my cheeks burn with embarrassment. "Stop it. Have you been in my shop?"

"Best candy ever," the surfer guy said again as he came back from putting the body in the ambulance. He bent down and picked up his bag, then held out his hand. "Rick Fender."

"Hi, Rick. Wren Johnson." I shook his hand.

"Nice to meet you, Wren," he said, then grinned. "Do I get a discount on the candy?"

"Come in while I'm there, and I'll see what I can do," I said.

"Perfect." He waved and walked back to the ambulance, where EMT Ritter closed the door and walked over to the driver's side. The two EMTs made an odd pair, as EMT Ritter was a large woman with square shoulders and Rick was lanky, like a guy who ate whatever he wanted but never gained an ounce.

"Well, I've got to get back to the store," I said to Jim. "You know where to find me?"

"I think perhaps you should come down to the station first," he said.

"Are you kidding me?" I asked, somewhat unnerved by the idea. I'd been by the police station, so I sort of knew where it was, but I'd never been inside. In fact, Officer Hampton was the only police officer I'd ever spoken to. The first time we'd met was at a chamber of commerce meeting. I was lucky enough to have never run afoul of the law. Until today.

"I suppose you can take the cat home," he said. "It would be too big a distraction at the station." He reached over and scratched Everett behind the ears.

Everett meowed as if he agreed.

Relief washed through me. "So I can go home?"

"For now," he said. "But don't go anywhere. Right now, you *are* suspect number one."

Everett and I left the beach. The wind was colder than I remembered. I felt like the business owners were watching me as I walked by. Suzy from Suzy's Flowers stared. I turned my sweater collar up. Mrs. Beasley of Beasley's Gifts watched me from across the street. I sent her a little wave, and she stepped back.

Then there was Wallace Hornsby from Hornsby Tailor Shop. He peered at me from behind his small, round glasses, and I sent him an uncomfortable smile. Everett meowed, so I hugged him. "It's okay," I said. "They're just curious." I paused and decided I was going to act as naturally as possible. So I put Everett down, straightened my sweater, and walked the rest of the way back to my shop. The last thing I wanted to do was act like a murder suspect. Actually, the last thing I ever wanted to do was find a dead body. I guess I needed a new last thing.

Connect with U s

Visit us online at
KensingtonBooks.com
to read more from your favorite authors, see books
by series, view reading group guides, and more.

Join us on social media

for sneak peeks, chances to win books and prize packs,
and to share your thoughts with other readers.

facebook.com/kensingtonpublishing
twitter.com/kensingtonbooks

Tell us what you think!

To share your thoughts, submit a review,
or sign up for our eNewsletters, please visit:
KensingtonBooks.com/TellUs.